CONOCIMIENTOS

PRESS

ERÉNDIRA

a novel

Rose M. Borunda

CONOCIMIENTOS

PRESS

Book design by ash good.

Published by Conocimientos Press, LLC
San Antonio, Texas

ISBN: 978-1-961794-04-7

CONOCIMIENTOSPRESSLLC.COM

CONTENTS

Eight Years Earlier

The Cruz family travels northbound on Interstate 5. The father and mother sit in the front. They're returning home after visiting family in Southern California. Naníta, the grandmother, sits in the middle of the back seat. The couple's ten-year-old son, Ariel, sits to Naníta's left side, reading a comic book. Their five-year-old daughter, Eréndira, sits to her Naníta's right and rests her head on the elder's shoulder where she falls asleep. After a few monotonous hours, the child wakes up and slowly opens her eyes.

"Are we there yet?"

Naníta answers, "Not yet, baby."

Eréndira sighs, snuggling back into her Naníta's soft body.

The child's eyes are drawn to the flat, barren land rolling by outside her window. "Naníta?"

"Yes, baby?"

"Who is that?" asks Eréndira as she looks out the window.

Naníta looks outside. She sees nothing but flatland.

"What, baby? I don't see anyone."

"She's right there."

"Who, baby?"

"The lady on the white horse."

Naníta looks hard but sees nothing. The mother in the front seat looks back at them—this is not the first time the child has seen a lady on a white horse. The mother and the grandmother nod at one another, and Naníta tells the child, "Go back to sleep, baby."

Present Day

"I hate my name!" Eréndira shouts as she storms through the front door.

Verónica, Eréndira's mother, is upstairs writing a justification memo that would encourage the college where she is a professor to hire four direly needed assistant professors for the following academic year. At the sound of Eréndira's voice, Verónica stops typing mid-sentence, but when the front door slams shut with a ferocity she has never heard, she jumps out of her chair, bounds down the stairs, and stops dead in her tracks at the sight of her unexpectedly disheveled daughter.

Eréndira turns to her mother and, through clenched teeth, blurts out, "I *hate* my name!"

"What are you saying, Eréndira? What has happened?"

"I. HATE. MY. NAME!" Eréndira emphasizes.

Locked eyes. Defiant stance. Mother and daughter freeze on the spot.

Verónica, unaccustomed to adolescent outbursts, takes in her gentle-natured child, scanning her rigid posture and frazzled hair, which is usually carefully combed with every strand in place. Soon, Verónica notices a dark streak oozing down the side of her thirteen-year-old daughter's neck.

"What is this?"

Verónica instinctively draws Eréndira closer and lifts her shoulder length hair to expose a deep scratch at the base of her hairline. Eréndira reaches for her neck and winces. Verónica grazes the spot where pain, previously numbed by adrenaline, now stings. Eréndira draws her hand to eye level to look at her blood-stained fingers.

"I hate my name!" Eréndira exclaims once again, as a consuming rage pushes a cascade of tears.

Verónica resists the urge to faint at the blood's vivid color. She takes a deep breath and steels her knees against the impulse to buckle. Her maternal instincts override these physical inclinations. Gently, she leads Eréndira to the downstairs bathroom and guides her to sit down on the toilet. With a washcloth soaked in warm water, Verónica dabs Eréndira's seeping wound. The sight of blood has also turned Eréndira's soft brown complexion pale and, in turn, compels her to submit to her mother's care.

Verónica's nausea dissipates, and she quietly probes, "¿Que paso, Eréndira?"

"What do you mean, what happened? You know what happened. We moved *here*! I hate this town. I hate my school. I hate these kids. There's no one else like me here. They look at me like I'm some sort of freakish unicorn!"

Eréndira's words sting.

"I know you miss your friends back home but remember why we moved. Your father had been commuting for way too many years. The hours on the road were affecting his health. We needed to get closer to his work, and fortunately a position came up for me at the university."

Eréndira sits silently, considering what should come out of her mouth next. She doesn't want to sound bratty, but she wants to burst out with the inconvenient and unspoken fact that she was essentially *notified* they were moving. She was never *asked* how she felt about being uprooted. She was preparing to enter the high school where her older brother, her mother, her maternal grandmother, and countless cousins had all graduated. There, Eréndira enjoyed the privileges of an upper middle-class family while also being immersed and validated for her Indigenous and Mexican American roots from both sides of her family. Her family was well known and respected but—*just like that*—her hometown disappeared in the rear-view mirror. She was plucked from all that was familiar and expected to acclimate to a community where she was not only the new kid in school but an outsider in this tight knit university town where most of the kids had grown up together. Their social groups were established and unwelcoming to a new kid—especially one whose ethnicity classified her as one of those 'sundown' people, meaning *you can work our kitchens, pick up our trash, and take care of the elderly, but be out by sundown.* She tries to soften her response.

"Yea. I know. You and dad got what you need, but this school sucks. You should have let me stay back home."

Verónica lets out a stomach-punch sigh and momentarily pauses her soothing strokes. "There is no way we would have moved here without you. Remember all the trips we made to visit the area and how many schools we thoroughly vetted. We even considered a private school for you. Your new school has so many more opportunities than what you would have had back home. The test scores … extracurriculars—"

"Test scores aren't everything," Eréndira abruptly interrupts.

"You're right. Test scores aren't everything. But here we are now, and we've got to figure out how to get through this. Whatever *this* is."

As Verónica continues wiping the blood from Eréndira's neck, hoping that the gentle strokes might soothe her daughter's soul, she begins to consider that perhaps people in their new community don't have much experience with those outside their circles. If this is the case, Eréndira would stand out and be perceived as some sort of exotic creature, which is just as bad as being labeled a freak.

Looking at her troubled daughter, Verónica questions their decision to move to this university town. *Perhaps it was a mistake?* She gently probes, "How did this happen, Eréndira?"

"It was a fight. If you can call it that. It had to happen. That bitch that lives down the street from the school was asking for it. She kept staring me down. When I walk by her at school, she says stuff to her friends. They start laughing."

Verónica cringes at the harsh language coming from Eréndira but does not shut her down, recognizing that it was more important, at that moment, to just listen and let her speak, uninterrupted. Nevertheless, the circumstances being revealed were bewildering. Softly, Verónica offers, "Eréndira. We have not raised you with violence."

"I didn't have a choice. They make fun of my name and do all kinds of stuff. All day. Every day!"

While Verónica finishes tending the wound on her daughter's neck, she pushes away the unease rising in her stomach. Eréndira's experience reminds her of similar attacks in her own youth. She did not expect this kind of mistreatment toward her daughter—today, and in a university town.

Prior to moving here, she and Victor heard cautionary stories from a few of their African American friends who moved out after their children were subjected to multiple hostile and racist attacks. They had fled to other nearby communities, taking their education and six figure salaries with them. The Cruz's assumed that it would be different for their beautiful child. Unfortunately, it wasn't. Now, their daughter would have to learn how to draw strength from her name rather than reject that coveted moniker, the same as that of a young princess who lived over five centuries ago. She, too, contended with violence, but of an unimaginable degree.

An iPhone buzzes and Eréndira looks at the screen.

"It's Naníta."

Naníta and Eréndira have a daily ritual where she calls Naníta when she gets home from school. In this way, Naníta knows that Eréndira has made it home safely, and the two maintain daily contact.

"Text her back," Verónica instructs, knowing that they need time to process what has just transpired.

"What should I tell her?" asks Eréndira.

"Just tell her you're home and will call her back."

Eréndira types the text while wishing she could transport herself to Naníta's warm embrace. In that sanctuary, maybe Eréndira could unload the heavy resentment that has planted itself inside her. She has never felt such anger. Its weight is a dark and unbearable burden. She needs her Naníta. Her grandmother. Her lifeline.

Her heart softens. Deep breath. Grandmother. Granddaughter.

Verónica does not want to pressure Eréndira to tell the story twice, as recapping the traumatic event would add more stress. She figures it is best to let Eréndira catch her breath, calm her soul, and compose herself, while they wait for Victor, Eréndira's father, to get home. Eréndira goes upstairs to put on fresh clothes and wash her face. Verónica turns off the computer, shuts the door to her home office, and starts to make dinner.

As soon as Victor enters the house, Verónica motions him to join her in the privacy of their bedroom. Despite a long day at the office, Victor quietly listens to his wife's emotional recounting of what transpired after Eréndira's arrival from school. Then, they call Eréndira to join them in the living room. The three sit across from a freshly lit fireplace. Eréndira angrily recounts what happened that day with her eyes cast down to the floor.

"I was walking home from school with my new friend, Melissa, and came across Susan. She's a bully. Every time I see her, she harasses me, and it's all because her ex-boyfriend has a crush on me, but I don't care for him. He has made advances, and I told him to leave me alone … that I wasn't interested in him. That made him angry. So, he told Susan I had made a move on him, which made her jealous and she came after me."

Eréndira looks up at her parents for their reaction. Both stay silent. Then, Verónica nods for Eréndira to continue.

"The fight happened a block away from campus. Me and Melissa were just chatting away. It had been a good day up until that point. I was sharing with Melissa how much I liked singing in the choir, and she was telling me how she was thinking of trying out for the fall musical when we ran into Susan and her mob of friends. We were half-way up the block from school when we spotted them on the street corner. At first, we didn't see them … because there were others ahead of us … going the same direction."

Eréndira chokes up.

Victor gets up and pours a glass of water. He hands it to his daughter and asks, "Could you have avoided these girls?"

Eréndira takes a long sip before continuing. "By the time I caught sight of her, it was too late to turn around. I would rather have avoided a confrontation, but if she saw me turn around and walk away, it would make me look weak."

"I see ..." Victor affirms.

Verónica interrupts, "Let her finish telling us, Victor. Then we can ask questions."

"You're right," Victor says, and then adds to Eréndira, "Sorry, mija. This is just so out of the ordinary. I'll try and keep quiet. Please continue."

Eréndira takes another sip of water. "Melissa had also spotted Susan and her clique, but when she saw that crossing their path was unavoidable, she whispered to me, 'Just keep walkin' and talkin' and don't mind her.' I did my best to do what Melissa said. I tried to keep the conversation going, but then the bully started in with her crap!" Eréndira's voice grows louder and faster as she repeats the bully's words. "'Hey Mex. We need someone to do our yard work this weekend. Our last worker got deported! You want the job?' Susan's friends laughed, which only emboldened her to keep it up. So, she did ... 'Hey you! What's your name? Aria? DeeDeeDa? Hey! I'm talking to YOU!'"

Victor affirms, "That must have made you angry, hearing her say those mean things?"

"She pissed me off! We tried to ignore her. Me and Melissa kept our eyes fixed on the sidewalk ahead of us and just when we were about to get past the bully, she stepped toward us and hurled another insult. 'Hey! Ask your mama if she wants to come work for us. We need a maid too!' The bully then turned to her friends, and they all laughed like a bunch of hyenas. Even with all that filth coming out of her mouth, me and Melissa kept on walking but then ... All I can remember is Melissa saying, 'Just keep walking'... when suddenly I couldn't move forward anymore. My upper body was pulled backwards. I remember seeing Melissa turn back to see why I wasn't by her side anymore, and the rest is all in slow motion. I didn't have control of my own body. Susan had grabbed my hair from behind and was pulling me backward. My instinct took over. I turned to face her, and, in a moment that happened too fast, I swung my right arm in a wide arc and planted my fist on her nose. It was a quick strike, just like I learned in karate. Blood spurted onto the sidewalk, and the bully's friends ran in all directions."

Eréndira pauses.

Victor and Verónica look at one another, not knowing what to say. Victor finally confesses, "Well, you know, Eréndira. We had you take karate so you would have the confidence and knowledge to protect yourself. Our hope was that you would not have to use it, but it seems like you did what you could to avoid this girl. She obviously didn't know what she was getting herself into. Now, you've drawn blood. What happened then?"

"To tell you the truth, Papa, I squared off on her like I was trained, but she was all hunched over with her hair covering her face. Other students ran up on the scene. It all happened so fast that everyone was left speechless. Melissa came up behind me. I guess she could see that I was pretty jacked up, so she took me by the arm and said, 'Come on. She's done. This is over.' I backed away, and once I was far enough away to be sure there wouldn't be another ambush, I turned my back on that bully and followed Melissa's lead."

Verónica cuts in, "But Eréndira … I saw what she did to you. That was bad enough. Still, it sounds like you did some damage. Did anyone attempt to help her?"

"I'm not sure what happened. As I was backing away, I saw other students gather around her. They just stared at the spectacle of the school bully crying on the street corner, her nose gushing blood and holding a handful of my hair!"

Victor, stunned by what Eréndira just said, abruptly shouts, "What do you mean she had a handful of your hair?"

Eréndira pulls her hair up, turns her back to her father, and, for the first time, Victor sees the gaping bald spot at the bottom of her hairline and the raw fingernail trails, "Damn that girl! She did this to you?"

"¡Cálmate, Victor!" Verónica urges.

"I am calm! You didn't tell me that our daughter was physically hurt!" He yells back. "Look what that girl did to our baby!"

"I know. It's not right, but . . . but as you can see, our baby is okay. Let her finish the story."

Victor's eyes seethe with anger. He takes his daughter's hand and says, "Sorry, Eréndira. I am so sorry this happened to you. I'll try not to interrupt again. Please, finish the story."

Eréndira takes a deep breath, recognizing that her father often showed his emotions more than her mother, but there was no way of protecting either one of them from the circumstances. She would need them both to move forward. She continues, "The students who came running to see what happened stepped back and let us walk away. Nobody said anything to us. They just looked at me with shock. Melissa turned to me and said, 'Damn! You took care of her. Where'd you learn to fight like that?' I told her I had a brown belt in karate. To earn the belt I broke a board with my fist, but I never thought I'd be having to break a nose. Melissa thinks nobody will be messing with me now but I'm not so sure."

Victor looks to Verónica before saying, "Why not? In my day, if the bully got what they deserved and was taken down, then that was the end of story!"

Eréndira squeezes her father's hand, "Papa, I wish you and Melissa were spot on, but my gut tells me the problems are only beginning. This all started as soon as we moved to this town. Having a name like mine marks me as *different,* and that's just a part of the bad attention I get."

Victor and Verónica understand why Eréndira did what she did, but also remind her that adults at school are there to intervene. Eréndira tells them that's what kids in elementary school might do but certainly not in junior high. Soon, Eréndira doesn't have anything else to say, so for the rest of the evening, she stays in her room, curtains drawn, and headset on, listening to heavy metal. She skips dinner. She has no appetite. This, until the doorbell rings. Eréndira gets up and looks down from her second-story bedroom window that faces the street. A City Police car was parked in front of their house. She hears her parents talking to someone—a man—at the door. They let him in. Then, Victor's voice calls for her from the bottom of the stairs. Once again, he summons Eréndira to come downstairs.

The following morning, Ms. Foster, the vice principal, arrived at her office. Promptly attending to the blinking red light of her voicemail, she entered the code. There is only one message, but as soon as the voice comes through Ms. Foster pulls the phone away from her ear. The woman is screaming so loud that the voice is distorted, "Ms. Foster! This is Susan Lane's mother. What the hell! You people are letting in these wild hoodlums, and one of them attacked my daughter! I want that girl arrested. I had to take my daughter to the hospital! I think her nose is broken!"

In the background, Ms. Foster hears an indistinct sound, like somebody crying, and the caller cupping her hand over the receiver, but still hears her shouting to whoever is in the background, "Shut up Susan! I'm leaving a message for your vice principal! Get another towel, and don't get blood on our white carpets! For heaven's sake!" The caller takes her hand off the phone, and the screaming continues: "Ms. Foster! I want that new girl arrested and kicked out of school! Do you hear me?"

The phone slams down so hard that Ms. Foster is left rubbing her ear. She has not even hung up the phone when she is buzzed by Lola, the front office clerk. Ms. Foster reaches down to turn on the intercom as Mrs. Lane barges into her office with her daughter trailing behind.

Lola runs in behind the two shouting, "Mrs. Lane! You can't just walk in like this! I told you to wait in the reception area!"

Susan's hair hangs loose over her face but fails to fully conceal her bandaged nose. Ms. Foster, trying to hold her composure, takes control of the situation. "Thank you, Lola. I've got this."

Lola gives Mrs. Lane a look of disdain before turning around to leave.

"Oh!" Ms. Foster addresses Lola once again, "Please shut the door."

Lola looks at Mrs. Lane, and then questioningly at Ms. Foster, "You sure?"

"Yes, I'm sure, and thank you."

As soon as the door closes, Mrs. Lane starts in.

"Ms. Foster!" yells Mrs. Lane, "I called you last night and have not heard back from you!"

Ms. Foster remembers the "Responding to Angry Parents" Training sponsored by the school district as she takes a conscious moment to deeply inhale and slowly let out her breath fully before speaking.

"Mrs. Lane. It's 7:30 in the morning and I just barely got to the office and heard your message."

"But I called you right after school, and you weren't here! In the meantime, my daughter was assaulted on her way home! It is the school's responsibility to ensure our children arrive home safely! Look at my daughter!" She motions to her daughter, who has seated herself in one of the chairs on the other side of Ms. Foster's desk. Then accusingly says, "What were YOU doing while my daughter was being assaulted?"

Ms. Foster has already had several encounters with Mrs. Lane, who is considered a frequent flyer at the school. Most of the faculty and staff have had an 'experience' with this helicopter mother who is known to cover for her daughter's behavior.

Ms. Foster, knowing this woman's track record, sustained a calm and patient tone, "Mrs. Lane. I was not aware that you had called until I got to work this morning. After school yesterday, I was supervising a volleyball game. It was a double header and I went directly home from the gym. Please sit down and, if I can ask Susan, what happened yesterday?"

Susan put on a baby voice as she told her side of the story. "That new girl, *Erandi*, or whatever her name is ... She doesn't talk much. I don't think she even speaks English. She has a crush on my boyfriend. He told me about it. He ignores her, but yesterday after school she came up and without any warning just punched me!"

Ms. Foster knows who Susan is talking about. The 'new' girl who quietly walks the hallways, seemingly keeping to herself, is now embroiled in a mess with Susan. Ms. Foster turns to Mrs. Lane, "I can assure you, Mrs. Lane, that I will investigate. And, yes, it is my responsibility to follow up even though the encounter transpired after school and off school grounds."

Somewhat mollified by Ms. Foster's assurances, Mrs. Lane spits out, "Well! *Those* people. You know how they are! Violent. It's to be expected. She's probably part of a gang!"

Ms. Foster holds her tongue at Susan's mom's not-so-subtly veiled insinuation. Her judgment is already biased because of Susan's reputation, as this is, most certainly, not Susan's first 'incident' with another student. Trying to conceal her own internal agitation to the woman's racist tone, Ms. Foster firmly says, "I will conduct a full and impartial investigation." This cues Mrs. Lane that the discussion is over, so the irate mother promptly stands up, takes her daughter by the arm, storms out of Ms. Foster's office without a good-bye, and slams the door behind her.

Ms. Foster hangs her head as soon as Mrs. Lane and Susan are out of sight. She will have to spend the rest of her Thursday morning cleaning up after what she expects to be more drama created by the school bully. She opens up Eréndira's contact information from her desktop computer and notes that her mother's phone number and work address are at the local university. The office number she calls picks up on the second ring.

"Good Morning. This is Professor Cruz."

"Hello. This is Ms. Foster. I'm Vice Principal at your daughter's school. I am following up on an incident that transpired after school yesterday."

"Yes. Thank you for calling Ms. Foster, and for following up. We were visited by City Police late last night. The officer responded to a complaint from the woman whose daughter attacked my daughter. The officer said he would be coming to see you today. He took a statement from my daughter after listening to her side of the story. He also took pictures of her wounds."

"Her wounds?" asks Ms. Foster. Susan had made it sound as if Eréndira was the aggressor and the fight had been one-sided.

"Yes, that girl and her friends have been picking on my daughter for weeks now. My daughter is new at school and doesn't have many friends, but she has never been in a fight before. That girl attacked her from behind. She left fingernail gouges on my daughter's neck and a gap on her scalp where she pulled out her hair. It is obvious that Eréndira was attacked from behind."

"I see. Well. I am sure that officer … What is his name?"

"Officer Franklin."

"Yes! I know Officer Franklin! We've worked together over the years. I'm sure he will be in touch with me today."

Noting the time, Verónica says, "I'm sorry but I teach a class in a few minutes. Unless there's anything else for now, Ms. Foster. Otherwise, I'll wait to hear back from Officer Franklin or yourself as to what will happen next with the girl who assaulted my daughter. Thank you for calling."

With the call over, Verónica packs her laptop, eschews the elevator, and walks down the four flights of stairs to the ground floor. As she strolls through the tree-shaded campus on her way to class, she considers whether the school will conduct an impartial investigation and treat Eréndira fairly. Her daughter never had any problems in their hometown, but, now having lived in their new neighborhood for just a matter of months, this incident had drawn a police car to the front of their home. The suspicious looks from their neighbors did not reflect well upon the newest family who happened to be the only people of color in the neighborhood.

Officer Franklin, as expected, arrives at Ms. Foster's office. Together, they interview Melissa, Eréndira's friend, as well as some of Susan's friends who, at the sight of a uniformed police officer, volunteer little but do tell the truth. In the end, the statements all corroborate Eréndira's rendition of what transpired the previous day.

That Thursday night, Verónica and Victor talk quietly while lying in bed. Neither sleep. They recognized that Eréndira had been forced into a situation where she had to defend herself and that she was not responsible for this unwanted attention. They worry … *How will the investigation go for their daughter? How will they keep their daughter safe from unwarranted abuse?*

Verónica's stomach churns.

Victor is at a loss for what to do next.

Eréndira quietly fumes and stares at the ceiling wondering what will come of all this turmoil. She wishes she could have stayed in her hometown where she knew everyone—where all the kids hung out together, went for swims, and sang karaoke with the goal of singing the worst to make everyone laugh. With her friends back home, it was never about laughing at someone but *with everyone.*

She can't remember the last time she had a full belly laugh and that makes her heart hurt. She turns up the music on her iPhone, trying to drown out the anger and hurt inside.

That night, as the prior one, no one in the Cruz family sleeps.

Verónica and Victor had moved their family from the Bay Area to the Sacramento region, while Naníta, Eréndira's maternal grandmother, had relocated to the Sierra Foothills. Though Naníta still maintained ties to friends and family living in the Bay Area, her move was prompted by witnessing how, day-by-day, the hills that sloped away from Mt. Diablo and eased into bountiful orchards were increasingly overtaken by housing developments and strip malls. Naníta didn't fault the newcomers to these homes for their encroachment upon the lazy agricultural town where she grew up, raised her daughter, and had a hand in raising her daughter's two children—Eréndira, and her older brother, Ariel. She understood the San Francisco and Silicon Valley workers, tired of living in condos and apartments, were seeking a slice of land to call their own. Naníta, too, desired a small piece of land where she could sink her hands into the dirt and connect with the seasonal cycles that are often tolerated, but not appreciated, when living in the suburbs. She also wanted to, once again, have some elbow room where she could plant a garden and hear the birds sing.

By the time the Cruzes had started their own move to the Central Valley, Naníta was already settling into her single-story home on a few fenced acres. The beauty of her new location just East of Sacramento was that she could more easily maintain contact with Verónica, Victor, and Eréndira, the grandchild that she has cared for almost daily. With Ariel living away from home during his first year of college, it was a priority for Naníta, known to her friends as Elizabeth, to be close enough for weekend get-aways or, if an emergency should arise, to be there for the Cruzes.

With everything happening in Eréndira's life, she can't get to Naníta's home soon enough. A sense of relief washes over her as soon as she gets into the car.

When Victor calls up the stairs to let Eréndira know they are ready to leave and she doesn't come down, he panics, "Verónica! Where is Eréndira?"

Verónica, already at the door leading to the garage, sees their daughter sitting in the SUV's back seat. "She's already in the car waiting for us!"

"Oh! Okay! Good!"

The Cruz family catches Highway 50 and heads east toward the Sierra Mountains in the distance. The drive up is an unusually quiet one, as the emotional overwhelm of the previous day's events lingers. Eréndira leans against the window, watching the gradual transition of urban, to suburban, to rural, as they leave behind the city and climb into the foothills. She smiles when she sees the El Dorado County sign.

With each passing mile, Eréndira takes in the changing topography. The sloping hills hold groves of oak trees, interspersed with gray pines, and occasional rock outcroppings. Cows and goats graze while intermittent ponds gave refuge for a great variety of fowl. Clouds billowing above appear almost within reach. Despite her previous sleepless nights, Eréndira feels slightly rejuvenated as each approaching hill towers over the last.

After an hour, the Cruzes enter Naníta's broad driveway. Eréndira, previously slouched against the side of the door, bolts up as they arrive. The vastness of the sky and the expansive hills embrace them even before exiting the car. Eréndira's shoulders relax, her jaw unclenches, and her heart eagerly anticipates the familiar sounds and sensations that she knows will soothe her troubled mind. Having Naníta at least this close is a blessing during challenging times.

In anticipation of her family's arrival, Naníta waits in a patio chair out front, happily observing the birds and the clouds. At the sight of her family coming down the long driveway, she joyfully jumps up and claps. Victor and Verónica are first to step out of the car, and she welcomes each of them.

While Eréndira waits her turn for her big Naníta hug, she scans the landscape that anchors her in a way she hasn't felt in days. Simply being in a space that isn't where all the turmoil is happening puts her at ease. More so, being with her Naníta calms her in ways for which she has yet to find words. Finally wrapping her arms around her Naníta, Eréndira deeply inhales the comforting scent of lavender and chili colorado!

Although Naníta, or Nánde, as Verónica calls her, was aware of Wednesday's altercation, Verónica has not told her the aftermath of the investigation conducted by the police officer and vice principal, deciding instead that she would let Eréndira share the outcome, in person, with her Naníta.

"Come in. So glad to have you here!"

"Thank you for having us over," replies Verónica. "I know you're barely settled in, and here we are. Anything we can do to help you unpack?'

"Yes!" chimes in Victor. "Now that we live in suburbia, I miss the open space. Put us to work."

"No worries. I'll have plenty for you to do soon enough. I'm getting my bearings on this property as it is! Soon, I'll have a list for you." Naníta turns to Eréndira, "How is my favorite granddaughter doing?"

"Naníta," says Eréndira, "I'm your ONLY granddaughter!"

"That's true. But you're still my favorite!" Naníta pulls Eréndira closer and plants a big kiss on her forehead.

"Aye, Naníta. You're always joking and kidding."

"That's true too! Look at you! So observant!"

Naníta takes her family on a stroll of the property, pointing out some of the highlights. Behind the house, a miner's dam cuts across the path of what is now a seasonal stream. Rock outcroppings, also known as tilt-ups, jut out of the ground like monuments, while an array of cottonwoods, oaks, and gray pines in various stages of growth shade the back acre.

After enjoying a delicious brunch on the back patio, Verónica and Victor pick up pruning shears and a pole saw. They figure they can use their time productively during their visit by trimming back trees and shrubs. As the two disappear into the area of the property that has seemingly not been manicured since who-knows-when, Naníta turns to her granddaughter.

"Your mother told me what happened. I know it is not your way to fight. You've always been happy-go-lucky, but if you want to talk about it, you know I'm here."

"I know, Naníta. I know I'm not supposed to fight, but that girl, or any other, won't be bothering me anymore. I did what I had to do. Like you've taught me. Always be kind—pero no te dejes—don't let them take advantage of you."

Naníta looks at her granddaughter for a moment then responds, "Just like your namesake."

Eréndira raises an eyebrow and gives her grandmother a quizzical look. She wonders but does not say aloud, *Who is this 'namesake' that her Naníta talks about and why was she named after her?* She doesn't know of anyone else with her name.

Eréndira sits quietly facing the back property while her Naníta pours a cup of mint tea. Naníta studies her granddaughter, noting an unusual trace of grimness in her face and stiffness in her body perched on the patio chair. Steam from the freshly brewed tea ascends from the cup and returns Naníta to the task of pouring. The gentle fragrance evokes memories of how she was taught the healing powers given by the plant people.

The tea Naníta pours for Eréndira is made from transplanted cuttings that flourished in the garden of Naníta's grandmother, Mama Lupe. Each time Naníta moved to a new home, she maintained the tradition of replanting cuttings from this medicinal plant. Requiring minimal care, the mint thrives in shady areas often fed by the run-off from garden faucets. The tea, like their family, has traversed the American continent so that many in the family lineage could enjoy its medicinal properties despite having lost the memories of its origins.

Eréndira's lineage is traceable to a land thousands of miles south of the Sierra Foothills and she knows only remnants of the life of her Great-Great Grandmother who immigrated to the United States from Mexico in the early 1900s. Known as Mama Lupe by over one hundred grandchildren, this distant relative was born in the late 1800s in what is known as Acámbaro, Guanajuato. She taught her granddaughter, Elizabeth, who instructed her daughter, Verónica, who showed her daughter, Eréndira, to ask the plant permission before removing any of its leaves.

When she was a child, Naníta would watch her grandmother stroll through her garden in her well-worn huaraches. Mama Lupe would pause and regard each plant as though acknowledging the presence of an old friend. When she got to the faucet, she would bend over and talk to the mint plant, which flourished under its drippings.

Finding this odd, Elizabeth (long before she was Naníta) had asked, "Mama Lupe. ¿Por qué hablas con algo que no puede responder?" *Why do you talk to something that can't talk back?*

Mama Lupe answered in the quiet tone with which she spoke to any one of the grandchildren from the constellation of her expansive family, a family now rooted, like the mint, in a land called the United States. She explained to the young Naníta, "It is necessary to engage with the plant people who live alongside us on this earth. Unlike us, who only touch the ground when we walk and stand, they have their feet firmly burrowed in the earth. This means that they are closer to the earth than even we are."

Little Naníta looked down at her feet and considered the fact that she didn't have roots like the plants. Only the bare bottoms of her feet were in direct contact with the soil. She tried to dig her toes into the rich soil of the garden but, unlike the many plants in Mama Lupe's Garden, she was unable to penetrate any level of depth. She understood, then, that the roots of the plants provided them with greater and more intimate connection to the earth.

Yet, this did not explain why Mama Lupe would be speaking to a plant, so the young Naníta probed, "Pero, las plantas no tienen oidos. ¿Cómo te oyen?" *But plants don't have ears. How do they hear you?*

With her attention still focused on the plants, Mama Lupe offered, "They, like all living things on this earth, feel our intentions. We must maintain good relationships with all living beings, including plants. Chiquita, you must remember that plants give us medicine to heal our bodies, and, for that, we must respect them and show our appreciation."

Naníta still did not fully comprehend the meaning behind Mama Lupe's answers. Nonetheless, she carefully watched the process by which her elderly grandmother selected leaves from the mint plant. She noticed that Mama Lupe examined the various stems and, after a lengthy inspection, cut only one or two leaves from each. This left many leaves untouched. In this way, Naníta learned from Mama Lupe's actions as well as her words. What stayed with Naníta was that balance is maintained with Mother Earth by not taking for granted the healing properties of the plant and by demonstrating conscious appreciation of her gifts.

Naníta remembered Mama Lupe's ever-present jar of mint leaves soaking in olive oil. There were occasions when she would see her grandmother going about her chores with leaves affixed to each side of her forehead. Mystified by the sight, she pondered whether her Mama Lupe was somehow communicating telepathically with the plant people.

For this reason, Naníta decided to ask, for certain, what was the purpose of sticking mint leaves on one's temples, "Mamá Lupe, ¿Por qué tienes esas hojas en la sien?" *Grandmother, why do you have those leaves stuck there?*

"Ay mi hija, siempre con las preguntas!" Mama Lupe went on to explain to her ever-inquisitive granddaughter that this practice drew out the negative energy. As Naníta grew older, she concluded that this was her Mama Lupe's home remedy for beating a headache!

Just as Naníta learned from Mama Lupe, she now offered Eréndira these teachings about the medicinal qualities of plants and the relationship among humans and all living things. In so doing, Naníta sought to draw out the negative energy inside the young woman who now sat at her patio table.

The two slowly sip the softly scented tea. The warmth of the cups against the palms of their hands provides its own source of comfort against the chill of the morning. Naníta thinks to herself, *No wonder this tea is called hierbabuena—good herb.*

Throughout her childhood, Eréndira had regularly sought the sanctuary of Naníta's presence, so with no further prompting, she gave Naníta a brief recount of the events leading up to the police officer's visit to their home. With circumstances so out of character for her granddaughter, Naníta was deeply concerned about the events of the previous days and their effect on Eréndira's well-being.

"So that's how it went down, Eréndira?"

"Yeah. Pretty much." Eréndira, tight lips and face hard, would not offer more. Naníta sensed that it was best not to push and that the rest of the story would come on Eréndira's own time and when she was ready.

"Hey!" Naníta says, seeking to change the energy. "Let's go down to the back of the property. I want to show you something. We can take our tea with us."

Eréndira sluggishly rises, but her reluctance to indulge her Naníta wanes as they walk down the path away from the house and past smatterings of oak trees, from young seedlings to mature adults vibrantly producing acorns. Many, unable to deeply extend their roots, are bent and crooked, while others bow with age. Eréndira's eyes fall upon rock outcroppings interspersed among the trees. The small mineral monuments grow out of the earth like the peaks of mountain ridges. Ancient and newly sprouted cottonwoods follow the stream that cuts diagonally across a flattened patch of lawn that Naníta has named, "The Shire" after the mythical lands depicted in *The Lord of the Rings.*

A breeze catches Eréndira's long, dark hair and lifts it as though it is a wing. The sun, yet to reach full height in the clear sky, softly touches down on her face. The angle of the warm light casts long shadows from her eyelashes across prominent cheekbones. She momentarily pauses and tilts her head, as though listening to music carried by the breeze.

Naníta continues down the path to the area past the stream where boulders of various sizes and shapes dominate the perimeter of The Shire. She waits for Eréndira to catch up and then leads her to an area below a bent oak tree.

Once Eréndira reaches her, Naníta pulls her close. They stand over a conglomerate rock peeking up at them, barely visible above the ground. "Right now, your mother and father are clearing debris and trimming overgrown trees. The few weeks that I've been here, I've been raking an overabundance of leaves and fallen branches that have accumulated for many, many years. I rake the leaves onto a tarp and drag them down to a pile so they can decompose on their own. In the meantime, the ground around these rock monuments begins to reveal much." Naníta points at their feet, "Take a look."

Eréndira looks down but doesn't know what she is supposed to be looking for. All she sees is a mishmash of rocks, thrown out in an ancient volcanic eruption and now stuck together like a puzzle. Eréndira frowns. She doesn't know what her Naníta is trying to show her. While she recognizes that this is one of the long-winded ways her Naníta explains life to her, she would rather, in this case, be told what it is she's supposed to be seeing. Looking away, she shrugs her shoulders and waits. This is her cue for Naníta to relent and tell her what she's supposed to be seeing.

Instead, her patient Naníta instructs, "Look closely. Where do you see patterns? Look at it as though you were looking at a picture."

Eréndira sighs, then draws closer to the bedrock. She catches the outline of a chiseled surface, focusing her eyes on the mangled mass. It is apparent that carefully placed incisions have produced patterns which, in turn, have created shapes. After tracing the incisions with her finger, she steps back to study the totality of what she is seeing. Her eyes widen.

"Holy shit!" she exclaims, immediately slapping her hand over her mouth. She knows her Naníta doesn't like foul language.

Naníta smiles and comments. "You see it. Don't you?"

"But Naníta! How did you see this?"

"How could I not see it?"

Eréndira kneels on one knee to get a closer look. She scans the exposed portion of the rock and discerns the outline of two faces chiseled onto the surface. With the outer edges of the entire tableau submerged in soil, the carved-out images appear to emerge from the ground.

Naníta continues, "With each tarp load of leaves that I haul off to the compost pile, it looks like the boulders, buried under layers of accumulated leaves and branches, are growing. The layers of decomposed debris buried what is here. Now that I am cleaning this up, the ground recedes, and the boulders are revealed. What is being exposed speaks to us about life before."

Eréndira tucks a strand of long hair behind her ear and looks up at her Naníta. "Before what?"

Naníta has never been one to give a straight answer, believing that developing her granddaughter's critical thinking requires piquing her curiosity. Just as she, as a child, probed Mama Lupe with numerous questions, her own inquisitiveness expanded her understanding and appreciation of the world.

Without responding, Naníta scans the property. Turning to her left, she sees beyond the back fence to the property boundary that marks the furthest end of her two acres. Beyond the fence is a ravine in which the seasonal stream cuts through the property and disappears around a bend. Eréndira follows Naníta's gaze, which is focused on the direction of the stream, then turns her attention toward her right.

Eréndira slowly gets up from her knees and climbs a narrow path to the dam. Constructed with flat rocks expertly fitted one on top of the other, the dam's height tops at least ten feet, but its size appears excessive for the tiny stream that emerges below it. The width of the dam, whose ends disappear into the side of the adjoining hills, speaks to a structure intended to hold back a force of water which was, at one time, much greater. It doesn't take an engineer to conclude that the current stream was once a larger river. Naníta and Eréndira, exchanging no words, conclude that the ground they stand on was dramatically different prior to the existence of the dam. Eréndira walks back down the path to join her Naníta's side.

"Naníta, you're uncovering the before … the before this dam was built?" She looks directly into her Naníta's eyes to bring her attention back to their exchange and to the rock tableau at their feet.

Not to be rushed by her impatient grandchild, Naníta responds, "Tell me what you see."

Refocusing on the chiseled image, Eréndira says, "There's what looks like a Native American person. Just his head. It's just his profile … looks like some kind of feathers on top of his head. He has some sort of decoration on his ears."

"Go on." Naníta encourages Eréndira. "What else do you see?"

Eréndira again kneels at the tableau to get a closer look. "There's another person, but not Native American. He has a black beard. He has on one of those hats that mom uses when she wears her regalia at graduation ceremonies. This one has what looks like a feather attached to the cap. A white feather."

"Yes. And how are they positioned?"

"What do you mean positioned?"

"How are they carved in the rock in relation to one another?"

Eréndira reexamines the total visible space, measuring about two feet in width and one and a half feet in height. "The Native American is up above on the right side of the image. He is looking downward toward the other face, the person with the beard, the one below… faces away from the Native American."

"Good! So, if you were to interpret this as a story, what might this scene be telling you?"

Eréndira stands up and surveys the two-acre property that her Naníta recently purchased. She scans her surroundings and how the home and fenced-in property are nestled in a little valley, surrounded by towering hills. From any of the hills on the western side of the property, there would be a clear view of the Coastal Range and the Sacramento Valley stretching in between. Eréndira turns to her Naníta, "I see you from above, but you don't see me because I'm on top and you're below."

"Yes!" Naníta, radiant with her granddaughter's interpretation, adds, "And, now that I see you, I can tell others."

Eréndira considers this interpretation of a tableau carved onto the face of a rock. "That's some deep stuff! This sighting by one of the other marks a moment so important that they made a picture of it."

"Yes!" exclaimed Naníta, "Because they didn't have cameras back then, they documented it on the rocks."

"Wow! So, it must have been a big deal when it happened! Makes me wonder what was going on."

Naníta places an arm around Eréndira as they both look down at the carved image. "Raises lots of questions…"

Eréndira and Naníta take their time making their way to the house from the back of the property. The snaking trail ascends, just enough, to compel Naníta to make an occasional stop to catch her breath. Halfway up the trail, the two take a short break. Eréndira turns around and takes in a sweeping view. "What is this place, Naníta?"

Naníta turns around at the sound of Eréndira's voice and, together, they take in the hills rising dramatically on either side of The Shire. It is evident that a raging river once carved out this valley and flowed into a canyon that extended beyond Naníta's property line. In this natural scene, the perpetual residents made themselves known.

A variety of birds fly up and down the valley, their paths crisscrossing over the stream. Eréndira and Naníta watch the birds dodge from one tree to the next as they jockey for the best positions on the branches of oaks and cottonwoods. The incessant rhythm of acorn woodpeckers pounding on thick trunks echoes in the corridor. White-breasted nuthatches scurry up and down branches while a breeze carries the cooing of mourning doves across the canyon. A small flock of flickers perch above Eréndira and Naníta; their orange tail feathers catch the sun's light as they launch toward another tree to escape an aggressive scrub jay. White-crowned sparrows and towhees fly circular in the air, snagging small insects on the wing. Several robins dig through a thin layer of leaves—their rustling mixing with the mockingbird's melody. Lizards scurry over rocks along the path while the croaking of frogs adds to the cacophony of nature's symphony.

Naníta and her granddaughter stand side-by-side in awe of the diverse range of birds. They have been warned about the abundance of rattlesnakes but also know that many creatures who crawl on the ground, including snakes, are harmless.

Finally, Naníta speaks. "For generations, these regions have been home to many of our relations. Also, it is where the people of the Original Nation left their history."

"History?"

"Yes. Of course. There are many ways in which people transmit their history from one generation to the next. What did you learn from your classes about the history of this area?"

Eréndira's face is expressionless. Her big brown eyes turn to the sky searching for an appropriate response. Finally, she says, "I don't know." But just as quickly as she admits to not knowing anything, she abruptly pulls her ever-present cell phone from her back pocket and starts clicking away.

Naníta assumes that Eréndira impulsively retrieved the phone because she had just received a text, so she leaves her granddaughter to attend to it. Despite her annoyance with the sudden intrusion to their moments together, she has become accustomed to the outside world barging in on her time with her granddaughter. Naníta tries to be tolerant of the short attention spans of even people her own age. She had begun to notice that conversations with new acquaintances were often devoid of focus, lacking meaningful and insightful exchanges. It is as though the art of conversation had become a tradition of the past.

Having been raised by elders, Naníta cherished personal connections and storytelling. She tried to quell her contempt for the ever-present dominance of electronic devices that seemed to pedal superficial values which, in turn, breeds shallowness. But in moments like this, she feels like a relic from the past. While she was not as old as the engravings in her backyard, she yearns for the majesty embodied by the tableau because it was purposeful in its communication. Despite its age, it still reached out from under the layers of debris. In its creation, it was meant to capture and tell future generations of a historical event in a medium that transcended time.

Naníta, concluding that her granddaughter's attention had been hijacked by the outside world, continues up the path, alone.

Just as she reaches the back patio of her home, Eréndira calls out, "Naníta! Wait a second! I found some stuff!" Eréndira's quick strides put her next to Naníta's side in a few seconds. She held her phone out in front of her and began reading, "The county website says this was 'gold country.'"

"Yes. True!" Naníta confirmed, and then silently forgave herself for judging her granddaughter so quickly, "And when would this area have been given that name?"

Eréndira's answer is more of a question than a statement. "1849?"

Naníta gives her granddaughter a pleased look. "Good! I'm impressed! And you act like you don't learn anything in school?"

Eréndira says, "I didn't learn that from school. At least I don't remember learning it. I figured that out from Sunday football."

Naníta's face contorts with puzzlement. "What does Sunday football have to do with the discovery of gold in this area?"

"Aye, Naníta!" exclaimed Eréndira. "You've heard of the San Francisco 49ers! You know … their mascot is this little squat guy with a wide hat, bushy beard, and suspenders. He's a gold miner." Eréndira's face beams a smile at her resourcefulness.

Naníta, sitting down at the patio table, rolls her eyes and says, "We both have a lot to learn. Don't we?"

They are suddenly interrupted by a loud skirmish between birds that can be heard from a long distance. From a tangle of oak branches, a red-tailed hawk suddenly appears, giving chase to a quail at top speed. A group of magpies sitting on the property fence watch the chase and appear to make wagers on who'll win the battle. High above it all, vultures with expansive wing spans dip with the drifts of high breezes and cast wide circles. They first appear as innocuous kites, but these same vultures will be the first to arrive and enjoy the carnage left by the battle between the hawk and the quail.

Naníta sighs at nature's daily interactions. What she and Eréndira are witnessing portrays bird behaviors played out, time and again. The predator hawk disrupts the home of another bird family, seeking to pillage. The protector quail puts up a fight to defend its family, but when the enemy appears to be too powerful, the quail entices the intruder to give chase and leads the danger away from the nest.

Eréndira draws instruction from the scene played out before her and applies it to the conversation at hand. She has an epiphany. "Naníta! I just figured it out. The images on the rock. It's an Indian looking down at a gold miner!"

Naníta silently considers Eréndira's conclusion for a few moments. "You think the person depicted on the engraving is a miner?"

"Sure! Let's have a look!"

"I'm getting tired, Eréndira. I don't feel like walking back down there again."

"No worries. I took a picture of it. See?" Eréndira pulls up her phone, opens the Gallery app, and taps on the picture she took.

"Ay, Eréndira. You're so quick with that apparatus of yours. I didn't even see you take the picture! You'd be a deadly gunslinger!"

"A what?"

Naníta sighed. She didn't want to explain and lose the thread of their conversation. "Never mind."

With heads perched over Eréndira's phone, they examine the image captured by her camera. To Naníta's surprise, Eréndira places her thumb and forefinger in the center of the screen, and then, with an opposing motion of her fingers, the picture magically enlarges. Eréndira shifts the picture again to focus on the tableau's lower image.

"You know, Naníta. I don't think that's Sourdough Sam."

"Sourdough Sam? Who's Sourdough Sam?"

"The 49ers Mascot! That guy with the bushy beard and hat."

"Ah! I don't think the people who lived here would be memorializing Sourdough Sam, but there is a story to tell here. In the meantime, Eréndira, do you want to tell me what happened at school? I didn't get to hear the whole story. Kind of like that hawk and the quail. I don't know how the story turned out!"

Eréndira, still in the patio chair opposite her grandmother, tilts her head away from the image and puts away her phone. "Yeah, I know mom told you about what happened with me and that girl. Once the vice principal and the cops got involved, more stuff happened."

"Yes … and it's what happened after they got involved that I don't know."

"Well …" Eréndira flicks her hair back, folds her legs, and settles back into her chair. "So. This is how it went down—"

Eréndira begins the account of what transpired with a deep breath...

"Fortunately, that asshole's friends made it right. They ended up telling the cop and the vice principal the real story. They backed me up, not her."

Naníta winces.

Eréndira immediately reads her body language and corrects herself. "Sorry Naníta. I know you told me not to say bad words. I'll start over."

Naníta silently nods, accepting Eréndira's apology.

"Okay. So, this is what happened. Remember I told you about the girl who had been hassling me?"

"Yes, her name is Susan?"

"Yeah. Her."

"What made her so angry with you? You've never had problems with any of your classmates before."

"It all started because of her boyfriend. Everyone knows he's a player, but she doesn't want to acknowledge that fact. Well, he tried to hit on me at a party, but I made it clear I wasn't interested. When I ignored him and told him to leave me alone, it pissed him off—" Eréndira stops abruptly. "Oops! There I go again! Sorry. No bad words."

Naníta replied understandably, "That's okay, 'Mija … you're trying. Keep on telling me what happened."

Eréndira continued, "So, to get back at me, because he's used to getting his way with girls, he told Susan that I had tried to make the moves on him and that's what set her off."

Naníta considers what Eréndira shared and interjects, "Interesting that a young woman would be wanting to fight over a boy. She must be insecure."

Eréndira took a moment to consider Naníta's comment. "Well, yeah. I guess she doesn't have much going for her."

"I suppose not. Perhaps she is not raised to have dignity."

"What do you mean?" asks Eréndira.

Naníta picks up an apple from the fruit bowl on the patio table and hands it to Eréndira. She then instructs her, "Stand the apple up on the table." Eréndira easily stands the apple on its bottom end, so it sits perfectly positioned on the table. Then, Naníta picks up a knife and with a swift and decisive motion cuts the apple down the middle. She hands the two halves to Eréndira and instructs, "¡Otra vez! *Again!* But this time, stand them up by themselves."

Eréndira gives Naníta a puzzled look and attempts to stand up the two halves on their own. They fall over. After several attempts, she stops and concedes, "It's not going to happen. They don't stand alone."

Naníta then instructs, "Now, try them together."

Eréndira places the two halves together and, in doing so, the apple stands. "Okay. So, this means what? Two parts make a whole?"

Naníta nods. "Yes, they are both equal. Notice. Your last name is that of your mother's … and it is the same as mine. Your brother has your father's last name which is the same as your father's father."

"Yeah. I always wondered about that."

"It's a tradition from our culture. The matrilineal side is just as important as the patrilineal. One is not less than the other. We depend on and support one another. Though we are equal, one could not stand without the other.

Eréndira leans back, folds her hands across her stomach, and stretches her legs out in front of her. "I get it. There should be mutual respect."

Naníta nods, takes a bite of one of the apple halves, offers the other half to Eréndira and says, "Continue with what happened."

"Her friends got called in, one-by-one, by the vice principal, Ms. Foster. My friend Melissa got called in, too. Ms. Foster was trying to figure out what happened. Melissa told them what she saw so I got backed right away. I wasn't sure if Susan's friends would tell the truth, but once they saw the cop standing next to Ms. Foster, they broke and told it like it really happened. Susan had been running her mouth all over the place, but her friends stopped repeating her lies."

Naníta stopped Eréndira with a question. "Why were the police involved?"

"Well, Susan's mother was going to press charges. I broke her nose after she attacked me from behind. They wanted to pin the whole thing on me. Plus, since it happened on the way home, the school would have had to suspend me."

"A lot at stake, Eréndira."

A broad silence interrupts Eréndira's retelling. Naníta turns to her granddaughter, who has not only stopped talking but is now looking down at the sliced apple in her hands. Her eyes well up. Her breathing grows deeper and quicker to hold back what is inevitable …. A trail of tears streams down her cheeks, and she begins to uncontrollably sob.

Naníta rushes to Eréndira's side and holds her granddaughter close. "Let it go, 'Mija. Tears are healing. It's our spirit's way of resetting, putting the pain behind us, so we can move forward. Let it flow."

After several minutes of pure release, calm returns to Eréndira's body. Naníta momentarily disappears as she steps back inside and returns to the patio, handing her granddaughter a tissue. Eréndira blows her nose and wipes the traces of tears from her face.

Once Eréndira catches her breath, she proceeds, "So, the vice principal figured out what happened. Susan not only started the whole thing, but she also heard about how every time I walk by her in the hallways, Susan started saying stuff. Even when we were in class—we have geometry together and when the teacher's not looking, she and her friends threw stuff at me."

"What did the teacher say?"

"Teachers don't say nada. They hear commotion, but they don't do anything!"

"Do you tell the teachers what they're doing?" asked Naníta.

Eréndira scoffed. "I can't be tattling. This isn't kindergarten, Naníta. When we get to junior high, we have to handle our own business."

"Lo entiendo." *I understand.* Naníta paused for a heartbeat or two. "What happened after the vice principal figured out that Susan was the instigator?"

Eréndira, now emotionally relieved, regained momentum, "So the rest just rolled out from there. Ms. Foster told Susan's mother that her daughter wasn't telling the truth and how her daughter had been harassing me. They even called me into the office. I had to show them the scratch mark on my neck and the spot on my scalp where my hair had been pulled out."

Eréndira paused, turned her head away from Naníta, and parted her thick brown hair, revealing a bald spot and a fresh scab for Naníta to see for herself. This time, Naníta's eyes sting with tears, and her jaw tightens at the sight of the wounds left on her precious granddaughter.

Eréndira continued, "So, the tables got turned on Susan. Now, *she* is facing charges if *we* want to file. Plus, suspension."

"Did they drop the accusations against you?"

"Yea. But she still got suspended for five days for starting the fight. Also, because she was saying racist stuff, it made her look bad. When she comes back from suspension, the vice principal wants to do some sort of meeting between us. I'm not so sure I want to sit down with Susan though. I've got nothing to say that I didn't already say with my fist."

Naníta lets the last sentence hang in the air for a while. She feels her granddaughter's anger but knows her well enough to recognize that it masks her pain. The transition to this new community has not been easy. Adults at this school seem not to notice or, worse, not care about the hostility that permeates the school culture. Eréndira has been forced into responding to violence with violence. Naníta fears that exposure to such chronic toxicity might change the nature of this generally kind-natured child.

A slight breeze breaks the tension. The words that conveyed the story and recreated the violent incident are carried away by the wind and given back to Mother Earth, where she will consume, cleanse, and return the air with goodness. Balance is restored.

Retelling the incident to Naníta is good for Eréndira's spirit. As she sips her tea, Eréndira considers how karate training provided her strength and confidence, but she wonders, does she have the skills to deescalate another attack or avoid confrontations? Her sensei trained her to use physical force as a last resort, but in a hostile culture, she fears she may have to use her fists once again.

As though reading her mind, Naníta says, "Tell me, Eréndira. I know you did the best you could under the circumstances. You've never had to use your training to defend yourself before. It's one thing to repeat defensive moves, over and over, in the Dojo. It's another to have to respond to an attack. It's in those moments that we really don't know what we would do, but in this situation, you broke her nose."

Eréndira looks down at her hands where her slender fingers and perfectly manicured nails that artistically interpret Chopin's piano pieces are picking apart the soiled tissue. "I know Naníta. I wished it hadn't happened, but she pushed me to it. I snapped."

"I understand. It was self-defense. She grabbed your hair from behind. That was cowardly on her part."

"Yeah. It was that, but I could have taken her down without breaking her nose."

"Dime, entonces, *tell me* .... What did it? What made you snap?"

"It was what she was saying. She was making fun of my name. Then, she was saying stuff like 'have your mom come and be my mom's maid.' That was it."

"¡Cabrona! She insulted us."

"Naníta! You're always telling me not to cuss!"

"Ah yes! I'm sorry, 'Mi hija! You're right. It slipped! Even I must be reminded sometimes! You know, I was with an Elder from the Cochiti Tribe a couple months ago. He was saying how our breath comes from our spirit. That is how we know we are alive. When we put words onto the breath, it reveals our spirit. What we say tells others who we are, spiritually. That is why we must consider what we put out into the world. Our words can carry goodness or they can pierce another human being like a bullet."

Eréndira did not always know how to respond to her Naníta's philosophical observations so she doesn't say anything for a while before picking up where she left off. "Okay. I get it. I was letting her get to my spirit. It got so pent up, it made me sick. It's like her ugliness contaminated me."

"That's right, 'Mija. Bad energy can be toxic, and it is everywhere, but we mustn't let it infect us like it just did me."

The two, grandmother and granddaughter, notice a lone turkey on a neighboring hill trying to rejoin the rest of the flock that has already flown onto her property. The turkey has forgotten how to use its wings and paces anxiously back and forth on the other side of the six-foot deer fence.

"You see that turkey on the other side of the fence, Eréndira?"

"Yeah, what about it?"

"It keeps getting left behind by the rest of the flock. It tends to trail behind the others, and when it does catch up, the other turkeys not only ignore it but often peck it."

Suddenly, from the top of the hill, the neighbors' dogs appeared. They spot the lone turkey and race down the hill to give chase, barking aggressively. The turkey starts to run and then suddenly remembers it has wings. With furious flapping, the turkey escapes the dogs, clears the fence, and lands safely on Naníta's property where it rejoins the rest of the flock.

"Wow!" exclaimed Eréndira, "That turkey can fly when it wants to!"

Abrupt squawking draws their attention back to the turkeys where several from the flock turn on the one that just joined them. Unprovoked, the turkeys peck at their fellow creature and chase her away.

Naníta completes her thought, "You have a right to protect yourself and to belong, but if people treat you disrespectfully and don't value you, it is their deficiency. The greatest crime in this world is cruelty. Kindness has guided our culture for years, but not all of humanity values this as we do. This understanding has defined our ongoing struggle to survive. Don't forget that."

Eréndira, with her eyes still on the turkeys, nods, "Looks like that turkey needs to find a nicer flock."

Naníta smiles at her granddaughter, pleased that she is learning lessons from the cues around her. "I know you're going back to more turmoil. After your mother told me what had happened, I was very worried for you. What concerned me most was that after the incident, when you got home, you told your mother that you hate your name."

Eréndira turns away from Naníta, knowing that her grandmother played a big role in naming her. She tries to handle her explanation with diplomacy. "Yeah. I said it. It wasn't one of my finest moments, you know, but that girl, Susan, cuts up on my name. No one has a name like it. The teachers can't pronounce it, so they avoid even saying my name in class. They can't be bothered with learning how to say a name that doesn't sound like everyone else's."

Naníta takes a moment to consider her granddaughter's experience. A bullock's oriole perches in the trees above. Though shy, its rattling call compels them both to look up and spy its brilliant yellow orange feathers peeking through the green leaves. Naníta regards the range of beauty in her surroundings before offering, "It can be hard living amongst people who have been raised on fear and conformity. They don't get out much, I suppose, so they see you as unusual. Remember, back home in the Bay Area? There are many young women who possess your beauty."

"Yeah, but even there my name was not like others …. like a Maria, Sofia, Erika, Isabel."

"No. You're right. Your name is significant. It's a tribal name."

"What?"

"The name is from our Purépecha Tribe. The name, Eréndira, comes from a Princess of our Tribe. She, too, like that quail we saw earlier and like what you had to do—she had to fight, and ultimately, she had to flee, but she did so with purpose."

Eréndira, piqued by this new information turns to her Naníta, "Like that turkey! She had bullies coming after her?"

"I suppose you can say that. You were named after her. Because she was so significant, it's important that you know her story."

Eréndira scoffs, "I already have her name. Isn't that enough?"

"In some ways, yes … but in telling her story, the Princess does not experience the third death."

"You're talking spooky stuff now, Naníta."

"Not spooky at all. The first death is when the life force leaves your body." Naníta motions with her hand over her heart and extends her palm up to the sky. "The second death is when your body is given back to the earth." Naníta motions to the ground before finishing her explanation, "and the final death is when we stop telling stories about the person. That is when they are gone from the memory of those who walk the earth."

Eréndira sits quietly considering Naníta's explanation of the three deaths when Victor and Verónica appear from the trail. After a full afternoon of yard work in The Shire, their shoulders sag and their steps drag.

Verónica stops halfway up the trail, looks up toward the patio, and shouts, "Nánde, you have anything cold to drink?"

Before replying, Naníta turns to Eréndira and says, "The story of the Princess will have to wait. I need to attend to your mother and father. For now, you have more to consider. You are in the prolonged aftermath of the battle taken on by the Princess."

Eréndira's eyebrows take on a quick arc. Naníta steps into the house to retrieve a pitcher of lemonade. Verónica arrives on the patio in time to catch Eréndira's quizzical face.

"What's going on?" she asks.

"Naníta started telling me about the Princess."

"What princess?"

"Princess Eréndira."

Verónica and Victor give each other a knowing look before Verónica says, "Yes. It is time you learned about the young woman from our tribe for whom you were named. First, let me show you something we found out on the property!"

Verónica opens her clenched fist to reveal a flattened shale rock. Naníta, who has returned holding the pitcher of lemonade, brings her gaze to her daughter's hand. The family of four gaze down at the rock embedded with the fossil of a shell.

Eréndira, eyes wide open, exclaims, "Wow! I wonder how that got here?"

In the Year 1503

The Purépecha kingdom consisted of three geographically diverse regions. The northern region included a sub-humid zone that fronted Chapala and Cuitzeo lakes. The central region, a moister band of cool forestlands, housed hundreds of pines and lakes abundant with fish. The hottest region was in the southern Rio Balsas area, separated from the Pacific Ocean by the Sierra Madre del Sur.

The kingdom's capital city, Tzintzuntzan, *Land of the Hummingbirds*, was a colorful vibrant urban center like the birds that made it home. Located in the central region, on the south shore of the northern arm of Lake Pátzcuaro, Tzintzuntzan was flanked by mountains to the east and the west. A robust population of 40,000 people inhabited the capital of a kingdom of 1.3 million people. It was here, in this thriving city, that Sesasi gave birth to Princess Eréndira in the year 1503.

Sesasi cuddled her newborn daughter and considered the many blessings surrounding the birth of her child. As members of the royal household, a cast of women specializing in a wide range of skills and ancient wisdom ensured that Sesasi and the child were comfortable and nurtured. Several women attended to the mother and newborn by providing fresh clothing, nourishing food, and clean bedding, while herbal specialists ensured that Sesasi drank teas known to enhance milk production. Most importantly, the circle of women bestowed only kind words and blessings to ensure that the young mother and her newborn were embraced with peace and harmony.

Sesasi was overwhelmingly grateful for the women's attention because the final months of the pregnancy were particularly challenging. The child's determination to break free of the womb compelled Sesasi to spend the last months of the pregnancy in her bed, dependent on the care of others. Enabled by their kindness and constant prayers to the Goddess, Sesasi carried her baby almost to the expected season. Though the child arrived early, Sesasi's prayers were answered. Her daughter was born healthy. For this reason, as she gently rocked the newborn, she silently gave thanks to Cuerauáperi, the Goddess who gives birth and is mother of all life forces, humans, animals, and plants.

Holding the strong-willed child against her chest, Sesasi wondered as to the nature of this child whose fortitude pressed her to enter the world with such determination. She gently wiped clean the afterbirth from the infant's body and, with a smile on her face, offered her a welcome greeting to the world, "Terútseme sani ixu, my child. What urged you to enter the world so early?"

The newborn coughed as though clearing her air passage to respond to her mother. At this moment, Sesasi said softly, "Jirestani … yes, *breathe!* Cuerauáperi has blessed us with your arrival. There is no rush to greet tomorrow. Today, my daughter, we cherish these moments in which we look upon one another."

The newborn, her eyes still adjusting to the light of the world, looked directly into Sesasi's eyes and rewarded her mother with an all-knowing smile for enduring a difficult pregnancy.

"Ah!" exclaimed Sesasi. "Look at that beautiful smile!" She held the newborn closer to whisper in her ear, "I shall call you, Eréndira. *She Who Smiles.*"

Sesasi reflected on the circumstances into which her daughter was born and her relationship with the child's father, Timas. Though Sesasi was not Timas' temba or wife, she held high status within the household because he was a Lord, and she had his enduring favor. As she admired the newborn who now suckled at her breast, she considered how her first encounter with Timas sparked the events leading to her present elevated status.

Sesasi's name means "pretty," and it was her physical beauty that initially captivated Timas when he laid eyes on her. Over time, his spell-bound attraction evolved as he fell in love with her and eventually brought her into the royal household. As the adopted brother of Zuangua, the Cazonci, the Ruler of the Purepecha Nation, Timas was one of the many consuls to the Cazonci and served as Captain of War. Thus, Sesasi and their newborn daughter enjoyed the privileges of the royal family. In addition to the benefits bestowed by their status, Sesasi's own lineage provided her child with a direct connection to a respected and valued warrior caste from the border town of Acámbaro.

Timas, as consul and Captain of War, was entrusted by Zuangua in the instruction and development of the Cazonci's four sons whose training considered that, one day, they could be called upon to lead the kingdom. The young men were provided for by the abundant tributes collected from the kingdom's four regional quadrants, but they were, nonetheless, expected to not just passively accept entitled privileges that came with their status. Instead, they were expected to recognize and appreciate the toil and sacrifices of those who maintained the kingdom by learning, directly, from them.

To this end, the royal sons, Tangoxóan, Tirimarasco, Azinche, and Anini traveled with their Uncle Timas to the furthest regions of the 45,000-square-mile kingdom where they worked with, engaged, and observed the various skills possessed by the kingdom's people. In their travels, they then developed their capacity as hunters, warriors, providers, and, ultimately, leaders who understood the sacred value of the earthly gifts provided by Cuerauáperi.

During one of the expeditions, Timas, traveling with his four nephews, had followed the Chignahuapan River to the town of Acámbaro. Strategically situated on the border facing their tenacious enemies, the Mexica, Acámbaro's warriors protected the interior of the kingdom. Zuangua recognized that maintaining strong relations with the people of Acámbaro was vital to the continuance of the empire, which is why Timas and the four brothers were charged with regularly visiting all the border towns and paying respect on behalf of the Cazonci.

Purépecha warriors had a reputation for being ferocious. This was due not only to their courage in battle but also because they were the only tribe in the entire region with knowledge of metallurgy. While other tribes on the continent made their tools and weapons from flint and obsidian, the Purépecha warrior's distinctive weapons were made of gold, silver, and copper. One of their weapons, the macana, was a sword consisting of multiple knives protruding from both sides which made for deadly encounters on the battlefield. The use of metal weapons elevated the Purépecha warriors' reputation as being particularly formidable in battle. Their enemies' weapons of wood and rock were no match in hand-to-hand combat.

Beyond access to deadly metal weapons, the Purépecha maintained and sustained the loyalty of their allies. Subsequently, the skilled warriors and archers from the borderland territories were rewarded for their military prowess by not being taxed or having to pay tribute. Their contribution to the Kingdom consisted of protecting the eastern perimeter of the kingdom abutting the Mexica kingdom. Zuangua wisely strengthened this relationship. His appreciation was expressed in gifts of turquoise, parrot feathers, beans, amaranth, and maize, which Timas and his sons delivered to the citizens of Acámbaro and to the other border towns.

It was during one of the tours of the border communities that Timas had a chance encounter with Sesasi on the bank of the Chignahuapan River. The moment which she and Timas first laid eyes on one another was vibrantly emblazoned in her mind. Recalling the specifics of what transpired just prior to meeting made Sesasi quietly giggle to herself as she cradled her newborn, Eréndira. The smile on her newly born daughter's face had brought back the memory of this fortuitous encounter, which she recounted to her in the calm after the child's entrance into the world.

Acámbaro, Sesasi's home of birth, is at an elevation of 6,400 feet and provides prime viewing of the surrounding territory. For those not accustomed to the elevation, the thinner air takes time for one's lungs to adjust. Timas, climbing the hills with the four brothers on their way toward this border town, became winded and faint as they followed the trail along the Chignahuapan River. When he doubled over gasping for oxygen, the younger brothers started to tease him. As the elder charged with providing instruction of the Cazonci's male lineage, Timas was expected to set an example for the young princes. That day, as he struggled to fill his lungs with air, was not one of his best.

Of the four brothers, Timas saw promise in the character of the oldest brother, Tzintzicha Tangoxóan, whose name means 'one who erects many fortresses and is courageous in battle.' While Tangoxóan had demonstrated courage and sturdiness, he was also known for his humility and gentle soul. For this reason, it was predicted that Tangoxóan may, one day, replace his father as Cazonci. Not being a man quick to anger or to engage in silliness, he did not join the younger brothers in teasing the elder. Instead, he quietly rested on the riverbank and passively observed the unfolding interaction between his siblings and his Uncle Timas.

With one knee on the edge of the Chignahuapan River, Timas cupped water from the river into his palm and took slow sips while ignoring relentless ribbing from the youngest, Anini. Timas closed his eyes and inhaled several deep breaths to refill his lungs with much needed oxygen while the two middle brothers jumped into the river and waded, waist deep, in the shallowest portions of the moving water. The brothers splashed each other while daring one another to swim the expanse of the river to the opposite shore.

Tirimarasco, the second oldest, addressed Anini, "Little brother, show us how fearless you are! I dare you to swim across!"

Anini, only in his mid-teens, looked at the wide river span and retorted, "After you, big brother! I will follow you!"

Tirimarasco grinned. "Ah, you are afraid!"

"No! Not afraid! I am cautious!" Anini ended his response with a splash that hit Tirimarasco's face with full force. This set off an exchange of splashing that engulfed them both in the chilly river water.

Still, the four brothers remained close to the shore on this unusually warm day because they knew, too well, that the undercurrents running beneath the deceptively calm surface could easily sweep away even the strongest swimmers. Over the years, many bodies had been pulled out of various rivers throughout the kingdom; bodies of those who underestimated the strength of unseen currents. Knowing the perils of the river, the brothers, even during their horseplay, dared not venture further into its deeper and darker reaches, despite their escalating dares.

Anini turned his attention to his uncle, who remained kneeling at the river's edge quenching his thirst and catching his breath. "Uncle Timas! If you keep drinking the water, where will the fish swim?"

Timas smiled at the youngest brother's ribbing and continued to drink. The other brothers laughed which only encouraged Anini, known for his humorous capers, to continue. "Uncle Timas! Careful! The river is draining!" Anini stepped out of the river, laid down on the bank and began flapping his arms and legs while shouting, "Oh No! Oh No! Uncle Timas! I am without water to swim in! What shall I do? Stop drinking the water! Please!"

The brothers roared at the sight of their comical brother. Timas gave his silly nephew a side glance and could barely stifle his own laughter at the sight of Anini mimicking a beached fish. Having visited this region several times before, Timas was familiar with the twists and curves of this river. Just around the next bend, he knew that the river went wide, and the currents flattened into a wide pool in which even a toddler could safely wade. This, however, was not known to the brothers who had yet to test their swimming skills on the Chignahuapan River. Timas figured this would be a good time to inject a bit of his own horseplay with the comical brother Anini.

With his altitude sickness subsiding, Timas suddenly stood up and shouted, "My dear Anini! I never knew that you were a fish masquerading as my nephew! Don't worry! Fish or human, I will save you!"

At that, Timas picked up Anini, tucked him under his right arm and walked into the river, submerging the youngest brother's body in the water but being sure not to dip his head under. The remaining three brothers watched the spectacle of the flapping youngest brother being carried into the river while the uncle continued to walk, and then swim toward the darkest recesses of its expanse. Their laughter subsided as they bore witness to their uncle and brother growing more and more distant as they were rapidly carried downstream.

After a few moments, the brothers cried out, "No! Uncle Timas! Turn back! It is too dangerous!" The brothers ran along the river attempting to keep the two bobbing heads in sight but the swiftness of the current outpaced them. Dripping with water and out of breath, the three brothers continued to follow the path of the river but lost sight of their uncle and Anini as they disappeared around a severe bend in the river.

Anini, holding tight to his uncle, whose arm firmly encircled his chest, screamed, "No! Uncle! I am sorry! Please, don't let me go! Please! Go Back! I don't know how to swim! I promise to stop teasing you!"

Timas expertly navigated the river's current with the stroke of one arm. He pulled both of their weight across the river's expanse and reassured his terrified nephew, "Hold on, Anini. Don't panic. Let your body go with the current."

Anini stopped resisting and regulated his breathing. Once he stopped fighting against his uncle's efforts, he realized that after they had turned the river's bend, his uncle was not only walking onto the opposite bank of the river but was fully carrying him like a baby. They walked onto the shore where the pair came face to face with Sesasi who, astounded, looked upon the unusual sight of one man carrying another.

Timas, struck by the beauty of this young woman who, up until his emergence from the river had been peacefully washing clothes, was dumbfounded.

Anini, also struck by Sesasi's beauty, suddenly realized how foolish he looked being carried like a baby. He was embarrassed to be caught in such a vulnerable predicament and, for once, was at a loss for words.

Sesasi, struck by the ridiculous sight of the two dripping men standing speechless before her, was the one who spoke first. "What strange fish have washed upon our shores."

At that, Timas dropped Anini, who landed like a freshly plucked fish from the waters. Anini immediately stood up, erect, next to his uncle, faced Sesasi, and attempted to present himself in a more dignified manner.

Timas could not help but smile at Sesasi's reaction to the sudden emergence of two men from the river. At that moment, he realized that she was not only beautiful but witty, as well. This made her that much more appealing. He promised himself that he would shake heaven and earth to have the privilege to see this woman again, if even just for one more day.

So this was the first encounter between Sesasi and Timas. Eventually, Anini, the jokester, would play a vital role in bringing the two together. He would also pass on the skills he learned from Timas to their newborn, Eréndira.

Sesasi did not know, while she was washing clothes, that the river had just delivered to her the adopted brother and the youngest son of the reigning ruler of the Kingdom. Yet, this chance encounter marked the beginning of her relationship with Timas. Over the months that followed, Timas repeatedly travelled from the Place of the Hummingbirds to Sesasi's home in Acámbaro, the Land of Magueys. He travelled as often as he could, finding pretense to visit the border city for any occasion. In this way, he could continually "happen" upon Sesasi.

No longer emerging from the river, Timas would visit the shore where he might stumble upon Sesasi, hoping to find her attending to the family laundry, while he feigned inspection of the kingdom's resources. Other opportunities for a chance encounter presented themselves in the marketplace, where Sesasi would be accompanied by her mother, haggling with local merchants over the price of vegetables to cook for the week's meals. On these occasions, Timas would step in and offer the merchant an amount she couldn't refuse. Sesasi's mother, Parakata, would thank Lord Timas for his generosity while Sesasi offered the suitor a slight nod of acknowledgement.

While their interactions were few and far between, the stolen glances and unsupervised exchanges between the two left Timas with the resolve to make Sesasi his temba, his wife. He knew that the next time he found Sesasi on the bank of the river, washing clothes and accompanied by female members of her family, he would only have a few moments to address her and state his case. Much would have to be said with few words.

As his regular visits to Acámbaro became more frequent, he eventually became well known to the members of Sesasi's community. He paid particular attention to charm the older women with compliments as he made his way to Sesasi's side. In this way, they had come to trust him and enjoy his presence. To one he would say, "Your uamba *husband* is such a blessed man to be so well cared for!" and then to another, "My, you beat those clothes so fiercely … you must be a valiant warrior as well!"

On one occasion, he left the women giggling before he kneeled beside Sesasi, who pretended not to care about his Lordship's presence. Timas, looking to gain her favor during the stolen moment, cupped water in his hands and turned to her.

"I have adored you since the moment I saw you. I don't know if I can continue life without knowing you are near. If you agree, I would like to join our lives for all time. Would you consider it?"

Sesasi did not respond. She looked out across the river to the hills, trees, birds, and the familiar rippling water. Timas held his breath awaiting any favorable indication from her.

Finally, she turned to him, bashfully smiled, and simply nodded.

Timas, so overjoyed, lost his balance and almost fell over. Without another word to Sesasi, he immediately returned to Tzintzuntzan and approached the Cazonci.

"Brother, I come to ask for your permission to marry a young woman from Acámbaro."

Cazonci Zuangua, following the traditions of royalty, asked his adopted brother, "And of what household does this young woman from Acámbaro belong that we would strengthen ties within the kingdom?"

Timas, holding his chin high, responded, "She is of the protectors of our empire. The daughter of a mighty warrior, an expert archer."

Zuangua, sitting upon the Cazonci's throne, rubbed his temple. He recognized that his brother Timas was of marriageable age but had not yet been committed to any of the royal families from the empire's regions. There were many principal families who would politically profit from having a daughter marry the brother of the Cazonci, even if it was an adopted brother. Zuangua looked upon his brother and responded, "I am sure, my brother, that you desire this young woman and that her father is a Quanga, a strong and valiant man, who serves us well on the frontier. But I must remind you, you are to be married to a woman whose lineage strengthens our political ties in the vast region."

Timas understood his responsibility to his family because of the status he held as a Lord and, especially, as the brother of the Cazonci. For this reason, he presented the only other option that would permit him to have Sesasi by his side. Perhaps he could not have her join him as his temba, his wife, but as the next thing closest, his concubine.

Cazonci Zuangua considered the benefit of having the daughter of a warrior from Acámbaro living within the royal realm. While Sesasi was not of the status to be a temba to his brother, she would, nonetheless, strengthen the alliance, and hence, the loyalty between the people of the Land of the Maguey and the royalty residing within the Place of Hummingbirds. Zuangua agreed to this second option and gave approval for Timas to arrange for Sesasi's family to be approached.

Timas was left to convince Sesasi that the compromise was their only option to be together. On his next visit to Acámbaro, he acknowledged to Sesasi that he could never be recognized as her uamba, which meant that she would not hold the honor of being his recognized temba *wife*, but they could, nonetheless, be within reach of one another. This was the only arrangement granted by the Cazonci that offered any possibility to be together.

Sesasi understood how marriages worked in their kingdom. Experience with historic events such as cataclysms and wars required an interrelated network that sustained their culture. As a young woman, she had to make the best decision for not only her own life, but for that of her unborn children. Because her father was a respected warrior of a community that bordered hostile tribes, she was at greater risk of being kidnapped by enemy forces if their town should fall under attack. Throughout her life she had witnessed countless tears shed for the young daughters stolen by men of enemy tribes. For this reason, there was constant and heightened preoccupation with protecting the women of her village. Given this reality, Sesasi concluded that it would be safer to live in the kingdom's capital rather than in her own town that was constantly under risk of being the battleground of first attack. Whereas arranged marriages strengthened the bonds of political alliances across the kingdom, she knew that they did not necessarily reveal the heart's devotion. A life with Timas meant fidelity to her safety and to that of their future children. For this reason, she agreed to Timas's offer. He was overjoyed.

Having both the Cazonci's approval and Sesasi's agreement to his proposal, Timas had to convince his nephew, Anini, to serve as his representative to speak with Sesasi's parents to seek permission and have her join him as a life-long partner. In marriages between the children of the Lords, a priest would normally accompany the members of the young man's family and facilitate the request for the young woman's hand. Given that Sesasi's family did not hold such status, a priest would not participate in this interaction. Thus, Timas entrusted the youngest royal brother, Anini, with the honor of approaching Sesasi's father with the request that Sesasi join Timas as his common-law wife.

Timas' request did not sit well with Anini. "Why, Uncle? Why do you ask me? I am the clown of the family. And, yet you ask me?"

Timas placed both hands on Anini's shoulders, trying to calm this young man whose voice had risen to a high screech.

"Why not you, Nephew? You are the one from our family that Sesasi knows best. She trusts you. You, being so good with words, would be most likely to convince her father to approve of our relationship."

"But think about what you ask of me! You ask me to approach your loved one's father to ask not for her hand in marriage but for her to be your common-law wife! He is one of the best archers in the kingdom! What if he is insulted by your offer and answers with an arrow through my chest?"

"Then appeal to Sesasi's mother!"

"What a sight that would be! Appealing to Sesasi's mother with an arrow through my chest?"

Timas shrugged and as consolation offered, "That would be a sight, no?"

Anini continued, "Look Uncle, I do not fear the mother! Unless she is yielding a macana! But either one, mother or father, to whom you ask me to plead your case, you, my uncle, send me on a very deadly mission!"

"Have more faith, my nephew. I will send you with many, many gifts."

"Faith, I have much, but life, I only have one! It seems that when I am with you, my uncle, I am constantly at risk of joining our ancestors earlier than I would care to."

"Oh, Anini. You still sulk about our little swim across the Chignahuapan River? That was many moons ago!"

"No! I didn't swim! You swam! I gasped and prayed!"

"But Anini. Think of this! Sesasi witnessed my devotion to your life!" Reenacting the event that transpired at the Chignahuapan, Timas continued, "Remember how firmly I held you as we crossed the span of the Chignahuapan and then I gently carried you onto the shore. Seeing this with her own eyes, she recognizes how important you are to me. We shared an adventure and I saw you safely to the end. I would not do this for just any flapping fish, would I?"

Timas bared a faint grin, and the memory of flapping like a beached fish on the banks of the Chignahuapan River brought a big smile to Anini's face.

"Very well, but if I come back dead, you know what the answer is! And, from that moment on, I refuse to speak to you!"

Anini bowed and proceeded with his charge. The following day, Anini sent a messenger to Acámbaro to request a meeting with Sesasi's parents. After several days, the exhausted messenger returned with confirmation that the delegation from Tzintzuntzan would be welcomed.

Within days, the courageous Anini, youngest son of the Cazonci, led a small delegation with servants to Acámbaro. Carrying gold jewelry, hummingbird and parrot feathers, corn, blankets, and copper jars filled with kidney beans, Anini hoped to be well-received by Sesasi's father, Irepani, whose name means "he who lays the foundation for life and home," and her mother, Parakata, whose name means "butterfly."

Anini, upon entering Irepani and Parakata's home, sat across from the puzzled parents, who were unsure as to the full nature of this visit from the Royal family. The gifts, laid at their feet, confirmed Anini's status within the royal kingdom but they, protectors of the frontier, were unaccustomed to such formal visits from the Cazonci's lineage. After Anini had been handed a cup containing refreshing xocolatl, he eased their curiosity.

"Thank you both, brave Irepani and your lovely wife, Parakata, for entertaining my request to visit you here today. I have traveled many miles from the capitol, Tzintzuntzan, on request of my Uncle Timas, brother to my father, the Cazonci. He sends his prayers of health and prosperity for you and your family."

Irepani was not a man of many words and was having difficulty understanding the intention for Anini's visit, so merely nodded in response.

Parakata, on the other hand, provided balance to her husband's reserved nature. "We are happy to receive you, Prince Anini, and I hope that the xocolatl is to your liking?"

Anini's shaking hand betrayed his nervousness. In full view behind the seated and muscular Irepani were his crossbow and a collection of spears and macanas that had likely ended many an enemy's life. At the sight of these deadly and prominently placed weapons, beads of sweat dripped from Anini's armpits. He was certain there was a puddle on either side of his chair.

Parakata, to ease Anini's obvious nerves, reminded him to take a sip of his xocolatl, but his shaking hand caused several drops to spill onto his lap. Immediately, one of Anini's servants jumped up to wipe away the liquid, but Anini did not want to appear coddled. He waved the servant away, pulled the soaked manta up to his mouth, and slurped up the xocolatl droplets. When done, he looked up at Irepani and Parakata, who now had matching raised eyebrows. Anini realized how foolish he looked—even worse than appearing coddled.

"Oh yes, my esteemed hosts, the xocolatl is so delicious that it would be criminal to waste such a delicacy!"

His compliment brought a gentle smile to Parakata, but Irepani still sat silently with a look of stoic astonishment. Anini cleared his throat and delivered the proposal, a speech that Timas had prepared, in which he promised his lifelong devotion to Sesasi's safety and love which extended to their offspring. Then the servants, on cue, placed even more gifts at Irepani and Parakata's feet.

Irepani said nothing and did not acknowledge or look at the gifts. His steady stare remained on the trembling Prince. It was Parakata, once again, who offered polite words.

"We thank you, Prince Anini, for these gifts and for presenting us with your Uncle Timas' proposal. He has made his presence known to us on several occasions, here in Acámbaro. We will confer with the women of our family and send our decision."

Anini rose to his feet. He did not want to spend any more time than necessary in Irepani's presence while the renowned warrior was within easy reach of his weapons. He excused himself and exited. Once Anini and his servants were out of hearing range, Irepani and Parakata looked at one another and broke out laughing.

After Anini's departure, Irepani and Prakata heard Sesasi's position as to why the offer was desirable. Irepani, resistant to having his daughter serve as concubine to Timas or to anyone, understood that these offers from the Royal Family to the warrior class were uncommon. If, however, the offer was denied, Sesasi would, most likely, marry another warrior of their region. Her life, like her mothers' would be constantly at risk living in a dangerous region where she could be widowed at an early age or possibly kidnapped by enemy marauders.

Next, Irepani and Parakata conferred with the women of the family. After hearing what was being offered by the Royal family and hearing Sesasi's position, they concurred with Sesasi. Life would be safer for her if she lived in Tzintzuntzan where its location, further away from borderlands, as well as the additional protection of the royal guard, ensured greater security.

Weeks later, the people of Tzintzuntzan were going about their daily affairs—carrying home baskets of fresh vegetables from the market, exchanging gossip, and admiring their neighbors' newborns—when they stopped, one by one, as they caught sight of a cloud of dust rising from the main road that connected them to Acámbaro. They were not sure what to make of the large approaching company. At first, they were dumbstruck, but as the entourage got closer, they began to panic.

Sesasi, adorned in the multi-colors of the Purepecha people, was accompanied by a phalanx of women from Sesasi's extended family. It was not the women, however, that frightened the people of Tzintzuntzan, some of whom darted into their homes looking to hide their children while others began searching for the royal guard. They were uncertain if they were being attacked by their own warriors, because surrounding the entourage from Acámbaro was a battalion of warriors in full regalia. They carried colorfully adorned shields, macanas, bows, and spears. Their faces were solemn, and the uniformity of their collective stature signaled a message of strength.

As the well-armed entourage crossed the perimeters of Tzintzuntan, it became apparent that this was not an attack. Timas, having been beckoned by a terrified servant, ran out onto the road with his sword in hand, but as he caught sight of the envoy, the tension left his body, and he was filled with pure joy. This battalion signified the allegiance of the people of Acámbaro to continue serving as protectors of the eastern border of the kingdom. This, in honor of the relationship between Sesasi and Timas.

More importantly, the accompaniment of a battalion of warriors symbolically signaled the threat of what to expect should the favored daughter of an esteemed warrior, Irepani, and his beloved wife, Parakata, not be treated well. Timas, a war captain, had received the same lesson taught to all Purépecha men. They are forbidden from abusing women. For this reason, he understood the unspoken message that if Sesasi were mistreated, the repercussions would be severe.

Turning to the people of Tzintzuntzan who had gathered behind him, Timas called out to the servants and instructed them to prepare food for the approaching company. Then, he addressed the members of the royal guard who stood by his side, armed and prepared to protect the capital. "Stand down. These are our relations. They bring the woman I love."

With an ear-to-ear smile, Timas received the envoy with open arms and, out of respect, nodded to each member of the battalion.

And so, began the lifelong relationship between Sesasi and Timas.

Recalling all that had led to the gift of her newborn brought an easy smile to Sesasi's face. How her own life was altered since Timas and his nephew, Anini, emerged from the Chignahuapan River! As she gazed upon her baby daughter, she wondered what life would bring for Eréndira and prayed that eternal peace and harmony would continue to surround her child as it had on the day of her birth.

The year was 1508.

Sesasi heard the Cazonci Zuangua's bellowing.

"Who is the mother of this child?"

The Cazonci's startled attendants jumped in response and the footsteps of every person belonging to the royal household raced toward the Cazonci. That is, all but one.

Sesasi ran in the opposite direction. She had been meticulously attending to her seed plot, but when she heard the Cazonci's booming voice, Sesasi realized she didn't know the whereabouts of her curious five-year-old, Eréndira. Overtaken with panic, Sesasi dashed into her home, looked under the blankets of the bed, sprinted the outside circumference of the home, then darted back inside to confirm, once more, that Eréndira was nowhere in sight and she had no idea where she might be.

A deep pang hit the pit of her stomach. Out of desperation, she lifted the blankets of the bed one more time, hoping that her daughter would miraculously appear. Still, no Eréndira to be found. She reluctantly turned toward the Cazonci's call, and, as she dashed out, she collided with Chuperipati, who had just arrived at Sesasi's doorway. The two women fell to the ground, but quickly recovered and managed to get back onto their feet, breathlessly regarding one another with hands on their own stinging foreheads, the point of impact.

Chuperipati's assignment within the royal home was not to be a conveyor of messages but to oversee the Cazonci's jewels. Given that she had the Cazonci's favor and was fond of Sesasi, she felt it best that she be the one to summon Sesasi, who was constantly called upon when her mischievous daughter got into trouble. As the two dazed women recovered from their collision, Sesasi surmised from Chuperipati's sudden appearance what Sesasi already knew.

Chuperipati confirmed, "Yes, it's Eréndira."

Sesasi took a deep breath to calm her stomach and steel her nerves. She then followed Chuperipati to the Cazonci's home where her curious child had wandered off without her mother's knowledge.

The women cut across the spacious palace patio, entered the Cazonci's quarters, and stood side-by-side in the presence of the Cazonci. He looked upon them with astonishment, a look they mirrored as their eyes fell on the five-year-old child, Eréndira, happily seated on his lap.

Cazonci Zuangua broke the silence. "What is this? Do the women have a new fashion?"

Chuperipati and Sesasi, puzzled by his observation, turned to look at one another and discovered they had matching bumps growing out of their foreheads.

Chuperipati said, "No, Cazonci, we accidently found one another with our foreheads."

Cazonci Zuangua, with relief in his voice, said "Oh! Well, I am happy to hear this because the look does not become you."

Chuperipati and Sesasi turned to one another and assessed each other's swelling lumps. "Yes, not very flattering. We were both rushing to respond to your call," said Chuperipati.

The Cazonci, with a quizzical frown, pondered for a moment how two women coming toward him would be rushing in converging directions, but he dismissed this confusing detail with a wave of his hand. "Look for yourselves. I have this child here …"— motioning with one hand to Eréndira who remained nonchalantly seated on his lap—"… I find her to be the most delightful creature. With so many grandchildren running about, I can't keep track of who belongs to whom. You, Sesasi, are you her mother?"

"Yes, Cazonci. She is my child."

"Ah! So, she is not a grandchild but the child of my brother, Timas! She is my niece! Very well then. I would like to take my brother's child on a deer hunting expedition. Tomorrow, we leave for the islands of Lake Pátzcuaro."

As soon as these words were spoken, a messenger was sent to the chief canoe maker, Hicharuta Vandari, to prepare the finest canoe for the Cazonci's trip to Lake Pátzcuaro. The household mobilized to ensure that the Cazonci was provided for in every way—food, blankets, weapons, and sufficient attendants to respond to his needs for this unplanned excursion. Similarly, the chief boatman, Paricuti, was charged with securing the finest rowers. All was set in motion so that the following day, when the Cazonci and Eréndira arrived at Lake shores, a fleet of canoes would be waiting for the entourage of servants, warriors, and extended family.

The next morning, the slow-moving procession traveled over pine and oak covered hills. Their destination, Lake Pátzcuaro, lay in a basin of volcanic origin, nestled in the region's highlands. The Cazonci, taking deliberate steps at the head of the group, occasionally looked over his shoulder at the many members tagging along. They sensed his urgency and hastened their steps to keep up with him. Once they arrived on the Lake's shores, numerous flat-bottomed canoes awaited them. The Cazonci and Eréndira were assisted by two young, athletically built men into an exquisitely painted canoe.

The Cazonci waved off the attendants who attempted to board his canoe. He instructed them to board one of the other canoes, and then motioned for his rowers to push off. The young men expertly propelled the canoe into the pristine waters with hardly a ripple. The Cazonci, not intent on waiting, urged the rowers to continue and, in doing so, ditched the entourage. The attendants and warriors, still loading their canoes with food, blankets, and other provisions for the day, realized they were being left behind and hastily jumped into the nearest canoes. The rush to catch up with the Cazonci resulted in chaos. Several fell into the shallow waters, and others stood trembling; not sure whether to swim out to the Cazonci's canoe or to reorganize themselves on the shores. Their clamoring could be heard over the lapping waters hitting the side of the Cazonci's rapidly moving canoe.

The Cazonci looked over his shoulder and saw the widening distance between his canoe and the entourage. A wide grin spread across his face.

Amazed by the big lake, Eréndira observed, "Cazonci, there is so much water here! Where does it come from?"

"Good question, my child. This is pure itzï. It is a gift. Janíkua *rain* falls from the sky and runs off the mountains and hills surrounding this body of itzï. Yet, as vast as it is, there is a larger body of water that lies to the direction where you see the sun set. It is there that our ancestors once lived."

Eréndira looked to the west and asked. "Our people came from another lake?"

"Yes, in a manner, my child, it is a grand lake. Our people, the first humans, came from an island that was once in the kómekua *ocean*."

"A kómekua?"

"Yes," the Cazonci answered, "A kómekua is a larger body of water than a lake with fish larger than any of the canoes you have ever seen. The waves from the kómekua are so strong and high that, when standing on the shores, they knock down even our strongest warriors! Our ancestors lived, for thousands of generations, on an island in that kómekua. It is said that it was a paradise where the first temples, palaces, and cities were created. The kómekua provided plentiful fish, and the sun brought bountiful crops. Our ancestors were so well-cared for that they did not need to toil for food. Because of this, they were able to devote time to music, medicine, astronomy, sailing, religion, and writing."

"It sounds beautiful. Why would our ancestors leave such a place?"

The Cazonci scanned the western horizon. "Our ancestors had tremendous powers. With their minds, they were able to float heavy stones through the air and transform the world around them. But wisdom and power must always be used for good and, sometimes people fall out of balance with nature and our relationship with the earth was put at risk. Over time, the people observed that the kómekua's water was gradually rising over the shores. They knew that their civilization would be overtaken by the waves. The lands were shifting everywhere, so they determined it was best to save the people. Sorrowfully, they knew they would have to leave the sinking island." The Cazonci motioned with the wave of an arm to the mountains surrounding Lake Pátzcuaro and added, "A great deal of the land you see now and even that which you cannot see was once under itsï. Where we are even now, sea-faring animals once lived. When the continents shifted, the animals of the kómekua either adapted to the rising land or perished into its soil. So, you see, while some land sunk into the depths of the kómekua, other areas, once covered by itsï, rose up from the bottom out of the kómekua and became the refuge for humanity."

Eréndira considered the power of shifting lands and rising itsï that submerged a land and forced an entire civilization to seek refuge. "So, Cazonci, is this why we are called, Purépecha, The Late Comers?"

"Ah, another good question, Eréndira. That is correct. Our people are called this because we are late comers to *this* land." Eréndira's puzzled look prompted the Cazonci to clarify. "Consider the name of this lake and of the site nearby, Pátzcuaro, Place of Stones. There was a ruined temple here long before our people arrived. Just as land and water shift, so do people."

Astonished by the Cazonci's rendering of what has transpired over millennia, she concluded, "There were others here before us. So, if our people did not come here from the island that went under the kómekua, where did we come from?"

"As has been passed down, generation after generation, we are told that the wise ones wanted to ensure the survival of our civilization. Seeing the itsï rising over the shores of the island, they urged the people, as they boarded their canoes, to go in different directions. This was humanity's best chance of survival. It was their hope that, in the best case, all would find sanctuary but, at the very least, some would find land. Our people eventually arrived on a large body of land to the south of here, a land called Anti."

Eréndira considered a southern land where distant relations once landed but concluded that her people, the Purépecha, must have made another migration. "And did the kómekua swallow the Anti too?"

"You are certainly intuitive, my child!" exclaimed the Cazonci. "The people of Anti, the high crest, are still there. They are our relations who created a great civilization… palaces, temples, agriculture. Think about how our ancestors were able to travel across a vast kómekua. Since the rising of the sun in the east, we have had large and reliable water vessels. After our ancestors fled and settled onto a new land, we began searching for the others. In time, our ancestors found people of other civilizations who had also survived the rising itsï and resettled. In the search up and down the coastline of this emerging land, our ancestors began to trade with others. Realize, our dugout canoes hold up to 70 people at a time. So, imagine, when the seas ran high, our ancestors began coming to this region. Even now, our people who still live in our southern homeland continue to make the journey, landing at a port where they stay for five or six months not too far from here. When the good weather returns and the seas are calm, they go back to Anti. These voyages, up and down this land mass, have existed for many generations. Our Kingdom, that which you know, started from a group of our people who followed the river from Zacatula, went upstream and found this region favorable. So, here we stayed. The changes that take place with land and itsï make it so that people must change as well. So, here we are, the Purépecha, the latecomers."

"I believe, Cazonci, that our ancestors were wise and brave people."

"And you say that why?"

"Well, it must have been hard to leave their island, but they did it to stay alive. It must have been hard to abandon their home."

"Yes, you are right. Given the circumstances, they had to overcome fear if they were to survive. They made decisions based on what they could control, but a large lesson came from that event. What might that be?"

Eréndira considered the horrendous reality confronting her ancestors that had caused people to flee for unknown horizons in hope of finding solid ground. She looked to the Cazonci and said, "Respect the powers of Cuerauáperi."

"Yes. Our people know what it is like to have to abandon a land to survive. Now, we are here and, after so many battles with our adversaries, we pray to remain in peace."

The Cazonci gently caressed Eréndira's cheek and then fixed his gaze in the direction of their destination. He directed Eréndira toward a distant peak and explained, "From here we can see a dormant volcano. It sleeps now but when it rose from the earth, it carved out this basin that catches the itsï from the surrounding area. The earth is bountiful, but we must remember that her cycles are more powerful than us. This is why we must live in harmony with the earth and be, ourselves, balanced in all ways." The Cazonci then motioned toward the lake upon which their canoe smoothly glided. "From these waters our best fishermen bring us nourishment, but we must only take as much as we need and not be wasteful of the gifts."

Eréndira, on any body of water for the very first time, leaned over the edge of the canoe and exclaimed, "My Cazonci! There is a little girl in the itsï!"

Cazonci Zuangua leaned over the side of the canoe to see what had caught the child's attention. Looking down into the crystal-clear blue water, his reflection appeared next to Eréndira's. With the sight of the two of them, together, reflected in the lake, Eréndira ascertained that the child in the itsï was her. She stuck out her tongue at the child in the lake and was amused by the fact that the child in the itsï did the same.

"Cazonci! Look! We are there in the itsï and we are here in the canoe."

"Eréndira. You view the world with such wonder. You make me see everything anew."

Suddenly realizing that their canoe had distanced itself from all who had accompanied them on this outing, Eréndira asked, "And what of the rest who came with us?" She looked back toward the wake of their canoe and the entourage was but a speck in the horizon. "Cazonci!" She exclaimed. "They have your bow and arrow."

The Cazonci took a deep breath, leaned back into the canoe, and extended his legs in repose. "Yes, they do but today, I do not feel like hunting."

"What is it you feel like doing?"

"Let me see … Today, I feel like seeing the white herons on the Island of Yunuén." With that said, the Cazonci instructed the rowers to head directly to the island. They rapidly skimmed over the Lake's expanse toward their destination. In the distance, Eréndira noticed multiple images gliding in circular motion on top of the water.

"Look! There are large butterflies swimming atop of the lake!"

The Cazonci squinted to block the glare of the sun bouncing off the brilliant water. "Oh yes! Those are the butterfly fishermen. What looks like wings from a distance is a large net that is balanced and laid across the top of the canoe."

The Cazonci's canoe seamlessly cut within closer view of the fishermen, but without disturbing them. Eréndira gazed at the grace of the men who, one to each canoe, set aside their oar, stood, and then dropped a large net into the lake while still gliding and maintaining their balance.

"Cazonci! The butterflies dip their wings into the lake and capture fish from the depths!"

"Yes, Eréndira. You recognize their skill as well as the beauty of their movement."

"Their movements are like a dance!"

"And your view of the world is poetic!"

As they approached Yunuén, flocks of white heron glided on the water just off the Island's shores while hundreds more rested on dry land. The Cazonci inquired, "So tell me, Eréndira, has your father told you about the Princess Hapunda?"

"No, Cazonci. Would you tell me about her?"

"Yes… she was a brave princess who lived on the beautiful Island of Yunuén. It is given the name of Half Moon because of its curved shape, like the moon. Princess Hapunda, daughter of an important nobleman, possessed the most cherished quality of kindness, but she was also very beautiful. Her beauty, however, came to the attention of Chichimeca invaders who were themselves hunting for deer upon these islands. These hunters spied upon her as she was strolling the Island's shores and decided to kidnap her so they could give her to their leader to gain his favor."

Eréndira was reminded of a story shared by her mother, Sesasi. "Yes, Cazonci! My mother has told me of how our women have been taken by our enemies where she comes from … Acámbaro."

"Yes, your mother's people protect those of us living in the interior of the Kingdom, but they do so at great cost. When Princess Hapunda was taken, her aunts and the others who were with her fought the Chichimeca warriors with what they had, but it was to no avail. The Princess was carried away. Her bloodied and crying relations ran as fast as they could to alert the Princess's family. Upon learning of her kidnapping, Princess Hapunda's family and the entire community on Yunuén cried out in sorrow. Her brothers, however, were angered at the audacity of the Chichimeca. They began preparations to chase down the Chichimecas and rescue their precious sister."

Eréndira, fully entranced by the story of Princess Hapunda, shivered at the thought of being taken by enemies whose intentions were beyond her scope of understanding at the age of five.

The Cazonci continued, "The Princess was taken to the Chichimeca's encampment where she saw that the Chichimecas were greater in numbers than her own people and had many more warriors among them. She knew, however, that, despite being outnumbered, her own people would not settle for this aggressive act of her kidnapping. More importantly, she knew that her own people did not have the capacity to stand up against the military force of the Chichimeca invaders. Surely, her people would suffer devastating losses should they launch an attack."

Eréndira's eyes widened at the thought of a whole village of Purépechas dying at the hands of invading people. Yet, they were willing to risk their lives for Princess Hapunda. Taking advantage of the pause in the Cazonci's story, she asked, "What did the Princess do?"

"At night, while the Chichimecas slept, the Princess snuck out of their encampment and, without making a sound, made her way to the shores of Lake Pátzcuaro. Hidden by a cloak of fog, she told the spirits of the lake about the tragedy that was to come if her brothers and others of her community attempted to save her. Her heart grew heavy with the thought of them violently losing their lives to the Chichimecas. After speaking to the spirits of the lake, she was startled when Lake Pátzcuaro spoke back to her." The Cazonci closed his eyes as he drew the rest of the story from his memory. "There she stood, at Lake's shore when in a deep male voice, the words rose from the water and advised the Princess that she was to throw herself into the lake and join him forever. Princess Hapunda was overcome with conflicting emotions toward the sacrifice the Lake asked of her. The Lake, sensing her fear and hesitation, assured her, 'I will protect you, my Princess. You must make yourself one with me.' Given her predicament, she could either accept the unknown as offered by the welcoming lake or stay with the warlike Chichimecas and face a life of abuse and torment."

Eréndira absorbed Princess Hapunda's courage into her being, considering what it took to come to a final decision. Hapunda had been put in a situation where she had to assess her circumstances and choose from two options in front of her. One choice, offered by the Lake, had an unpredictable outcome. The other choice, staying with the Chichimecas, meant a life of enslavement and, very likely, the death of her community as they would surely attempt to rescue her.

The Cazonci continued, "With that, Hapunda jumped into the waters and when she resurfaced, she emerged as a white heron, to live forever in the lake and be nourished by its peaceful waters. Upon her decision, the people of her village knew she had escaped her captors and was safe from their mistreatment. Now, when you look upon this Island, you can see more herons who have, since that day, arrived. They continue to grace this lake to this day."

Eréndira watched flocks of herons fly above their heads. Their numbers were so many that they cast elongated shadows upon the Cazonci's canoe and at times momentarily blocked out the sun. She thought about the Princess's decision. Rather than accept the life of a captive, she escaped the Chichimecas and transformed into a graceful heron. As Eréndira observed the diving herons plucking fish from the waters, she arrived at a key understanding about the Princess.

"Cazonci! The Princess did not take her life, but the Chichimecas most likely believed that she did."

"Yes, my child. You are perceptive, like your father who, though a Captain of War, knows that there are many ways to defeat an enemy! Brute force is not always the answer to the violence inherent in humanity."

Eréndira warmed at the mention of her father, and shyly offered, "There are many ways to protect lives."

The Cazonci gazed out for a moment at the distant islands in the lake. "Yes, my child. The person intent on violence has one intention: domination and, sometimes, complete annihilation. As human beings we can and often respond in a like manner. It takes deep calm and reflection to consider other ways to respond to the violent nature in others. In this way, we also bring less harm even to ourselves."

Eréndira contemplated what the intensity of war would do to people. "Violence blinds."

Cazonci nodded. "Yes. And when attacked, we must consider and respond in ways that preserve life and culture. Consider this, Eréndira…"—the Cazonci motions for Eréndira to again look over the side of the canoe into the waters of Lake Pátzcuaro—"…like our reflection in the itsï, things are not always as they seem."

On the Way Home from Nanita's

Eréndira pulls out her iPhone to look up 'Princess Eréndira.' Immediately, a Wikipedia article pops up with a few paragraphs, which Eréndira quickly reads. She then calls out to her parents who have been sitting, quietly, enjoying the scenery as they drive through the hills, the pines and the oaks, back down toward the valley.

"Mom! Dad! I found something on the internet about the Princess that Nanita was talking about!"

Verónica says, "Oh yea. Nanita never got to tell you what she knows about the Princess, with getting our dinner together and then finding that fossil. What does the internet say?"

"Not a whole lot, but it sounds like she was something else! She was just a little older than I am when the Spaniards got to Mexico. This is confusing, though. Didn't Nanita say that she was from our tribe?"

"Yes," says Verónica, "From your Nanita's side of the family; we are Purépecha."

"In this story it says that the Princess was Tarascan. That doesn't sound anything close to Purépecha."

"That's not surprising. What happens, sometimes," Verónica explains, "is that there is what a people call themselves, but then others might call them something different. So, when outsiders encounter those who call you by another name, the outsiders then use the name given to you by others."

Eréndira considers her mother's explanation. "Give me an example."

Verónica quietly tries to think of an example. Then, Victor, who is driving, briefly makes eye contact with his daughter in the rearview mirror. "I have an example. This is from my side of the family."

"Okay. What?"

"Well, everyone knows us as 'Apache,' but this isn't what we call ourselves. The word means 'enemy' which is what we were to many other Native American tribes in the Southwest. That word, Apache, comes from the Zuni who, most likely, saw us as their enemies at one time."

"But I've heard you say we're Apache."

"Well, yea… after a while, people just take on the names given to them by others without even knowing its origins or what it means."

"That's awful!"

"Why do you say that?" Victor asked.

"Why should you let someone else give you a name that isn't yours? Especially a name that is so negative? It's demeaning! People should be called by what they call themselves."

"That's true, but I can tell you, we call ourselves Ndee."

"Okay. And what does that mean?"

"The people."

Eréndira considers this for a moment before saying, "I like that name better. But, you know, what else?"

"What?" asks Verónica.

Eréndira holds up her iPhone as they continue down the highway, "This write-up on the internet says that Princess Eréndira may have killed herself. Why would Naníta want to name me after someone who took her own life? That carries some bad energy!"

"Is that what it said for certain?" asks Victor.

Eréndira reopens the Wikipedia article and reads aloud, "There are many theories as to what happened to her. Some of which include suicide by drowning, leaving to train others for war, and that she killed herself for falling in love with a Spanish monk. One legend even claims that she was kidnapped by her own people and put into a temple so that the Spaniards should not find and kill her."

"That's interesting," Verónica offers.

"What part?" asks Eréndira.

"Well… the part about her committing suicide by drowning. Are you sure you have the right Princess? I remember your Naníta told me the story of a princess who was kidnapped by an enemy tribe. It was an interesting story that sounded like magical realism. It makes you think about the circumstances that the Princess was in, and then you had to read between the lines."

Verónica pauses for a moment, tapping her finger on her lap while she tries to drum up the name of this other Princess before relenting. "I can't remember the name of this other Princess. Let me text your Naníta and see if she can send me her name."

Verónica quickly sends a text message to her mother asking the name of the princess from the story that Elizabeth has told her several times.

After a minute or two, Naníta responds, Hapunda."

"Oh my, look at that!" exclaims Verónica. "Your Naníta, as much as she detests using the phone, she keeps it nearby! She got back to me right away." To Eréndira she says, "Look up Princess Hapunda." Verónica shows Eréndira the name sent to her by Naníta so she can see the correct spelling.

Eréndira clicks away and pulls up the story. After reading, she tells Verónica and Victor, "It says that this Princess lived on an island in Lake Patzcuaro. She was kidnapped by another tribe. She snuck away from where she was being held, went to the Lake, and started telling the lake her situation. Then, the Lake, through a thick fog, spoke back and urged her to get in the water." Eréndira pauses. "That's weird. A lake talks to her and tells her to jump in?"

Victor and Verónica give each other a quick glance, a half-smile, and shrug their shoulders.

"So, what happened?" Victor urges her on.

Eréndira continues to read the article directly, "After going into the deepest end of the lake she emerged, reborn into a mighty white heron and forever stayed around her beloved Patzcuaro flying and feeding from it for all eternity."

"What a coincidence."

"In what way?" asks Eréndira.

"Well… think about it. Two Princesses from the same tribe have similar stories. One was kidnapped and got away by the cover of the fog in the Lake. She then transformed into something else. If you consider the circumstances, Hapunda's story conveys a strategy that avoided harm to her people and to herself. Then, Princess Eréndira was likely fleeing after fighting with the Spaniards and training others to fight them. You think these two young women really went on to kill themselves? Sounds like the people of the tribe made up a story to conceal the whereabouts of these two young women. They protected them."

Eréndira considers the similarities in the two stories. "Wow. I wonder if Princess Eréndira knew the story of Princess Hapunda."

"What are your thoughts, Eréndira?" asks Verónica.

"Well, it's like you said, Mom, read between the lines. Maybe Princess Eréndira disappeared and made it look like she took her life. If Princess Hapunda became a heron... maybe Princess Eréndira came out of her situation differently."

"She transformed..." offers Victor.

"What do you mean she transformed?" asks Eréndira.

Victor explains, "The story is a metaphor. She became a different person. Circumstances in people's lives can make you call up ways of being that you didn't know you had within you. You rise to the occasion."

"Maybe she just blended in with the herons, but the birds could also be a metaphor in that she rose like a heron!" adds Verónica.

"Whoa! That's deep!" exclaims Eréndira.

"And another thing," continues Verónica, "didn't you say that another theory about Princess Eréndira was that her people hid her?"

"Yea... they hid her in a temple so the Spaniards wouldn't get her." Again reading from her iPhone, "...so that the Spaniards should not find and kill her."

"Soooooo..." Verónica says, "if you were to interpret that, what was it that she was doing that made the Spaniards so angry that they wanted to kill her?"

"Yea, and despite her being considered worthy of death by Spaniards, her people choose to protect her from them. That means they valued her so much that they put themselves at risk for her," adds Victor.

The three of them sit quietly as they descend into the valley, considering the clues in the coded information that Eréndira read out loud.

Verónica broke the silence. "So, it could be that when it says she was hidden in a temple that, like Princess Hapunda, she was someone held in high regard. Only the people of high status were placed in temples, but that would be only after their death. So, if they were hiding her so she wouldn't be killed the reference to the temple could mean that she was elevated in status but considered figuratively dead. It's a cover to protect her."

Eréndira considers all the factors weighing in on the possible outcome of this young Princess for whom she was named and the varying renditions of her story. "Wow. This is deep! It reminds me of that fossil you found. A shell fossil up in the hills. Who would have thought that the land where Naníta lives was once under water."

"And… that image on the rocks that your Naníta showed you. Did you ever figure out who those images are?" asks Victor.

"The one on top is a Native American. I thought maybe the one below was a gold miner, but Naníta didn't think so. I took a picture."

"Oh yea?" asks Verónica. "Let me see?" Eréndira pulls up the picture she took of the petroglyph and hands her mother the iPhone.

Verónica opens the image to take a closer look at the etched images and then zeroes in on the lower of the two. "You know what? That looks like Juan Bautista de Anza."

"De Anza? Like the trail?" asks Eréndira.

"Yes. Under Spanish direction, he led an expedition looking to expand those missions further into northern California. I had to teach about this when I was an elementary teacher." Verónica clicks away on her cellphone, pulls up an image, and hands it to Eréndira.

"Wow!" Eréndira holds her mother's phone next to her own. "It does look like him! Like the stories of the Princesses… gotta read between the lines. Looks like the people who once lived where Naníta now lives also left us with their own stories… but they put theirs on the rocks!"

"Yes!" agrees Verónica. "And there are other reliable sources. You'd be surprised what is captured in books and even rocks that tell us what happened a long time ago. Unfortunately, what is commonly taught in our schools doesn't really convey these perspectives."

Eréndira's thoughts return to the de Anza image etched on the rock. Is it possible that his intrusion into Northern California was captured in the rock etching by the Sierra Miwok?

Then she quietly revisits the many questions about the Princess for whom she was named. What did Princess Eréndira do that made the Spaniards so angry and intent on killing her? What, ultimately, became of her? Did she have to abandon her people to escape death? The circumstances faced by the Princess, remind Eréndira of her own circumstances. While no one is intent on killing her, unfortunately, she must return to school the following Monday and face the aftermath of all the conflict she had with Susan. Her stomach turns. *Maybe*, she tells herself, *I'll change my patterns and, instead of hanging out where I usually do I can do some research in the library. Who knows? Maybe like the lone turkey, I can find a nice flock to hang out with!* Plus, this would be a good distraction from all the turmoil. If her mother is correct about the image being de Anza, then she can call her Naníta with any new information.

As they enter the outer city limits, Eréndira remembers how her Naníta told her about the medicinal qualities of the mint tea that they had enjoyed earlier that day. It had calmed Eréndira's stomach and eased her nerves.

"Hey mom?"

"Yes, Eréndira."

"Can you ask NEandíta for a cutting from the mint plant next time we visit?"

"Sure. What are you going to do with it?"

"Plant it in our new yard."

"Good idea."

On her walk to school, Eréndira considers ways to avoid what certainly awaits her—the talk in the hallways, the classrooms, the cafeteria. Social media was slammed over the weekend with all that happened last week. Her fight with Susan, the vice principal getting involved, the police investigation, students being interviewed, and then, Susan's suspension. Melissa said the gossip was blowing up her Instagram account and that Susan ran her mouth with a bunch of lies.

As Naníta would say, "a bunch of mitote—nonsensical chaos!"

Melissa, being Eréndira's closest and only friend, had received numerous texts. Melissa hardly knew some of these classmates, but they all wanted to know more about the new girl on campus who took out Susan with one punch. The rumors flying around were outrageous, ranging from Eréndira being a judo master to being a gang member. Some were saying that Eréndira put Susan in the hospital while others were saying that Eréndira had been handcuffed and jailed during the investigation.

To sidestep the ridiculous chatter and the shifty looks, Eréndira times her arrival on campus just before the first bell rang. Still, she can't escape what awaits her. Walking toward her first period class—A.P. Bio—she attempts to offer as little attention as possible to noticing the way students look at her. Some students gawk, other students jeer, some students give long side glances, some half smiles and, if she isn't mistaken, she thinks she catches some giving her approving nods.

Just before stepping into her classroom, one lanky boy wearing a Disney sweatshirt runs by her in the hallway and calls out, "Hey… new girl!" Eréndira turns around somewhat startled. He gives her a thumbs up before disappearing into a classroom down the hallway.

Eréndira isn't sure what to make of the mixed reactions, but she is sure that despite her best efforts, she has made a name for herself, though not in the way she would have preferred. She wonders, *What does this all mean?*

At lunchtime, Melissa and Eréndira meet at the end of fourth period at their usual meeting place, the back wall of the library away from the various cliques that routinely stake out various areas of campus. In this little hide-away, they can talk, quietly eat their bag lunches, and escape *the looks* of their classmates. With their backs leaning up against the library wall, they are barely a few bites into their sandwiches when two girls appear at the far corner and approach them.

One asks, "Hey, can we sit with you?"

Melissa and Eréndira look at each other as though expecting the other to respond. They are both baffled by the request, but Melissa says, "Yea, sure, why not?" They scoot over and make room for the two girls. The four look at one another awkwardly until one finally offers introductions.

"Sooooo, HI! I'm Rosalee!" She extends her hand out to Eréndira and Melissa, who each take turns shaking her hand. "And, this is my sister, Luisa." On cue, Luisa repeats Rosalee's gesture of good will and shakes hands with Eréndira and Melissa.

With the formalities behind them, Rosalee and Luisa focus on their meal from the cafeteria. After quietly examining the various wrapped items, they dig in. Melissa and Eréndira notice that their clothes are out of style, their shoes worn down, and their backpacks are clean but a bit tattered.

"So," begins Melissa, "Where did you get those backpacks? I haven't seen any of those old school backpacks since I was in kindergarten."

Both girls blush. Eréndira sends Melissa a hard look, raised eyebrow and tilt of the head. Her silent way of saying, *Be nice.*

Melissa recalibrates and offers, "What I mean is… I bet those are collector's items! Kind of like those old pennies that are worth more than a penny!"

Eréndira gives Melissa a look of approval.

"Oh! I didn't know that!" says Rosalee. "Our mother got these for us."

Rosalee doesn't want to offer more information. The circumstances by which their mother obtained the backpacks as well as their food, furniture, clothes and much of what they own embarrassed her. Most of what they have is purchased at the local thrift store or given to them by local charities.

Rosalee is usually in the company of her younger sister, Luisa. She hopes to make friends with Eréndira and Melissa and does not want to call attention to the fact that she and her sister live in a migrant farmworker camp at the outer orbits of the community. They have struggled to make friends since enrolling in school and have found themselves walking the hallways and occupying desks as out-siders. Rosalee weighs how much to reveal to others about their lives and figures it best to redirect attention away from her and her sister.

"So, where are you from?" Rosalee directly addresses Eréndira.

"I'm from the Bay Area. Moved here right before the start of the school year."

Melissa offers, "I'm from L.A. I've been here for a few years. My mom works at the University."

"Your mom is a professor?" asks Rosalee.

"No." answers Melissa. "Eréndira's mom is. My mom is an of-fice manager for one of the Deans. After my parents divorced, she moved the two of us up here. She got tired of L.A. traffic. Life's a bit slower here, which she likes."

"Oh, sorry to hear about the divorce. You must miss your father?"

"Yea. It took a while getting used to him not being around but at least I don't have to hear them fighting with one another any-more. I talk on the phone with him almost every day and I go down for holidays, so we stay in touch."

"That's nice. At least you have a dad to talk to."

"You don't have a father?" Melissa asks.

Rosalee admits, "We don't know. He came up here to work when me and my sister were little. He would send money to my mother and then, it suddenly stopped. When my mother was no longer hearing from him, she got worried, and she came up looking for him."

"Did she find him?" asks Eréndira, intrigued by the circumstances.

Suddenly feeling like she has said too much, Rosalee tries to deflect and wrap up the story. "No, but she got sponsored by our uncle, her older brother and his family. She saved up a bunch of money and brought me and my sister to live with her."

Rosalee doesn't share more details because, in truth, their mother had to pay a coyote to smuggle the girls across several borders and thousands of miles. It was a dangerous journey of which, fortunately, Rosalee and Luisa have vague recollections of travelling in buses, car trunks, and walking at night across a treacherous desert.

Sometimes at night, Luisa has flashbacks of fast-moving bod-ies, lit by the light of a silvery moon. They are running, looking to hide from vehicles whose headlights illuminate shrubs, cactus, and boulders on dirt roads. She has vague recollections of being crammed into dark small spaces in moving vehicles with her sister and other people she didn't know. The stale air in cramped quarters with others made breathing nearly impossible. She remembers being told to hush by a man charged with her safe passage and admonished to hold tight onto her older sister's hand. By learning to be silent, Luisa and Rosalee learned how to stay undetected.

Luisa's silence, however, has become a fixed feature, a way of surviving. Her sister, Rosalee, on the other hand, is very social but has an aversion to being in small spaces. Luisa wishes her sister wouldn't talk so much because personal information seems to spill out of her when least expected. Luisa understood that many people in the U.S. don't extend compassion to anyone from "south of the border" regardless of the circumstances that compelled them to come at such great risk.

"Where are you and your sister from?" asks Eréndira.

"El Salvador," answers Rosalee.

At that moment, the sisters notice other students exiting the cafeteria. Luisa nudges her sister who acknowledges the prompt.

"Oh yea," says Rosalee, "We must return the lunch boxes to the cafeteria. They recycle these." The two sisters get up and put their backpacks on.

"Nice to meet you!" offers Eréndira.

"Nice to meet you too. Thanks for letting us have lunch with you," says Rosalee before she and her sister move toward the cafeteria.

Once the sisters are out of ear range, Melissa says "That was weird."

"What do you mean?" asks Eréndira.

"I was in P.E. with the older one, Rosalee, and she never spoke to me. I wasn't sure if she spoke English. And the younger one, I've never heard her speak."

"Well, I don't know about Luisa, but Rosalee apparently speaks English quite well."

"Yea… you know, people call them 'the scavengers."

Eréndira raises an eyebrow over the derogatory term.

"Why is that?"

"Well… they're headed to the cafeteria. When everyone else is done eating, they walk up and down the rows of cafeteria tables. They pick up the left-over packaged food left by other students. Goes right in their backpacks."

"They must be hungry," says Eréndira.

"They must be poor," adds Melissa.

"There's nothing wrong with being poor," Eréndira retorts.

"I didn't say there was! I'm just telling you what people are saying! You sure are touchy!" Melissa observes.

"Sorry. I don't mean to take it out on you. Just seems like, today, everyone's been acting strange around me. Before, I wasn't noticed and if I was… it was always with a weird look like I was dropped in from outer space. Like they didn't know what to make of me. Now, I am noticed but I'm given a wide berth like they are afraid of me, or, like these two girls, they want to be friends."

"Well… that's easy to explain."

"Oh yea? Well, alright, explain then."

"You took down Goliath," says Melissa, as a matter of fact.

"You mean Susan?"

"Yea… everyone knows she is such a bully. She picks on everyone. People who make friends with her suck up to her, so they won't get picked on. Think about those two sisters. They get food thrown at them. They ignore the taunting and act as if they don't care but you know it must bother them. Most people laugh or pretend they don't see what's happening. Even when Susan and her friends yell out, 'Hey Mexicans… go back to where you came from.'"

"That is awful. It's not their fault they are poor. And they're not even from Mexico. They are Salvadorian!"

Melissa agrees, "I know. Pretty ignorant. They assume that everyone with darker skin is from Mexico. Susan started in on me when I moved here. I told her that I was Italian. Then, she left me alone."

"Well… I don't care where Rosalee and Luisa are from. They seem nice to me. My Naníta has a saying, 'It is better to be bien educado y pobre than mal y rico.'"

"Which means?"

"It translates into something like… 'it is better to be poor but of good character than a rich person of bad character.'"

"Naníta is your grandma?"

"Yea."

"Is her name Naníta?"

"Of course not. Her name is Elizabeth. Why would you think that?"

"I am taking Spanish, you know. Isn't the Spanish word for Grandmother, 'abuela'?"

Before Eréndira has a chance to fully consider Melissa's question the bell rings and lunchtime is over. It is time to move on to fifth period. Eréndira and Melissa pack their plastic containers away in their backpack.

Eréndira asks, "Hey, I'm going to the City Library after school today. I got to do some research. Want to hang out?"

Melissa looks baffled. "Library? Like, where they keep books?"

"Yea. The City Library."

"Okay. Sure. Why Not? I'll text my mom and let her know. She won't believe me! I don't think I've been in the City Library. I only go to this one here at school when our teacher brings us here. I'll have to get a note from the librarian so my mom doesn't think I'm lying."

The two joined the stream of students moving toward their classrooms. Before her friend parts, Melissa turns to Eréndira, lowers her voice, and says, "You're not going to the library to hide out from Susan? Are you? You know she was suspended so she won't be back for a few days and, I heard she was doing independent study until the bruising from her broken nose goes away. She doesn't want everyone to see her like that."

"No. It's nothing like that. Ms. Foster, the V.P. is supposed to be getting us together when she does get back. I have some stuff I'm looking up for my Naníta."

"Alright then. See you back here after school."

Eréndira makes her way down the hallway to her choir class, ignoring the continuing side glances of classmates. Given what Melissa told her about Rosalee and Luisa, she is curious as to how the two sisters have been able to put up with the mistreatment by others in the school. More importantly, she wondered why no one has stopped all this behavior that seemed to be endemic. Her Naníta would say that the behavior is that of people who are mal educados.

Eréndira knows that there is so much more to Rosalee and Luisa's story than what was revealed during their lunchtime exchange. The circumstances of their being in this community and this school runs much deeper than what is on the surface. As she moves from class to class, she looks for Rosalee and Luisa in the hallways, but she doesn't see them. She hopes to reconnect with them again while pondering to herself, *What do people get out of being so cruel?*

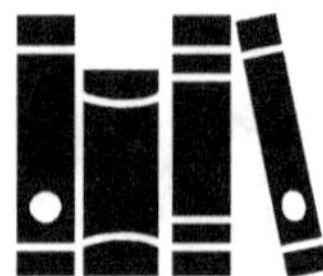

After school, Melissa and Eréndira sit at a computer terminal in the city library.

"What are you looking for?" asks Melissa.

"I'm looking for anything that can tell me about that Bautista guy."

"Who are you talking about? That guy in your choir class?"

Eréndira stops clicking on the computer and turns to Melissa. "Why would I be looking up Mario Bautista from Choir on a Google search when I can just turn around and talk to the tenors from the soprano section?"

Melissa shrugs.

"So, this is what we're doing—when I was visiting my Naníta last weekend, she showed me a petroglyph she uncovered on her property. I'm looking up this guy to see if he's the one on the petroglyph."

Eréndira pulls up the image she captured on her phone when she was at her Naníta's, shows it to Melissa, and explains, "My mom thinks it might be this Juan Bautista de Anza, a Spaniard who was one of those people making missions here in California."

"If it's him, what's his face doing on a rock?" asks Melissa.

"That is what I'm trying to figure out, but first I gotta see if it is possible that it is him. This means uncovering whether the Sierra

Miwok had contact with this Juan Bautista de Anza, so I'm looking up where he went. If the Sierra Miwok had any encounters with him, then they might have marked the sighting by engraving the encounter on the rock."

"Oh! So, what's the big deal with this guy?"

"Well, there's a trail named after him. It's the trail that the Spaniards took when they came up from Mexico. The Spaniards were worried that the Russians, the Brits, and the U.S. were going to expand into this area so this de Anza guy got permission to lead an expedition to Northern California and decide where to build some forts so they could fight off any other countries trying to make claim on this territory. Of course, nobody bothered to ask the California Indians if they were okay with this. Instead, the Indians were enslaved and forced to build the missions which supported the soldiers at these forts."

"Wait a minute! Where'd you hear all this? That's not what happened! Enslaved Indians? Who told you all this?"

"My mom. She used to teach elementary school. Some of the parents didn't like that she taught the truth about why the missions were built and what was done to California Indians in them. They just wanted their kids in her classes to make that stupid model of a mission like they did when they were kids."

"Hey! I made one of those missions!" says Melissa indignantly.

"Well… yea. Then, your teachers weren't giving you the full story."

Melissa sits quietly not knowing what to say. While she processes this new information Eréndira continues, "My mom told the parents that she wouldn't lie to their children, that they deserved better. Then, she told them that if she were to teach them lies then they would go through life believing lies. When she said that, it made the parents' mouths drop open. She told them it is better to teach to the heart, so children become compassionate and that when they get older they will make better decisions because they know the truth. Who's gonna argue with that? Right?"

"Well. This is the first I've heard of enslaved Indians at the missions. And yea… I made one of those missions in fourth grade, but I never thought twice about how the Indians were treated. We were given the impression that they chose to be there." Melissa pauses for a moment before continuing, "It kind of pisses me off that I'm just hearing this. I believed my teachers."

Eréndira stops typing on the keyboard and turns to her friend who is coming to terms with the fact that she has not been given an accurate rendering of history. "Well… it's not your fault you weren't taught right."

Melissa's face reveals betrayal. She slumps into her chair, crosses her arms and says, "And I liked my elementary teachers. Why would they lie to us? We were just gullible kids?"

Eréndira carefully considers Melissa's question before answering. "I don't think they know they're lying. Or, if they do, sometimes they are afraid to tell the truth because they might get backlash from people who feel embarrassed or responsible in some way for all the crap that happened. They would rather just bury the truth."

"What would it matter if the truth came out? It's not like this generation is responsible."

"True that." Eréndira acknowledges while considering why there might be resistance to the truth. "Well… think about it. People coming from Europe set their mind on taking all this land. That meant clearing out the people who were already here. Then, that land gets passed down, generation after generation, so there are people who inherit a crap load of land and wealth. If the truth came out the people living on this land would have to ask themselves how they ended up with so much and maybe wonder at whose expense they got what they have. They'd have to consider the cost for the people who were here first."

"What about the people who were here first? They're gone!"

"What do you mean, they're gone? Gone where?"

"Hell… I don't know but you don't see them around."

"Are you thinking aliens came down and took them all away?"

"Not out of the question! I haven't seen one. Have you?"

"Melissa! What is it you expect to see?"

Melissa stops to consider what happened to the California Indians, confronting her own misconceptions and musing over her belief that because she hasn't seen anyone walking around donning feathers and deerskin that California Indians no longer exist.

Eréndira sees her friend quietly processing this for herself, so she offers, "Teaching the truth is important for all of us, not just California Indians. That's why my mom was willing to stick her neck out as an elementary teacher. She has a bunch of books she keeps at home. She uses them to make her own lesson plans. I'll bring you one so you can see what people say took place in the Missions." Eréndira then redirects Melissa to focus on the computer screen. "Look… here's some info online. It's about the Trail being a National Historic Trail. It says that over 240 people, a multi-ethnic group, left Nogales, Arizona on a 1,200-mile journey. They were headed for San Francisco." Eréndira clicks on a drop-down menu that leads to "County Guides" and then explains to Melissa, "We know that de Anza founded the site of the fort in San Francisco, but I am wondering if he ever got close to the Sierra Foothills where my Naníta lives. Look at this! It's a map!"

The two, sitting side by side, lean toward the computer screen. A detailed California map shows the route taken by de Anza and, sure enough, it reveals a detailed expedition that deviates away from San Francisco and ventures into the central region.

Eréndira reads out loud a portion of de Anza's camp diary dated April 7, 1776: "'…we set forth on the march continuing northwest along the Sierra mentioned, and having traveled about two and a half leagues and crossed two arroyos with a little water and a growth of trees which reaches to the shores of the southern estuary, we came abreast of a large grove of pines or redwoods, and after about another league and a half of travel we found ourselves in front of the mouth of the port of San Francisco.'"

"Wow!" exclaimed Eréndira. "Do you know what that means?"

Melissa shrugs, "Uh, it means they couldn't find a decent coffee shop?"

"No, Silly! This means that they were in a part of California where they weren't that far from the Sierra Miwok… the people living in the foothills."

"Yea, but they were still far enough where they couldn't see one another. I don't think people had high powered binoculars back then. Did they?"

"Well… no, but when you are up in the foothills and look west, you can see the coastal hills. De Anza, and his expedition could probably see the Sierra foothills. There wasn't any pollution and smoke from fires like we have now."

"Okay. So, looking at this map. It looks like de Anza made it as far as Antioch, but we still don't know how he would have contacted any of the Indians who were up in the hills," Melissa points out.

"Well… let's read on and see what else is here."

Melissa's eyes land on a passage she begins to read aloud: "Ah! Here's more! 'We ascended a high hill to see what we could see. The first thing we noticed was that the river which we had thought would turn to the east, continued to the east-northeast, and that from here upstream it appeared to us to be more like a large lake than a river. This impression was supported by the fact that up to now we had not seen the current which was reported on the first journey, and that the water appeared to have an ebb and flow, and also by the fact that we had not found any flotsam, and that the surf continued. From that hill we saw to the east and to the north an interminable plain without any groves, and to the northeast the snow-covered Sierra which we mentioned yesterday.'"

"So, apparently, they were able to see the Sierra's from a high hill! Let's check another de Anza Entry… let's look at this one from when they were passing through the San Francisco area. It's dated March 31st."

Melissa reads on, "'Today in passing we have seen six villages, whose inhabitants, not accustomed to seeing us, fled like wild beasts. Notwithstanding this, about forty heathens have come close to us and I have given them presents. The last one whom we encountered discovered us about forty paces away, and although less than five steps from where he was there was a place where he might have hidden, such was his terror that he lay down in his tracks…I tried to relieve his fright and to get him to stand up, but for a long time I was unable to succeed… I thought it best to leave the unfortunate fellow alone.' I wonder," says Melissa. "why the Indians got so freaked out at the sight of these Spaniards?"

Eréndira definitively answers, "Probably because they had heard from other tribes further south of the crap that the Spaniards were doing to them."

Eréndira prints out the information from the website and jots down a few notes. She is about to log out when Melissa stops her.

"Wait… there is a bit more here about that area in the East Bay…. It talks about the Antioch/Oakley Regional Shoreline where there is 'a plaque placed on the edge of the shore on the east side of the fishing pier. Near this camp on April 3rd, there was a friendly exchange with members of a Bay Miwok village.' That's interesting. There was a shoreline of some kind, and this is where they connected with some Miwok from the Bay."

Eréndira says, "I think a lot of California used to be under water. There was more water here a long time ago than what we have now. If de Anza was stopped by the tule marshes from going any further, how did the Sierra Miwok see him, up close and personal enough to make an etching of his likeness on a rock?"

"Dang, girl. It's like we're getting close but something's missing!" Melissa checks the time on her cell phone and adds, "Look. I've got to go. Are you going to tell your grandmother what we found?"

"Not yet. I'm going to dig some more and see if I can make a stronger connection. There were a couple of names of people travelling with de Anza… Font… Garces… It looks like their diaries are included on this website."

"Why are you looking all this up here in the public library? You could have done this at home."

"Yea… but they have archives here and other stuff that is not on the website. Like this publication that I checked out before you got here. It's about the Expedition but seems to tell it more from the Native perspective."

Melissa's eyes grow wide as she looks at the publication that Eréndira holds in her hands. Eréndira can see that Melissa has taken an interest in this research, so she offers, "Look… I've got a bunch of homework tonight, so I won't have time to read this. You want to take it home tonight and we can talk about it tomorrow?"

"Yea! That works for me!"

At that moment, Eréndira gets a text. Her father is home from work, and he is wondering where she is. She quickly texts back, "Library. Be home soon."

Turning to Melissa she says, "Crap. My dad's home from work already. I lost track of time. Let's go!" The two jump up, place their belongings in their backpacks, and head for the doors. Eréndira reminds Melissa, "Don't forget to get a note from the librarian so your mom knows we were here and not out messing around."

Melissa walks straight to the librarian behind the check-out desk and asks her to write a note to her mother. The young woman, with wire framed glasses, gives Melissa a knowing smile. This isn't the first time she has been asked to vouch for a student spending time in the library. The librarian signs her name, stamps it with the official library seal, and writes in the date and time. Eréndira watches Melissa hurriedly pass through the double glass doors, reaching for her phone to make a call, as she makes her way out.

In the meantime, the quest to make the connection between the Sierra Miwok and Juan Bautista de Anza will continue and Eréndira is grateful to have this welcome distraction. In a matter of days, she will be required to sit down with her nemesis, Susan, and iron things out. However, now she knows more of who Susan is and what she has done to Rosalee and Luisa. She dislikes Susan even more than the day she busted her nose. The seed of anger seethes when she thinks of the inhuman cruelty. As Eréndira walks home in the late afternoon, she wonders how Susan learned to behave this way.

As she enters the front door, Eréndira's father promptly greets her while he is preparing dinner.

"Hey Eréndira! Is that you? I'm in the kitchen."

"Yea! It's me. I'm a bit late. Was at the library. Where's mom?"

"She teaches a night class on Mondays. Remember? Her class is out by 7:00. She should be home by 8:00 or so. How was school today?"

"It was okay."

A guarded answer, Victor surmises, that tells him nothing, so he digs deeper. "Any backlash after everything that happened last week?"

"No. People left me alone," Eréndira answers, somewhat deflated that this sensitive topic that she would like to avoid is brought up. But then she perks up and adds, "But I did make two new friends!"

"Oh yea? Who are they?"

"Two sisters from El Salvador. They sat with me and Melissa at lunch."

"Oh. Cool! Sooooo… you were at the library?"

"Yea. I was at the library. Don't act so shocked!" Eréndira retorts defiantly.

"Well… it's just that you never went to the one back home." Victor defends.

"Yea. That's true but the one here is bigger and has more stuff. It's more like those University libraries that mom used to drag me to when she was working on her doctorate."

"So, what kind of stuff does this library have?"

"Well… like archives where they keep old stuff… printed stuff that came out before computers."

Victor takes this opportunity to give their new town a positive spin. "Sounds like there are a few good things about this community then, right?"

Eréndira hesitates before answering. "Yea. I guess."

"Well, you're home just in time for dinner." He proceeds to serve dinner directly from the pans on the stove while she pulls out silverware from one of the drawers. They settle in at the dining table and Victor inquires, "Tell me more about this library. I haven't had time to check it out."

Eréndira tells Victor about Melissa's and her efforts to confirm that the petroglyph on Naníta's property is an image of a Sierra Miwok looking down at de Anza. With excitement in her voice, Eréndira explains that if her mother's guess is right, then they can conclude that the Sierra Miwok were, like Naníta says, chronicling history on the rocks, making the petroglyph historically significant.

"That's great, Eréndira. Hit your mother up again for what she might know about that expedition. I know she's been distracted with settling into our new home and her new position at the University, but she used to teach this stuff. It's her sweet spot."

"I will, pops! And can't wait to tell Naníta too!"

Eréndira retreats to her room after helping Victor clean the kitchen and preparing a plate for her mother to have a late dinner when she gets home. She starts her homework and resists the temptation to get on-line and check social media. Melissa had warned her that the gossip has been ugly and much of it is racist. She even suggested to Eréndira that she just ignore it all for a while, promising that, eventually, "Susan and her swamp-dwelling friends will find someone else to pick on." Eréndira figures this is sound advice, for now.

Upstairs in her bedroom, looking over song lyrics that her choir has been rehearsing, Eréndira hears the garage door open. Out the front window she sees her mother's SUV pulling up to enter the garage. Verónica uses the automatic garage door clicker to promptly close the garage door behind her. Since the police visit to interview Eréndira the previous week, neighbors have been gawking at their home. She figures it better to give them less to see so as not to feed rampant imaginations.

Eréndira runs down the stairs, anxious to share what she learned about de Anza with her mother, but, when she gets to the bottom of the stairs, she overhears her parents in the living room. Her mother asks her father about Eréndira's day and if anything else has happened. He confirms that nothing else transpired and that their daughter spent the afternoon in the library. Their conversation reminds Eréndira of the turmoil and her stomach starts to churn. She wishes she had some of her Naníta's mint tea. She quietly retreats back up the stairs without greeting her mother, puts on her headphones, and listens to music.

Past 9:00 p.m. Verónica knocks on Eréndira's door. By then, she has dressed down and has had a quiet dinner while watching a sitcom with Victor. She knocks several times before calling out, "Eréndira, are you awake?" Eréndira, still wearing her headphones, doesn't hear the sound and doesn't answer. Verónica opens the door, pokes her head in, and spies Eréndira sprawled out on her bed reading song lyrics.

Peeling off her headphones, Eréndira utters, "Hey mom. I didn't hear you."

Verónica enters and says, "It's okay. So, school was good today?"

"Yea," answers Eréndira glumly.

"Your dad said you were doing some research at the library. You're looking into de Anza? What did you find?"

Eréndira perks up at the reminder of her newfound interest and much needed distraction. She reaches for her backpack and pulls out now crumpled printouts of the information gleaned at the library. She unfolds the papers and lays them on her bed as she explains, "I found out that de Anza's expedition didn't just end at San Francisco. He did sort of a loop around the Bay and ended up as far east as Antioch and Oakley." She shows her mother the specific text, pointing out where it states, *They reached the site of Antioch, and encountering impassable Tule marshes, headed south back towards Monterey.*

Eréndira adds, "He came across several tribes who lived in the Bay Area. We even saw that he came across a people called the Bay Miwok, but it doesn't say anything about the Sierra Miwok."

"A ver. *Let me see.*" Eréndira hands her mother the printouts—she reads the excerpts before saying, "Oh yea. Moraga where St. Mary's College and the city is named for him. That's where I did my master's degree. Ah! Font! Yea, I remember Pedro Font. I read his translated journal. We can credit him for being one of the first to bring homophobia and racism to California."

"What?" Eréndira asks.

"Well, the Spaniards, at that time, were culturally very misogynistic and their clergy were extremely conservative. The Spaniards, once on this continent, didn't think highly of the people with whom they came in contact. You can tell by how de Anza referred to the Indians, 'wild beast' and 'heathens.' Font, a Chaplain, accompanied de Anza. His job was to map out the Bay Area and help pick the sites for a fort and the missions. The Indians were to be enticed, caught, whatever it took, so they would serve the Spaniards' needs.

The Indians had every good reason to get as far away from these men as they could!"

"You're saying that Font was a chaplain, but he wasn't such a good guy?"

"That's right. The Spaniards, at that time, brought their prejudices and a lot of bad intentions. The clergy talked about converting people on this continent to Christianity but, really, it was all about conquest and securing land for the royal crown. The Indians, up and down the continent, were forced to work for the Spaniards. Even our people were forced to do the mining, agriculture, building structures… everything. The missions were an extension of the encomienda system that was established in Mexico. So, as the Spaniards made their way up the coast from Mexico, the Indians were captured, stripped of their culture, land, everything… no wonder those people fled."

"That's what I figured. I had to tell Melissa a little bit about this because she didn't learn this, but you said you read Font's journal?"

"Oh yea… I can get a translated copy of his journal. The university library might have it, and, if not, I can order it from another campus or maybe even buy a copy and have it delivered here to the house. Let me check when I'm back on campus tomorrow but I do remember…" Verónica trails off to look over the excerpt, once again, and her eyes fall on notes that refer to a *friendly exchange with members of a Bay Miwok village*. She points to that excerpt for Eréndira and says, "See this? It says this encounter happened on the Antioch/Oakley Shoreline. That's waaaayyy East Contra Costa County. I kind of remember something I read from that journal when I was in the teaching credential program. It said something about de Anza's group trying to get up to the Sierras, but they didn't have the watercraft to transport their horses and wagons and all the stuff they had. So, they couldn't get to the foothills."

"Bummer," says Eréndira, deflated.

"Why so?" asks Verónica.

"If Font's journal confirms that de Anza and the rest of the Spaniards couldn't get up to the hills then the Sierra Miwok wouldn't have been able to see de Anza. That means that the image on the petroglyph at Naníta's probably isn't him. That puts us back at square one."

Verónica considers Eréndira's line of thinking, then offers, "But you're thinking that de Anza had to get to the foothills to be seen by the person that made that petroglyph. Let me offer you another possibility...." Eréndira perks up and Verónica continues, "Tribes weren't static. They traveled, traded and inter-married with other tribes... that's how de Anza got up and through California. They took routes that were already here and led by tribal people familiar with these routes that came up from Mexico. What I would say... is that there were Sierra Miwok who saw de Anza while he was on his," Verónica motions air quotes when she says, "'expedition' and then when they returned to their home up in the hills, they told others of what they witnessed and chronicled the encounter on the rock."

"Yea. That makes a lot of sense but how did they get from the Antioch/Oakley area to the hills across the water when even the Spaniards couldn't do it?"

"Ay... Eréndira. Give the California Indians more credit. They had expertly made canoes that could carry lots of people. They could easily get around the choppy waters of the San Francisco Bay so imagine them getting across a lake?"

"That's right. You and dad found that shell fossil. There used to be more lakes and rivers here."

"Yep... where we are, right now, was under water back then. More like a lake and marshes... plus, riverways that they could have used to get upstream."

"There was something that Naníta said about the petroglyph. The way it was positioned."

"What did she say?"

"She said that the Native American was positioned on top, looking down on the Spaniard, who was looking away from the Native American. It could mean that the Native American was up on the hills and the Spaniard was down below. If the Spaniard is turned away, as he is in the petroglyph, but the Native American is on top and seeing de Anza, it means that the Spaniard may not be aware that he has been seen by someone from this Tribe."

"There you go." Verónica smiles at Eréndira. "You are seeing and interpreting history from the perspective of the people who were already here."

Eréndira considers this shift in perspective. She thinks about the derogatory words that de Anza used to describe the people he came across and how these words are so readily available for others to read. Then, she remembered how Melissa had been taught that the Missions were nice places where Indians enjoyed being, learned how to construct buildings, and do farming while readily accepting the missionaries' religion.

"You know mom. This makes me think of all this bullshit I'm going through."

"In what way?"

"Well... Melissa told me there's a bunch of gossip and lies on Instagram."

Verónica takes her daughter's hands in hers, examines the long fingers and polished nails, short but manicured. "You know Eréndira... there are three things you can always count on."

"I thought there were only two... Dad says, 'death and taxes.'"

Verónica laughs then says, "Well... those are two but there are also three other ones: night, day, and the truth. Even when the clouds obscure the stars and even the sun, night and day are still there. It's the same with the truth. Gossip and lies can try to obscure but the truth is always there, and it will eventually come out."

Eréndira looks down at her mother's hands holding hers.

"There's a lot of clouds out right now? Obscuring the sun and the moon?" asks Verónica.

Eréndira nods. "Yea. I guess, but clouds don't hang around forever."

"That's right. The skies will clear up." The two make eye contact and Verónica squeezes her daughter's hands. Then, Verónica exclaims, "Oh my! It's almost 10:00! We'd better get to bed. ¡Besitos!" She gives Eréndira a kiss on the forehead, gets up, and leaves her daughter's bedroom.

Eréndira gets under her covers, turns off the lamp by her bed, and tries to imagine what life would be like without so many clouds to contend with. She pictures a young Indian man seeing the

Spaniards who were treated like guests at a Bay Miwok ceremonial gathering. Then, perhaps, is it possible that a young man from the Sierra Miwok tribe jumped into a canoe and paddled across a great lake? Maybe he then arrived in the foothills and told the people of his community what he saw. After he told everyone of this encounter, he's then instructed to chronicle the incident on the rocks. People gather around after he has chiseled the image and he repeats the story of who he saw, time and again, for all to hear so they may learn of what is coming. He speaks his truth. The truth.

Eréndira, too, wants her truth to be heard over the drone of lies being told about her. As she lays in bed waiting for sleep to come, she reminds herself, *I need to call Nanita and tell her….* Then, her mother's words come back to her, "Give the California Indians more credit." She wonders, *Did they carve out the trails that connected Mexico to California and yet de Anza's name is attached to them? How far and wide did those trails go?* As she dozes off, she considers her own shift in thinking… that even she has underestimated California Indian agency.

Despite her mother's teachings, she, like Melissa, was only considering one point of view and it was casting a shadow on how she interpreted all that she was uncovering. She needed to consider the perspective of the California Indians who were on the receiving end of other's attacks. Similarly, she didn't want others to believe what was being put on social media about her. Drifting into slumber, Eréndira wonders if there is a lake into which she, like Princess Hapunda and, perhaps, Princess Eréndira, can jump into and disappear from it all.

It Was the Year 1516

"Sesasi is coming! And she brings us Eréndira!" shouted Parakata. Despite her husband Irepani's cautions, Parakata runs down the road toward the colorful procession arriving from Tzintzuntzan. Parakata had planted herself on one of the western facing hills of Acámbaro. This was the day, as she and Irepani had been notified by a messenger sent by the Cazonci, that her daughter and grand-daughter would come back for a visit from the Purépecha Capitol.

It had been thirteen years since Sesasi left her parents, Parakata and Irepani, in the border city of Acámbaro to join Timas in the kingdom's capital. During those years, messengers carried information between the two communities, which was how Parakata and Irepani stayed connected with their daughter. Despite the prolonged wars with the Mexica, messengers, at the risk of capture, exchanged valuable information between the nobles. They also passed on information to thwart attacks from outside forces. In previous years, the news that came from the border were alarming as there had been intensive conflict but now, the roads between Tzintzuntzan and Acámbaro were considered free of danger.

Sesasi's father, Irepani, undoubtedly had a hand in securing peace within the kingdom. While he was known for his valor on the battlefield, he was also recognized for his tenderness and commitment to spiritual balance. Irepani's job entailed training soldiers, purecutis, but he, himself, was a qhuacarati, a warrior. Military service was considered a religious devotion and Irepani's role as a leader meant modeling the highest standards of conduct to the younger members of his battalion, which included not only Purépecha but also Otomis and Chichimeca warriors who had given their allegiance to the Cazonci Zuangua.

The younger warriors under Irepani's watch collected firewood for the temples where they prayed to the solar deity, Curicáueri, the representation of fire, and to the female deity, Xarátanga, the earth mother who swept away impurities. In their prayers they asked for strength and courage during battle because if the son of an elite captured an enemy fighter, he earned titles of distinction. With first capture, a warrior became a quangapahua, warrior of the morning.

A warrior's commitment to protecting their communities was strengthened by attending the feast of Hiquándiro, which was held in Tzintzuntzan. This was where qhuacaratis and purecutis were prepared for battle and reminded of the code of conduct: obedience to their commander, fighting without retreat, and sexual abstinence. This last requirement meant that women, including Parakata, were prohibited from traveling to Tzintzuntzan with their husbands. Their presence created too much temptation. Abstinence was one of the sacrifices made by warriors in their devotion and preparation for battle.

Irepani's status as a qhuacarati obligated him to model self-discipline. In this way, he maintained order with the younger warriors and soldiers who were inclined to distraction and easily wandered from their spiritual preparation and ultimate mission. Because he was charged with closely supervising his young warriors, he was not able to see his daughter, Sesasi, and his new granddaughter, Eréndira, on the occasions when he was in Tzintzuntzan for the Hiquandiro Feast. Deviance from the codes of conduct would be a poor example to the younger warriors. Nonetheless, it hurt knowing that Sesasi and Eréndira were so physically close when he was in Tzintzuntzan, but he rationalized that the best way to demonstrate his love and devotion for them was to train warriors and soldiers who would best protect them. The strongest must protect the most vulnerable, and, for this reason, true warriors fought to the death on the battlefield.

Fortunately, a new era of peace had arrived and the roads within the Kingdom were now safe after an extensive six-month war that ended in a sound defeat of the Mexica. This meant that Sesasi could reunite with her family, and Eréndira would finally meet her maternal lineage in Acámbaro. With the announced sighting of the caravan arriving from the capital, Parakata could not contain her joy. It had been too many seasons since she held her daughter, and all she knew of her granddaughter, Eréndira, was that all who knew her found favor. A palm-sized greenstone carving of Eréndira's features when she was ten years old had been delivered several years prior by messengers. The beautiful image capturing her soft features, large eyes, and prominent cheekbones was kept on the family altar.

Now that the war with the Mexica was behind them, Parakata's legs could not carry her fast enough to reach the approaching caravan. She was surprised that at her age she could run as fast as she did in her teens when she had to flee marauding Mexica warriors. While Parakata ran toward the arriving caravan, she slowed down to determine who rapidly approached her from behind. Heavy footsteps pounding the ground were soon upon her. In an instant, Irepani, with the speed of a jaguar, ran past her. The force of the wind in his wake was audible. Seeing him outpace her in the race toward the approaching caravan she shouted, "Irepani! You told me not to leave the boundaries of Acámbaro and here you are leaving the boundaries yourself!"

Irepani yelled over his shoulder, his words carried by the wind, "Yes! But you would not mind me! So, I am running ahead to make sure the road is safe for you!"

Parakata stopped in her tracks and placed her hands on her hips. "But what is there to fear? The roads have been made safe! You assured me!"

Irepani turned around to face his wife but ran backwards to not lose his momentum that was taking him closer to his daughter and granddaughter. "My fear is having to suffer one more day. It has been so many seasons! I long to see my daughter and meet my granddaughter!"

"Ay, Irepani! I, too, miss Sesasi! Wait for me!" She continued her sprint toward the caravan.

"I've waited thirteen years! Catch up my dear butterfly!" He held out his hand to Parakata who took it and, together with hands clasped, ran down the road to greet their daughter, Sesasi, and meet their granddaughter, Eréndira.

Sesasi, in the midst of the caravan, spotted the two figures running at full pace toward them. The royal guards, at the front, were not sure what to make of what they saw. They could make out a man who was, from appearances, the build and status of a warrior, but his demeanor, running together with a woman, was out of character. The royal guard stopped the procession, alert to enemy spy incursions and their devious plots to trick Purépecha forces. Could these two running toward them, as though being chased by evil spirits, be enemies cloaked in Purépecha clothing? They were charged with delivering the Cazonci's gifts but also responsible for protecting Lord Timas and his family. Out of caution, the archers kneeled, drew back their bows, and prepared to let their arrows fly. Behind the archers, more soldiers formed a line to protect the caravan. Their spears, held firmly in both hands, pointed in the direction of the two people running toward them.

Sesasi, with Eréndira closely behind, moved toward the front of the procession, stepped in front of the archers, and motioned for them to lower their weapons. To the royal guard she announced, "Those two are my nánde and taáte!"

With that, she broke into a run toward her parents with Eréndira keeping pace behind her. The three, Parakata, Irepani, and Sesasi, collided into a full group hug. Parakata held Sesasi's face in her hands while Irepani placed his lips on the side of Sesasi's head and deeply inhaled her essence.

After a prolonged moment of holding one another to be sure they were not dreaming, Parakata broke her grip on Sesasi and turned to the thirteen-year-old who had been patiently observing the reunion. Parakata, laying her eyes on her granddaughter for the first time, addressed her directly.

"No wonder your mother called you Eréndira! Look at that beautiful smile!" Parakata held her arms open to Eréndira who stepped into her grandmother's embrace.

The caravan that delivered Sesasi and Eréndira also brought gold, silver and turquoise jewelry, pottery, and blankets—all made by the best Purépecha artisans. The Cazonci, grateful for the loyalty and courage of the people on the border, rewarded them for their strength and strategy that led to the recent defeat of the Mexica. After a night of celebration in Acámbaro, members of the caravan, along with Timas serving as the Cazonci's Emissary, resumed the procession. The following morning the caravan, minus Sesasi and Eréndira, set its direction south for Maravatio, then to Taximaroa, where the townspeople and military played a pivotal role in the recent victory over the Mexica. After distributing gifts to people along the border, Timas would return to Acámbaro for Sesasi and Eréndira and, with the royal guard, escort them back home to Tzintzuntzan.

The ensuing weeks would give Sesasi time to catch up with family while Eréndira got to know them. Eréndira had been told frightful stories of Otomi's and Chichimecas who kidnapped Purépecha women and had killed many of their people, but in Acámbaro, the Otomi and Chichimeca regarded Acámbaro home. In the evenings, gathered around community fires, Eréndira entertained her family and the community with stories of the Cazonci's gentleness, generosity, wisdom, and playful nature. This endeared the people of Acámbaro, who lived in constant vigilance and regularly risked their lives for the good of the kingdom.

One morning with the sun barely casting rays upon the sleeping community of Acámbaro, Eréndira awakened to her grandmother, Parakata, sitting by her side and looking down upon her. Parakata gave the morning greeting, "Najtsï na eránsku! I did not mean to startle you, my lovely child. I gaze upon you so I can engrave your image in my heart. Your mother will be visiting with her siblings and their children for the day. What would you like to do?"

Eréndira sat up, rubbed her eyes, and with certainty in her voice responded, "Please Naníta, my mother has told me, countless times, of when she met my father. I'd like to see where my father and my uncle, Anini, emerged like a washed-up fish from the Chignahuapan River."

Parakata smiled at the thought of the familiar and humorous story. "That, my child, is what we will do today."

The two quickly packed a lunch and made their way down the winding path that took them from Acámbaro, situated on the elevated hills, to the shores of the Chignahuapan River. Once they arrived at a river bend, Parakata laid out a blanket and the two settled in for their first meal of the day, ichusïkuta and t'atsïni, tortillas and beans.

"So, Eréndira, this is where they met!"

"How do you know it was here, Naníta?"

"Because this was your mother's favorite place to go. She loved having time away and being alone. Here, she could watch the birds, spot the fish jumping above the surface, and listen to the rushing water making its way to the ocean."

"That is a side of my mother that I do not see."

"What do you mean? That she enjoys being in nature?"

"No, that she spends time alone. In Tzintzuntzan, she is always in the company of others."

"Well, you must understand that where we live it is not safe. Your Tatíta being who he is, reminds us, always, to be cautious. Here, in Acámbaro, one never knows when Mexicas or others have snuck by our sentries. A woman, alone, is easy prey."

"Yes, Cazonci Zuangua told me about Hapunda!"

"Ah! So, you know that women are highly regarded and sought after. For this reason, we must be vigilant. If we are taken, it can cost the lives of many men who attempt to recover us. This places great responsibility on the entire community to watch over us, even your mother."

"Is that the reason why Tatíta Irepani is hiding in the bushes behind us?"

Parakata laughed, knowing that Eréndira had not been fooled by Irepani. When Parakata and Eréndira left home before the sun had fully cast its rays upon the hills, Irepani sprung from his bed, threw on his clothes, and followed them. All the while, he attempted to maintain distance so his wife and grandchild would not be aware of his presence.

Parakata, in a hushed tone, said, "Yes. Pretend you don't know he's there. It would hurt his feelings if he knew that we knew he is there hiding."

Eréndira leaned toward her Naníta so her words would not be drowned out by the rushing water and whispered, "He has been following us since we left home."

"Yes, yes… and it is not so much that he is afraid that something will happen to us, it is that he wants to be near you. There were so many times when he was in Tzintzuntzan knowing that you and your mother were there, but he could not deviate from his responsibilities of overseeing so many young men. He must stay focused. This is a great sacrifice, and it tears at his heart." Parakata held Eréndira's hands in hers before continuing, "Seeing you and your mother gives him so much joy and reminds him of why he makes the sacrifices he must make as a qhuacarati. And, if he should die in battle, he knows why he devoted his life to it. It would be for you, me, your mother, and all the others."

"It has been thirteen years, Naníta, since I was born. What has changed so that I am able to come and visit you now? We should have come earlier. We have soldiers to guard us."

"I know quite a bit about the history of our conflicts with other tribes but the expert in our family…" Parakata subtly nodded her head toward the bushes where Irepani was nodding off under the warmth of the rising sun. "He's gazing upon us from behind the bushes. Let's do this, I am going to pretend that I must water the earth and accidently come upon him. I will, then, flush him out like a rabbit! Next, I will act surprised and invite him to join us. That would make him so happy."

"Good idea, Naníta! I'll sit here and enjoy the river, pretending I don't know he is there."

With that, Parakata got up, turned toward the bushes where Irepani attempted to remain discreetly hidden, but his growling stomach made him wish he had brought deer jerky to nibble. At the realization that his wife was walking toward him he abruptly bounced up and, in doing so, disturbed a flock of birds nesting in the bushes. This was Parakata's cue to call him forth while feigning surprise.

"Who goes there?"

Sheepishly, Irepani responded, "It is I, Irepani. I was just going for a stroll, getting some exercise." Irepani emerged from behind the bushes. He looked over his wife's shoulder to have a closer look at Eréndira sitting on the blanket. She rewarded him with a glowing smile. "Oh! Eréndira! You are here with your Naníta!"

"Yes, Tatíta. I am so glad to see you!" Eréndira feigned surprise. "Please come and join us." She motioned to the vacated spot on the blanket where her Naníta had been sitting. "We have beans and tortillas if you are hungry."

There was no need to repeat the invitation. Irepani promptly stepped toward the blanket and plopped down next to his granddaughter. In the morning light, an orange radiance reflected off Eréndira's jet black hair. Her skin, a deep brown the color of earth, glowed golden. Since Sesasi and Eréndira's arrival, the two had been constantly whisked away by the many extended family members so Irepani had not been granted time with his precious granddaughter. It reminded him of the ache in his heart of being separated from them, all these years. His eyes welled up in tears.

As Eréndira passed him his first meal of the day, she noticed the tears. She mistook his tears as disappointment. "Tatíta! I am sorry that we have nothing else to offer you than the tortillas and beans!"

"Oh no, my grandchild," Irepani chuckled. "The beans and tortillas are wonderful. Seeing and hearing you reminds me of your Naníta and your mother when they were much younger. You carry their beauty with humility. I listen to you when you speak with the others at night around the fire and share stories. Your words, spoken like music, reflect such dignity."

"Thank you, Tatíta. You and Naníta taught my mother well."

Parakata, having pretended to relieve herself behind nearby bushes, rejoined the two on the blanket and addressed her husband, "Irepani, your destination for your morning stroll was so timely, Eréndira was asking about why it took so long before it was deemed safe enough for her and her mother to visit us here on the border."

"Oh yes!" Irepani, wiping away tears, settled into the events leading to the era of peace. "In the time of my grandparents, our people desired the land known as the Toluca Valley. It is a valley abundant with gold, silver, copper, and even greenstone and salt. This is important to us because our people work with metallurgy. My father's and grandfather's generation fought a seven-year war with Mexica allied forces over access to this valley. Skirmishes were constant and with each encounter, the tension between our nations worsened."

"I see, often, in Tzintzuntzan, the beautiful jewelry, weapons of metal, and have tasted the salt, but the greenstone? What is its use? It is only a stone." Eréndira asked.

Irepani pulled out a rock from a pocket in his manta. From the greenstone could be discerned a carefully carved image of Eréndira. While displaying the rock he explained, "When we were unable to arrange for your safe passage during the more recent times of turbulence, your Naníta and I requested, through the messengers, for a carving of your image so we would have the likeness of you here. Greenstone gives to harder rocks. This allows us to send messages or information that can be carried by the couriers. This carving of you, was a gift."

Irepani passed the palm-sized carving to Eréndira. She examined the likeness, flowing hair, large eyes, and soft features. She turned to her grandfather, "So the Toluca Valley had great significance."

"Yes, and other regions as well. The conflict over these regions started with skirmishes and led to a full-scale war. This is what was told to me by my Tatíta."

"So, Tatíta," Eréndira addressed her grandfather, Irepani, "how did we finally win?"

"There were a few years in which the Mexica had a general by the name of Tlacaelel. He was fed up with our people's efforts to gain control of these rich lands, so he brought together 32,300 formidable warriors from many tribes." Turning to Eréndira to emphasize the next point, he stated, "The lesson here, Eréndira, is to grasp when and where strength of mind and spirit can be stronger than brute force."

Irepani paused and took a few bites of his tortilla. Eréndira, held in suspense, didn't move or probe. She sat quietly while Irepani chewed his food. They watched a beaver pop out of the water as though curious to hear the story firsthand.

After Irepani swallowed, he continued, "The gathered Mexica forces came en masse. We knew we could not place all our warriors on the front line in a face-to-face battle. This would leave the rest of the kingdom unprotected. So, we positioned only a small number of our warriors at Taximaroa, the entryway between the Purépecha and Mexica Kingdoms—these warriors were but a decoy. The Mexica forces engaged this small battalion of Purépecha warriors and easily chased them off, but this was part of the larger plan. With what appeared to be an easy victory, the Mexica became arrogant. Their forces then moved across Purépecha territory toward the capitol and when they made camp, the might of all our warriors fell upon them. The overwhelmed Mexica forces fled in two groups. One retreated toward Taximaroa, the direction from where they came, the other group sought refuge in the Toluca Valley, but there was no protection for what came upon them. The Purépecha warriors overtook them. It was a slaughter."

Eréndira tried to imagine what so much death looked like. Tens of thousands of human beings. "Tatíta! That is a lot of death."

"Yes, Eréndira, and the Mexica ruler, Axayacatl, became despondent and humiliated by so much loss but he learned his lesson and did not mount another attack on our people in his lifetime."

"That was in the time of your amámba and taáte?"

"Yes. My taáte, he, too, was a qhuacarati. In his lifetime, Acámbaro was a small village, but since that war, this and many other cities on the Eastern border have protected the Purépecha Kingdom. We are fortunate to have Otomi and Chichimecas on our side. They found disfavor with the Mexica and joined us, as allies. Taximaroa, south of us, continues to be the Central Point of the Purépecha Border. In turn, the Mexica also created a Western front. We face one another like vigilant neighbors even though we continue to trade with one another and conduct diplomatic relations."

"I have seen them, Tatíta. I have seen the Mexica diplomats and even the merchants in Tzintzuntzan. They never directly see the Cazonci, and they are always watched by our warriors."

"Yes. Because of the ongoing skirmishes we do not trust them. We have messengers and translators who accompany them from the border to the capitol. These are usually Otomís who know our language and speak Nahuatl, the language of the Mexica. They are only allowed entry through Taximaroa where our officials interview anyone seeking entry. If allowed to enter the kingdom, they are escorted to their destination. As you have seen, they are never given an audience with the Cazonci. But, while we have attempted to maintain some shred of diplomacy, skirmishes along the border continued. This lasted for a generation until they began attacking territories that encircled our Kingdom. It appeared they were testing our boundaries, all along our southern border to the Pacific Ocean, looking for weakness."

"And then came the Tlaxcalan warrior Tlahuicole," Eréndira offered as entry to the continuance of the story.

"Yes, so you have heard his name," said Irepani.

Eréndira confirmed, "Yes. My taáte impressed upon me and my amámba of the imminent danger because of Tlahuicole. We were afraid for you, Naníta, and the rest of our relations. For our safety, my mother and I were whisked away to an island in Lake Patzcuaro."

Irepani threw a stick into the river before he said, "It was good that you knew. He was an impressive warrior who led full assaults on Taximaroa, Maravatío, Tzitaquaro, Tzinapicuaro and, of course, Acámbaro. We could never let our guard down. Women and children could be taken at any hour. The attacks were relentless."

Eréndira excitedly offered, "I have heard that my taáte, the captain of war, came up with the strategy but, it was here, Tatíta, that his plans were carried out. I would like to hear from you what happened."

"Just like the rocks, Eréndira, a stronger one can wear down a weaker tone. This is why we instill so much spiritual preparation and obedience with our soldiers. A person with a strong spirit can overcome a person with only a strong body."

Eréndira sat silently as she processed her Tatíta's last words. "A spirit with purpose endures. A body fatigues."

"Yes, Eréndira. But, think of it this way, the body is of the earth. It wants to live. When facing the risk of death, it yearns to live. We are committed to a higher calling; protect our Elders, our women, our children. If we retreat, if we surrender, then our spirits have acquiesced to the needs of the body. We do not let fear of death alter our calling to protect our loved ones."

Eréndira looked out at the hills, now illuminated by the rising sun. The rushing Chignahuapan River playfully bounced over boulders and around cottonwoods rooted on the banks. Flocks of birds descended onto the shores, scratching for seeds. She was surrounded by a cloak of pure joy, but she knew that moments of peace, such as this, were hard earned.

"It is fear, Tatíta. Isn't it? Our spirits must overcome fear."

"Yes, and what else must we do when we are called upon to engage in what we would rather not do? Such as killing other humans."

"Use our heads!"

"You are wise, Eréndira. The use of brute force does not always reflect strength but like a harder stone, we bear into their vulnerability, their lack of discipline."

"So, the story that came to us is true! We used strategy to defeat them, once again?"

"Yes. They apparently did not learn from past events. Once again, we staged a force at Taximaroa. It wasn't a large force but large enough to make it look like we were putting forth a defensive battle. Our forces then retreated into the interior but..." Irepani then raised a finger to emphasize the point, "left behind that which would tempt them to lose their focus."

Eréndira beamed as the recounting of what had transpired just the year before unfolded before her.

"Tell me the rest, Tatíta! I am fascinated!" exclaimed Eréndira.

"So, here we are now, in the Land of Maguey! Acámbaro! And what are we able to leave behind for the Mexica, thinking that they have, of their own accord, overtaken the city?"

Eréndira laughed as she came to fully understand the chain of events, "The Purépecha left behind octli, a wine... made from the akámba maguey... akámba as in Acámbaro!"

"Yes. And lots of it. Your taáte is a smart one! We left stores of octli everywhere for them. The Mexica soldiers got inebriated as they celebrated... thinking they had won the war. Little did they know, they walked right into our trap. We watched from afar and waited while they drank and drank. They sang and shouted and counted themselves victorious too soon. Once they fell asleep, in a drunken stupor, our warriors descended upon them like tukúrus upon mice. The bones of those slaughtered were left in the Toluca Valley. They are still there as a reminder to the Mexica."

"And you were there Tatíta!"

"Yes. I was there, my child."

"Don't let him fool you, Eréndira," Parakata cut in. "His role was to oversee the younger ones who transported the octli. Once the Mexica men were inebriated, there wasn't much fighting. It was mostly chasing drunken and bewildered warriors! Not once did your Tatíta have to touch his bow!"

At that, Irepani and Parakata both laughed at the image of the Purépecha warriors in pursuit of intoxicated, fleeing Mexica warriors. This was a further reason for why Purépecha culture rejected abject drunkenness. Harsh punishment was enacted upon those who did not abide by these cultural expectations.

"Yes, but Tatíta, you were able to repel the Mexica and bring peace to our people."

"Yes, my grandchild… but remember, it is because we are disciplined and balanced, spiritually, physically, and mentally! It has been known since ancient times when our ancestors were forced to abandon the land of Mu, deep in the ocean, that ego, greed, division leads to destruction. There are forces within humans that we must resist. When they surface in our enemies, we must be prepared to defend ourselves. So, tomorrow, while you are here with us, you will begin training with me."

"You will train me to be a warrior?" asked Eréndira with enthusiasm.

"You are of a warrior lineage. To be balanced you must have skills to protect yourself and others. We hope you may never have to do so, but every woman in the border can yield a sword."

"Then, Tatíta I shall master the sword, and pray that I will never have to use it. May eternal peace reign!"

"I love you, my Granddaughter." Irepani hugged Eréndira.

Parakata smiled upon the two, forging in her mind the image of her husband and granddaughter in full embrace. She relished this rare moment of tranquility. She knew that, soon, Sesasi and Eréndira would return to Tzintzuntzan. She prayed that they would see one another, once again, under this veil of peace.

Repetitive drumming told of strange vessels arriving off the shores of Tabasco. The rhythms rang across the valleys, bounced off hillsides, echoed through canyons, and transmitted a dire message from one kingdom to another. The drumming sounded an ominous alarm.

Five large vessels, propelled across the water by large wind-catching wings, carried men from another land. They were sighted in Thirteen Rabbit Year (1518) off the Gulf Coast seashore. The Chontales were the first to encounter these peculiar men wearing clothes made of metal. As was the custom, the Chontales peacefully welcomed these unusual men as they disembarked from their vessels and presented them with gifts. The outsiders, in examining the gifts handed them, were particularly impressed by utensils made of gold. Little do the Chontales know that their act of generosity will prompt their demise.

The gold excited the strange men who returned a year later. The outsiders once again dropped anchor on the same shores, but, this time, subjected the Chontales to a brutality that was eventually meted out to anyone who impeded the goal of these men: the acquisition of material riches for themselves and the King and Queen of Spain. The leader of this expedition was Hernán Cortés.

In February of 1519, while the drumming rang across the continent, Eréndira, now sixteen years of age, had received foundational combat training from her maternal grandfather, Irepani. She could wield the macana, launch a spear with precision, and masterfully shoot an arrow. The Cazonci, after observing her agility with these weapons upon her return to Tzintzuntzan from Acámbaro, was so impressed that he arranged for Eréndira to continue advanced combat training. He did not ignore the persistent warnings from other parts of the land portending the presence of peculiar people and unusual events. While he held no expectation for Eréndira to join the ranks of soldiers, he anticipated that should Purépecha defenses ever be threatened, that she could defend herself and those of the royal family. Eréndira was whisked away to the islands of Lake Patzcuaro, where her Uncle Anini was charged with bolstering her skills as a balanced warrior.

Eréndira's daily regiment entailed navigating canoes across the chilly waters and taking daily swims so that, eventually, she had the strength to singularly cover the distance from one island to the next. In case she was pursued by the enemy on water, she worked to expand her lung capacity to hold her breath for long periods under water. She spent hours repeating drills with various weapons, practicing hand-to-hand combat with the guards assigned to protect her. She was taught military strategy so she would know which weapon and tactics to employ under various circumstances.

One evening, after rigorous training, Eréndira, her Uncle Anini, and the accompanying guards rested on the shore of an island enjoying a meal freshly caught from the lake. Anini recounted the story of when he first met Eréndira's maternal grandparents, Irepani and Parakata,

"You should have seen the look on Irepani's face when I spilt the xocolatl. I didn't know what else to do but to slurp it up! Your Naníta, Parakata, was so gracious but Irepani…"

"Uncle Anini!" interrupted Eréndira.

"What is it, Princess?" Anini's voice turned serious. Eréndira suddenly stood up, put up a hand signaling everyone to be silent and tilted her head to catch a distant sound carried by a light wind. Anini and the guards looked to the East from where the urgent drumming originated and passed over them like a tukúru in flight.

"Uncle Anini. It has been a year since we have heard such drumming. What does this mean?"

"Not good. It is ominous. We should get rest." To the guards he instructed, "Put out the campfire. Best that we do not attract attention." Promptly, the guards followed Anini's orders. To Eréndira he said, "Tomorrow we move to another Island. First light, we erase all traces of our presence here."

Before Eréndira, Anini, and their guards departed the island, a breathless messenger sent by the Cazonci arrived by canoe. The

Cazonci summoned Eréndira and Anini to immediately return to Tzintzuntzan.

Eréndira was apprehensive over events that threatened to penetrate the borders of the Purépecha Kingdom. Those closest to the Cazonci whispered in grim tones. While the Royal realm still appeared to be safe, Eréndira detected unease in the Elders voices and a veil of foreboding on the faces of those closest to the Cazonci. Noting an unusual number of healers coming and going to and from the Cazonci's home, Eréndira sought her mother as soon as she could.

"What is it mother? What is happening with the Cazonci?"

Sesasi, unsure herself as to what has befallen the people of the kingdom, said, "Much has transpired while you have been on the island. Drums warned us that someone is coming."

Alarmed, Eréndira asked, "The Mexica?"

"Yes. They did come. But the forewarning was not about them. Oddly, the Mexica came asking for help."

Sesasi sat Eréndira down on one of the cushions in their home. Her daughter had been gone for months of training, and Sesasi spent these precious moments bringing Eréndira up to speed with events that foretold imminent danger.

"An envoy of ten, sent from the Mexica ruler, Montezuma, presented themselves at the border city of Taximaroa. They asked, with a sense of urgency, to speak directly to the Cazonci. When he was notified of their request, he instructed that they remain in Taximaroa and be treated well during their stay. The Cazonci wanted them detained there to ensure that deception did not follow them. Once it was apparent that they came with good heart, they were allowed to present themselves to him here in Tzintzuntzan. The Nahuatl interpreter, Nuritan, accompanied the Mexica envoy. The Cazonci's lords and sons joined the meeting but disguised themselves so as not to be recognized by members of the Mexica envoy."

Eréndira observed, "The Cazonci thinks ahead. It was wise that the royal family identities be concealed. While there is peace between our nations, distrust remains."

"Yes, and for that reason, while the Cazonci met with the envoy, he repeatedly tapped the ground with an arrow held firmly in his right hand."

"Ah!" exclaimed Eréndira. "To remind them of our dominance. What happened next, amámba?"

"The Cazonci told Nuritan to ask the Mexica's what they wanted and why they came.

Members of the envoy laid before the Cazonci gifts sent by Montezuma: turquoise, jerky, green feathers, ten round shields with golden rims, rich blankets, belts, and large mirrors. Then, the Mexica spokesperson conveyed, through the interpreter, how peculiar people, accompanied by Tlaxcalans, an aggrieved people who had turned against the Mexica, had attacked the Mexica by surprise."

"That is what the drums spoke of? War… but this time, provoked by others against our enemies."

"Correct, and now, the Mexica are engaged in warfare with these peculiar people and their allies, the Tlaxcalans. The Mexica have killed some of these men who ride large deer and are killing others who are on foot. These peculiars carry something that makes sounds of thunder and kills all, leaving not one. The Cazonci, suspicious of the Mexica and their stories, offered the Mexica envoy to rest for a day or two. Then, he brought in all his advisors and recounted these bizarre events reported by the Mexica. The Purépecha have never been asked to supply military aid. This was a highly unusual request given the ongoing animosity and conflict between our two kingdoms. The Cazonci could not discount possible treachery in this request, so he decided to proceed with caution. The Cazonci's advisors concurred with his assessment, appreciating his caution."

"The Cazonci is wise!" observed Eréndira. "What has been decided to determine whether this is another attempt by the Mexica to overtake us?"

"The Cazonci set forth a plan by which to uncover, for himself, what is taking place in the Mexica Kingdom. After collecting gifts from our Kingdom to be delivered to Montezuma, he sent Purépecha messengers to accompany the Mexica envoy on their return. While the gifts were graciously accepted by members of the Mexica envoy, they were visibly disappointed. They had hoped for the Cazonci's commitment of an alliance against these peculiar people."

Eréndira considered their reaction. "They could have feigned disappointment. What of our assigned messengers? What if they were held captive? I have been told the stories of Mexica treachery!"

"You think like the Cazonci, Eréndira! He proceeded with caution, so he executed another means by which to determine whether there was truly a verifiable threat in their region or if this was all merely a Mexica ruse. After the Mexica envoy rested for a day and departed for their kingdom, accompanied by the Purépecha messengers, Purépecha warriors were sent on a separate road toward the Mexica kingdom to see what they could learn."

Sesasi waited for Eréndira to process these grim circumstances that had now set the kingdom in a restrained state of alert. After a few moments, Eréndira, still a novice in military strategic training, concluded, "This is peculiar. When have the Mexica ever asked for our alliance? Is it a trick of some kind?"

"We don't know for certain but there is more you must know. Soon after the Mexica envoy returned to their capital, accompanied by our own messengers, the Cazonci gave audience to a desperate messenger from one of the eastern coast tribes. The bedraggled and weary man carried a palm-sized carved skull made of fire rock, engraved with the image of a tukúru, the owl."

Eréndira's eyes widened. She had been learning the art of communication using symbols. "The tukúru carries an ominous warning. The rare rock represents the destructive force of fire. The skull, a symbol of the afterlife." She looked to her mother and sternly said, "An unusual and imbalanced source brings death."

Sesasi looked at her daughter with admiration. "Yes, you have learned well. The Cazonci is attempting to ascertain what has transpired but the message on the rock is clear, an unusual source of death comes."

The two, mother and daughter, sat silently in one another's presence for some time. Eréndira was sorry to have missed the arrival of this messenger and that of the Mexica envoy. Her training took precedence over these events but, still, the Cazonci had summoned for her return. While the drumming had provided a warning, the messenger from the Eastern coast was confirmation that events were dire.

"Amámba, where is this messenger from the Eastern shores? Is he still here?"

Sesasi sadly said, "No, the Cazonci offered him to stay and rest but the man, exhausted as he was, insisted on carrying the message as far north as he could. He claimed that he would travel to as many other kingdoms as he could and when his body no longer could, he hoped that others would carry the skull rock further on. He told the Cazonci that other messengers from his tribe headed South and West to warn all who would give audience of what is coming. Two of our best warriors escorted him to the northern borders of the kingdom. He disappeared into the pines, carried by an urgency that only he understood."

"The man has a strong spirit, doesn't he, amámba?"

"Yes, Eréndira. Whatever he has seen and heard drives him to warn others. This, being his only mission in what remains of his life."

Eréndira, grasping the severity of these yet to be understood events, sadly confirmed, "This means we will not travel to Acámbaro and visit Naníta and Tatíta. I so desperately wanted to see them."

"Me too, Eréndira. Me too. I miss my family but let us see what our warriors uncover. They will see, with their own eyes, and hear, with their own ears, what has befallen the Mexica people, if any-thing." Sesasi continued conveying the events leading to Eréndira's being summoned. "A few days later, the Purépecha warriors sent on the different route toward the Mexica Kingdom returned. They captured three Otomis along the route and asked them of any news from the Mexica capital, Tenochtitlan. The Otomis, filled with dread, reported that, most certainly, the Mexica had been con-quered by others unknown to them and that the foul odor of dead bodies reeked throughout the Mexica capitol. Out of desperation, the Mexica were seeking allies even from their traditional enemies, in hope that others might come and liberate them from these out-side intruders. This was reported to the Cazonci who then gathered the lords, once again, to hear what was reported by the Purépecha warriors. He said to them, 'It is true. The Mexicas do not deceive us. Peculiar beings have come from other lands. What shall we do? This is a serious matter.' There were no answers, no conclusions, no way forward but soon after, the messengers who had accompanied the Mexica envoy returned with more gifts from Montezuma. More importantly, they brought accounts of what they saw with their own eyes which they conveyed to the Cazonci… the messengers said that after arriving by canoe to the Mexica capital, they were received by Montezuma. They told him that they were sent by the Cazonci, to report what they could learn about the presence of these peculiars. Montezuma understood that the Purépecha messengers were there to verify, with their own eyes, that the events reported to the Cazonci were true. They were then sent to Texcoco where they climbed to the top of a mountain. From that vantage, they saw a clearing that the peculiars occupied. The Mexica proposed that we, the Purépecha, fight together. They want our Purépecha archers to strike from one side of the clearing while the Mexica warriors attack from the other. They suggest that by joining forces that we can ensure the demise of these intruders. When the messengers returned to speak with Montezuma and told him that, yes, they believed what their eyes saw, he said 'Return to Mechuacán for you have seen the land which we wish to give to you if you join us. This matter which we beg of your Master, what answer can he give except that you will all come?'"

Eréndira considered how desperate Montezuma must be to ask for an alliance with their traditional enemies. She asked her mother, "What has the Cazonci decided to do?"

Sesasi shrugged then responded, "The Cazonci heard the messengers and the promise of land. Still, he did not want to commit his warriors to die for an enemy whose motives and promises could not be trusted. After conferring with his advisors, he, once again, refused Montezuma's request. Despite a new source of danger existing on their lands, the Cazonci refused to accept an alliance with the Mexica."

Eréndira, took in all that her mother reported, stood up, and gave her mother a hug. Then she set off through the door.

"Where are you going Eréndira?"

"I am going to see the Cazonci."

"But he is not well!" Eréndira stopped at the door upon hearing this. She had never known of the Cazonci being ill. She turned back around and said to her mother, "Why would he summon me and Uncle Anini to return from the Islands? If he is ill, there is more reason for me to see him."

Eréndira crossed the spacious patio that leads to the Cazonci's quarters but was abruptly stopped at the entrance. One of the royal guards blocked the doorway that she had so casually entered many times before. Taken by surprise at this, Eréndira challenged the guard, "Who are you to stop me from seeing the Cazonci?"

The guard responded, "It is by instructions of the high priest that no one enter."

"That is impossible. I have always been granted the companionship of the Cazonci."

"I know who you are, Princess. You are daughter of the Captain of War, Brother to the Cazonci... who is ill."

Eréndira was taken aback to hear the word *ill* attached, once again, to the Cazonci.

Defiantly, she addressed the guard, "Stand aside! The Cazonci, himself, has summoned me!"

Chuperipati, just having conferred with the Cazonci, came upon Eréndira defiantly facing off with the Royal Guard as she exited the Cazonci's quarters. She overheard Eréndira's last statement and interceded. "Let me see if the Cazonci will see you, Eréndira. I can't promise you that he will. He is very ill."

Chuperipati returned shortly and motioned for Eréndira to enter. The Guard moved aside, bowing his head to Princess Eréndira as she stepped by him. Chuperipati pulled Eréndira aside and cautiously whispered, "He has stated for you not to draw near to him. We do not know what has befallen him."

Eréndira acknowledged with a nod. She entered the Cazonci's room and was engulfed by the aroma of copal burned by her people when praying. Yet, there was another distinct odor intermixed with the familiar. It was the smell of rotting flesh.

Several attendants stood by the Cazonci's cot where he lay motionless. Upon seeing Eréndira enter the room he motioned for her to stop.

"Go no further, my child."

"Cazonci… What is it? What is it that has overtaken you?"

Before the Cazonci could answer, he began to vomit. An attendant by the Cazonci's side ensured that he did not soil himself. Another attendant wiped his face and, with a fresh cloth, dampened his forehead. His body was covered with red bumps that were filled with a milky fluid.

Another attendant standing by the door whispered to Eréndira, "He has tepari pamangarata, something hard on the body accompanied by exhaustion. It started with a high fever. He complained of his back, his head hurting. He was very fatigued. Then, a rash broke out on his face and upper arms before spreading all over his body."

The Cazonci recovered some strength and turned his head to get a better view of Eréndira. "My child. Your presence brings the warmth of the sun to my heart. As much as I love you, I don't want you to see me like this."

Uncontrollable tears streamed down Eréndira's face. "Who did this Cazonci? Who did this to you? Was it the Mexica?"

The Cazonci waved off the attendants who continued absorbing a milky fluid that oozed from red bumps throughout his face, arms, and legs. "No. No, Eréndira." To the attendants he said, "Please. Let me sit up and address the Princess." The attendants helped him swing his legs over the cot so he could sit up and face Eréndira.

Seeing the Cazonci in this condition, Eréndira tried not to show her shock. She stood with her feet firmly planted and her body erect but the stream of tears betrayed her emotion.

The Cazonci cleared his throat and in a barely audible voice, "Their women are fighting."

Eréndira did not have the context to understand what the Cazonci was saying, "Who? Cazonci? Who is fighting?"

"The Tlatelolca women, fighting on behalf of the Mexica. They fight the peculiars who have spears that spit fire and iron bolts. The Tlatelolca and Otomis war leaders were dying. Many were afflicted with this pestilence. The Tlatelolca warriors, those who could still lift their swords, fought to the end. Then, the Tlatelolca warriors were vanquished. That is when the women took up arms. They put on the warrior's regalia, fighting, and raising their skirts so they could give chase and capture these peculiars."

"Cazonci! What are you saying? What has happened? Who are these peculiars?"

"Something we have never seen before. Hear me now, Eréndira. These peculiars are not to be feared. These peculiars wear a skin of metal. Even the large deer that they ride are protected by this metal. But know, Eréndira, that the Tlatelolca had skull racks of those they killed. These peculiar creatures and the deer they ride are not invincible."

"What sort of deer is this, Cazonci, that they can be ridden?"

"Our messengers were told that these deer are trained to fight. A warrior who falls to the ground is trampled under the feet of these creatures. When attacked from all sides, these deer kick forward and kick back, twirling in a circle, and causing grave injury to attacking warriors."

Eréndira tried to imagine confronting such an animal. "We don't know of such a creature. How are we to defend ourselves against these peculiars riding ferocious creatures?"

"With courage, my child. Do not let fear defeat you. The large deer can be overtaken and defeated. The Tlatelolca had the heads of two of these creatures on their skull racks."

The Cazonci directed final instructions to Eréndira, "For now, you must survive this pestilence. These peculiar people bring with them a curse that afflicts the Mexica and, now us." He coughed before he asked, "Remember the story of Hapunda?"

"Yes, my Cazonci!" Eréndira understood the Cazonci's reason for reminding her of the story he shared on a beautiful afternoon when she was but a child, and they had canoed across Lake Patzcuaro. "You have taught me well, Cazonci."

"Yes, my child, and your taáte, Timas, your amámba, Sesasi, and even your Naníta and Tatíta in Acámbaro have taught you well. Mind them closely. Go now."

With that, the Cazonci laid back and Eréndira left his presence for the last time.

Within days, the Cazonci perished. His death preceded the passing of many in his household, the highest priest of the temples, many of the attendants who attended to the Cazonci in his final days, and then, the Purépecha people began to show signs of the affliction.

The Mexica, once again, sent another envoy to the Purépecha with the hope that their appeal for an alliance would be accepted. This time, upon their arrival, they were received by the Cazonci's eldest son, Tangoxóan, who had reluctantly taken the appointment to replace his father. Distraught over the deaths of his father, his relations, those of the household, and of their kingdom who had succumbed to the life-taking disease, tepari pamangarata, he lashed out at the ten Mexica's who presented themselves, once again, pleading for help.

Tangoxóan's anger and deep distress for the deaths in the Purepecha Kingdom foretold a perilous future. The cumulative effect on Tangoxóan was heaped upon the Mexica envoy. Rather than agree to an alliance, he told them to take their petition directly to his father. They fully understood what this meant. They would be executed. Given the destruction taking place in the Mexica capital, Tenochtitlan, their lives were at risk no matter what. They had no other options. They had gone to the Purepecha as one last effort to change the outcome of this invasion by outsiders. Instead, they went to their death. They accepted Tangoxóan's decree with a sense of resignation and asked that it be done quickly.

In the meantime, escorted by a small contingent of warriors, Timas arranged for Eréndira and Sesasi to be transported by canoe, under the cover of fog, to a secluded island in the middle of Lake Patzcuaro.

Before School

When Eréndira barely wakes in time for school the following morning, the stillness in the house tells her she's the only person on the second floor. Since her brother went off to college, silences in their home seem more pronounced. She misses hearing the Michael Jackson music he played so loud it shook the walls, serving as her cue that it was time to get up. She shakes off the sleep fuzzies and makes her way down the stairs, expecting to find her parents having their morning coffee. Instead, she finds only her father in the kitchen, cleaning up dishes from an early breakfast.

"Hey Dad! Mom's not here? I thought she got to go in late today."

"Good morning, mi'ja! Your mom left early. She had business to take care of ahead of office hours. I made you a lunch… in the fridge, and I'm off to catch the city bus."

Victor plants a kiss on Eréndira's forehead, puts on his blazer, grabs his briefcase, and yells back as he steps through the front door, "Don't forget to lock up!"

Eréndira, still in a sleepy daze, is glad that he didn't bring up the uncomfortable topic of Susan. As it is, she has a full day ahead of her in classrooms and hallways of a school where she has yet to find a niche for herself. The previous night, her parents consented to transferring her to a private school if the toxic behavior continued. Given this option, Eréndira agreed to take each day as it comes.

On her way to school, Eréndira texts Melissa, "Hey! What Up? Meet at our usual spot?"

"Sorry. Taking day off. Doin' essay for English class. Mom got me a book from campus. Changed my topic, so a big redo. You'll ♥ it!" Melissa responds.

Eréndira's heart sinks when she thinks of what her day will be like without her best and only friend. She replies, "☹"

Eréndira's anxiety builds as she moves through her morning classes and agonizes about not having someone to sit with during lunch. She hopes that maybe Rosalee and Luisa will show up and spare her the embarrassment of having to sit alone. Back home, this would not have been a problem as there were lots of people of different backgrounds and interests to hang with. She remembers sitting with friends at lunch with a full view of the quad and watching kids from the skater crowd show off their athletic feats in front of the band geeks who, in turn, took out their instruments and improvised music to the skaters' stunts.

On other days, Eréndira sat in the library talking with kids from the journalism club after their monthly publication came out. They often interviewed students whose families immigrated from other countries—Mexico, Italy, the Philippines, Portugal, and so on—and would publish unique stories, rhymes, or sayings. One of her favorite published sayings was from a friend she met in choir, EunMi. Her family was from South Korea. Everyone thought EunMi was extremely shy but Eréndira knew this was not the case.

One day, after Choir class, Eréndira and EunMi were chatting as they were headed toward the cafeteria and Eréndira decided to tell EunMi that people thought she was shy. EunMi took her time to consider what Eréndira had just shared. Then, she took Eréndira's arm in hers and motioned to her ears and mouth as she said, "I was taught there is a reason why we have two ears and one mouth. We should listen twice as much as we talk." In this way, Eréndira learned that it wasn't that EunMi was so quiet. It was that people just needed to shut their mouths long enough for EunMi to respond because when people spoke with her, she didn't interrupt or talk over them. She listened. While Eréndira was accustomed to gathering pearls of wisdom from Naníta, she was so moved by EunMi that she told her friends in the journalism club about her. The following month, EunMi was interviewed, and her quote made the club's publication.

As Eréndira walks alone through the halls of her new school, flashbacks from her old school keep her company. She realizes how much she took for granted in her classmates' jovial nature. Not only did they readily accept newcomers, but students would commonly greet and hug one another in the few minutes between classes. Now, she must bear the mixed bag of reactions—half smiles, side glances, nods of acknowledgment, glares. All this because Susan went running her mouth and then attacked her. Eréndira shakes off the memories because it makes her heart ache. She promised her parents she would take it a day at a time at this new school, and she will.

Lunchtime arrives. Eréndira must decide what to do with herself. *Eat alone? Sneak off campus and escape the eyes of my classmates? Duck into the library, surround myself with a bunch of books at an unoccupied table, and pretend I'm engrossed in a research project? Sit in one of the classrooms that teachers make available for students with nowhere better to be?* She decides to go with the familiar, back of the library.

As Eréndira takes her next step in that direction, she feels a tap on her left shoulder. She turns around to Rosalee's smiling face. This time, she has not only her sister, Luisa, with her but a whole group of students.

"Hey! There you are!" says Rosalee.

"Yes! Here I am!" says Eréndira. "What's up?" Eréndira quickly scans the group of students standing behind Rosalee.

"We were wondering if we could have lunch with you and your friend...." Rosalee tries to remember—

"Melissa!" prompts Eréndira.

"Yes! Melissa! Can we join you today?"

Eréndira looks at the group of about ten students standing behind Rosalee and asks, "All of you?"

"Yes! All of us!"

"Well, of course!" Eréndira, relieved that she will not have to eat alone, adds, "Melissa's not here today, but I was headed over to where we were yesterday." Eréndira motions with an arm toward the rear of the library.

The students, carrying cafeteria lunch boxes or lunch bags from home, follow her to where she and Melissa meet for lunch. For the next forty-five minutes, with their backs leaning against the wall of the library, Eréndira chats with these new friends who have rescued her from having to miserably eat by herself. She learns that these classmates are themselves, or their parents or grandparents, from other countries: Pakistan, Ukraine, Vietnam, Brazil, Israel, and Taiwan.

Lunchtime passes quickly for Eréndira and her new friends, so they are startled when the bell marks the end of their time together. Eréndira quickly uploads as many of their phone numbers in her iPhone as she can. Some have their own cell phones while others use a landline that they share with the rest of their family. They all commit to meet the next day for lunch.

As they go their separate ways, Eréndira is, once again, tapped on her shoulder. She turns around but this time it is not Rosalee. It is her sister, Luisa. Though Eréndira had not heard much from Luisa, the words that come from her as the two of them stand facing one another are unmistakably clear.

Luisa says, "We want to start a club and would like you and Melissa to be in it."

"Okay? … What is this club about?"

"A club that brings people together to do kind things for others. We have been thinking of this for a while. Then, we heard what happened to you. We know you didn't start that fight with Susan. Her and her friends have done the same to us. They treat us bad. We thought it was about time we started sort of a counter force," says Luisa.

Eréndira is dumbfounded as to how the outcome of her unwelcome altercation has led to this invitation. "I don't get it. I landed a good punch on someone who asked for it. How does that make me a candidate for a kindness club?"

Luisa lets a moment pass before answering. Her thoughtfulness reminds Eréndira of her friend EunMi, who would have paused just like Luisa did before saying anything and not just let words fly out of her mouth. Luisa steps closer to Eréndira and explains, "You stood up to meanness. Nobody has done that. Now they're afraid of you."

Rosalee joins in to add, "And, now a line has been drawn."

Eréndira is speechless. This seems to come out of nowhere, but she now understands the undercurrent of thumbs ups and half smiles that she has been getting from students who she doesn't even know. Apparently, they know her and what she did. Unknowingly, her actions demonstrated overt resistance to an undercurrent of cruel behavior that has been tolerated but has harmed many.

Luisa patiently waits for Eréndira's response while she searches for the right words to convey her mixed feelings. Applying what she learned from her friend, EunMi, she finally honestly offers, "I don't know what to say. Can we talk about this some more later?"

"So, you'll think about it?" asks Luisa with a hopeful tone in her voice.

"Yes, of course I will." Eréndira assures her and then says, "Let's talk during lunch tomorrow. Maybe Melissa will be here then."

Luisa's face lights up with an ear-to-ear smile. Rosalee takes her sister by the hand.

"Come on Luisa. We'll be late for P.E." They half run toward the gymnasium.

Eréndira feels her phone buzz. It is a text from her mother that reads, "Sorry to miss you this morning. Left early to get to the library and get that book, Font's translated journal. Somebody beat me to it. Checked out last night. Sorry. See you tonight. Working late again."

Eréndira texts back, "Thanks for trying. See you later. 😊"

Afternoon classes drag on. Eréndira can't wait to FaceTime Melissa on her way home and tell her about Luisa, Rosalee, and their group of friends. Plus, she wants to hear Melissa's thoughts on the club they are proposing to start.

Finally, school lets out. As she walks home, Eréndira Face-Times Melissa, who comes on right away in a bright mood.

"Hey Girl!"

"So, what were you doing today?" asks Eréndira.

"I told you. Redoing a homework assignment."

"No Way! You took a day off just to do an assignment?"

"Well yea... my mom didn't believe that I was at the library with you. Even after I held the librarian's note up on the phone to show her! So, I told her what you and I were looking up about that de Anza guy. She knew I was draggin' my ass on this primary source essay for my English class. Everyone read Anne Frank's journal last year so the teacher wouldn't let us do that. Once my mother heard me taking interest in something other than K-Pop, she couldn't help herself. After work she went off to the university library and dug up this book. It is a translated journal from that guy, Font, who was with de Anza. She checked it out and brought it home…"

Eréndira stops in the middle of the sidewalk as she exclaims, "No! No Way?"

"Yes, Way. What's the big deal?"

"My mom went to the library this morning to get *that* book. It must be the only one in the University library. She said someone had checked it out."

"Ha! Well, girlfriend," Melissa puts on her sassy tone, "I've got the book and once I started reading it… speed reading through some of the boring stuff, of course, I couldn't believe it."

"What are you talking about? Believe what?" Eréndira steps off the sidewalk to let a current of students walk by.

"I'll tell you what?" Melissa says teasingly, "I'll email you the draft of my essay and you can see for yourself."

"You already wrote your freakin' essay on this Font guy?"

"Welllllll, not exactly a full blown essay, but I stayed up all night putting sticky notes on the interesting stuff!"

"So, what did it say?" Eréndira asks in exasperation.

"A LOT! 500 pages of stuff! Most of it is boring… a bunch of details, but it's also what is in between the lines."

"What do you mean?"

"It's what they don't say or what they say but don't realize that this Font dude is telling on himself."

"You're not making any sense. What do you mean he's telling on himself?"

"It's hard to explain. You'll have to see the sticky notes I put in there." Suddenly, Melissa cuts the conversation. "Sorry Eréndira. I gotta go. I promised my mother I'd make dinner if she let me stay home from school to work on the essay. My grade right now is hanging on the edge of a C so I gotta get this essay right. For now, just read my notes. I'll send it in a bit! See you tomorrow!"

"But wait!" Eréndira shouts into the phone but Melissa has already signed off. She didn't even get a chance to tell her about Luisa, Rosalee, and the rest of the group that she had lunch with and more importantly, what Luisa was asking of Eréndira. That would have to wait.

For now, she needs to get home and call her Naníta. Whatever it was Melissa read in that translated journal, it was so intriguing that it kept her up scanning through a 500-page book for the last 24-hours. Eréndira tucks her iPhone into her backpack and quickens her steps. She gets home before her dad and, as she always does, sends a quick text to her Naníta.

"Home, Naníta! Talk soon. Got homework. ♥ U!"

Her Naníta, attentive and waiting for Eréndira's communication at this time of day, promptly responds, "♥ U 2!"

After reading her Naníta's text, Eréndira heads straight to the fridge, gets a bottle of juice, and takes the stairs, two at a time, up to her room. She opens her laptop, connects to the big screen, sits back in her comfy desk chair, and clicks on to her email, where she finds a recently sent message awaiting her in her inbox from Melissa.

"Essay yet to come!!!! For now... Some notes!" Eréndira opens the attachment which reads:

```
Melissa Ghilarducci
English 9
Assignment #2
```

Notes on Font's Diary

```
Font's journal translated from Spanish to English
by a U.C. Berkeley professor. Considered primary
source document.
Spaniards arrive in what is now called Mexico in
the early 1500's.

Spaniards claim everything from Chile, in South
America, to the northwestern part of the America's
as theirs.
```

Spaniards feel threatened by Russians who start building trading posts on Pacific coast.

Spain sets a plan where Franciscan friars are to "convert and civilize the Indian, and soldiers to guard the country and protect the missionaries" (p. v).

In 1775, an expedition led by Juan Bautista de Anza is made up of 177 people; 30 soldiers, their families, muleteers, Lieutenant Moraga, four families of settlers, and the chaplain, Fray Pedro Font who kept a journal. They go up the coast to figure out where to build more missions. They had 590 mules to carry the luggage.

On journey Spaniards come across "Indians of the Channel," (Quabajay Tribe)
Indians seemed distrustful of the Spaniards. Font wrote, "saw very few women close at hand, for as soon as they saw us, they all hastily hid in their huts, especially the girls, the men remaining outside blocking the doors and taking care that nobody should go inside" (p. 251).

Font pokes around the Indian's village, despite men trying to block him from doing so. He gets into a hut to look inside and see how it was made and how they lived. No one invited him in, and he admits to not asking permission but he went in anyway. One of the Indians saw him wander in, uninvited. They shut an inner door on him so he couldn't go further. Spanish soldiers had been to this village before. There was one especially bad one called "Camacho." Whatever this Camacho guy did to the Indians must have been done to the women because the Indians now called every soldier Camacho and kept asking if this Camacho guy was coming again.

Expedition continues north. Confronted by a group of Indians armed with bows and arrows. Font writes that they came out "running and shouting and making gestures, as if they wished to stop us, and signaling to us that we must not go forward." (p. 323). These people don't attack but about thirty follow Spaniards in single file and ran, one behind the other, in single file, until they got ahead of the Spaniards. Font says that they stopped and "began to shout and even to shriek, making many gestures and signs as if they were angry and did not wish us to go forward. Then, seeing that we continued our way, without paying any attention to them, they again started to run to get ahead of us. Then they went through the same performance of shouting and talking very loud and fast, although we understood nothing of what they said" (p. 324). These Indians were Costanoan.

Later, the Spaniards came upon some Indians who were friendly and, through sign language, were trying to tell the Spaniards to stay put but the Spaniards continued. Instead of being grateful for being well received, Font describes the people as "ugly." Font writes "They appear to be gentle Indians, and it would seem possible to form of them a good and large mission." (p. 329)

Font records many times that they came across abandoned villages. Font wrote, "we saw some ruinous and abandoned little huts, but the only Indian seen was at a distance and running for as soon as he saw us, he fled for the brush of the Sierra like a deer" (p. 414-415).

Font wrote, "In all the journey we did not see a single Indian, although we found some tracks of them, and in some places a few signs and traces of ruined huts and small villages" (p. 417). Font writes that he believes the people have gone to the sierras because they are known to, in seasons where there is piñon and acorns, to head up to the mountains.

The expedition got as far as what we now call the Bay Area.

Eréndira closes her laptop, now understanding what Melissa meant by reading between the lines. Apparently, Melissa found primary source information that addressed her doubts about her own miseducation. Yet, Eréndira is still left with questions about the connection between the two images on the petroglyph in Naníta's backyard. While Melissa's essay seems to focus on the interactions between the Spaniards and the California Indians themselves, there is no mention of the Sierra Miwok. Eréndira pulls out her iPhone and sends Melissa a quick text.

"Read your notes. Interesting stuff. See anything about Sierra Miwok having contact with Spaniards?"

Dinnertime approaches, and Victor arrives home from work. Eréndira helps with dinner and over their shared meal she tells her father how her network of friends suddenly expanded that day. As Eréndira runs through all the details of who she met, where they are from, and what they would like to do, Victor tears up. Eréndira quiets at the sight of her father wiping his face.

"What's wrong Papa? Did I do something wrong?" Eréndira is confused by his reaction.

"Not at all. I'm just so happy. Your mother and I have been so worried about you. We just want you to be happy and safe."

"Ay, Papá." Eréndira gets up from her seat, circles around the table and hugs him as he continues to wipe his tears away. "You're so caring, but don't worry about me. I'm a big girl. I can take care of myself."

"Of course you're a big girl. It's just that we have worked so hard to get you into the best schools and provide every opportunity we can, but I wonder, sometimes, if our career advancements have taken priority over what's best for you and your brother."

Eréndira doesn't know what to say. Her parent's careers have never been a topic that she and her brother have ever weighed in on. Yet, she feels her father's heavy guilt in this moment for moving her to this community where she has experienced so much conflict. It was never their intention to place her in a community with so much hostility. They sincerely thought that the move was best for everyone. How were they to know otherwise?

She assures him, "Don't worry papá."

"We do worry. Promise me though, if this mistreatment continues and the school does nothing… you tell us immediately. ¿Prometido?"

"¡Prometido!"

Eréndira and Victor seal the promise with a pinky shake and proceed to clear off the table. While Victor sets aside a plate for Verónica, Eréndira checks her phone. Melissa has sent a text.

"No worries. I got your back. Left sticky notes in the book that might help U. Meet before school tomorrow."

Eréndira rereads the text several times. Melissa, in her reading of Font's journal, has found some clues to Eréndira's search for the connection between the Sierra Miwok and de Anza. Her hope restored, she quickly sends a text to her Naníta.

"Hey Naníta! Hot on the trail… might have connection between Sierra Miwok & Bautista. Will tell U more when I C U."

Naníta, enjoying an evening walk in the hills, feels her cell phone buzz. She smiles when she reads Eréndira's text, pleased to see her granddaughter pursuing a line of inquiry that will help her make sense of why the world is the way it is and why people are the way they are. With all that is happening to her, there are big lessons about human behavior.

She texts back, "Wonderful! Can't wait to learn what you find!"

As Eréndira finishes her homework she hears the garage door open. Her mother is home! Tonight, she will have good news to share with her mother; the book her mother tried to check out for her will be in Eréndira's hands the following morning, and she has found a whole new group of friends. There are not one, but two bright spots in her week.

Overshadowing the good, however, is the looming fact that Susan's suspension will soon end. In a few more days, Eréndira will have to sit across from Susan with the Vice Principal moderating. After Eréndira learned from Luisa that Susan and her cronies have bullied other students and spread lies, Eréndira's anger toward Susan has grown. *How*, Eréndira wonders, *could someone become so cruel?* She tries not to hate her, but the seed is there. Yet, Luisa, her sister, Rosalee, and the rest of their friends want to start a club that promotes kindness.

As Eréndira hears her mother's slow and tired footsteps come up the stairs, she tries, like her Naníta has taught her, to put aside the negativity and focus on what is good. Besides, she figures that her mother, like her father, could use some good news and it was time to share the knowledge she and her friend had collected.

Melissa and Eréndira agree to meet the next day before school. They know where to find one another… behind the back wall of the school library. Eréndira arrives first, anxious to see for herself the book that Melissa's mother checked out of the University library before her own mother could get to it. Their meeting feels oddly clandestine, as though they are doing something illegal, when their interest just revolves around the content of an old book! Melissa comes around the corner of the library, carrying herself with a sense of confidence that Eréndira has not seen.

"Hey Girl!" Melissa shouts out in greeting.

"Hey! I'm glad to see you!" Eréndira returns.

"Did you miss me?"

"Of course! But you gotta know… I've got a surprise for you!"

"Okay. Now, what are *you* talking about?" asks Melissa.

"It's your turn to wait in suspense! You'll see at lunchtime! Just be here today. No more skipping out!"

"That's a deal. And, just so you know, my paper is almost done! Aaaaaannnnnnnnnnnd…. drum roll please!" Eréndira drums on her thighs to produce an impromptu drum roll. Melissa reaches into her backpack and pulls out a thick, blue leather-bound book. "Ta-Daaaaa! Here it is!"

"Wow!" exclaims Eréndira. "That looks old!"

"Yep! It's about a hundred years old!"

Melissa hands the book over to Eréndira. Upon opening the cover, a loose piece of paper flutters to the ground.

Melissa bends over, picks it up, and says, "This is a list of page numbers I kept for you. As I was reading through the journal and finding what I needed for my assignment, I found stuff that will help with what you're trying to uncover—the connection between the Sierra Miwok and de Anza. I'm done with it so you can keep it 'til it's due back." Melissa tucks the loose piece of paper back inside the cover.

Eréndira slowly runs her hand over the cover and says, "Thank you sooooo much!" as she carefully tucks the book into her backpack.

"Don't mention it! Off to class! Gonna talk to the teacher about getting an extension on that essay! She gave me a D on my first assignment, and, honestly, that was generous!"

"Maybe she'll give you a double E on this one!"

"There's no such thing as an E!"

"Sure, there is!" Eréndira offers, "EE for Enthusiastic Effort!"

"Now who's being the silly one?" Melissa turns on her heels before she turns the corner, Eréndira shouts out, "Hey! Don't forget to be here for lunch! I've got a surprise for you!"

Melissa gives Eréndira a thumbs up before disappearing around the corner.

For some reason, this day suddenly feels different for Eréndira. She had not seen Melissa so enthusiastic about going to class. At one point, she worried that Melissa might be headed to alternative education as she has hinted, several times, about taking that route. Usually, just getting her to class was a daily challenge. They met when they were both walking aimlessly through the hallways to kill time during lunch. After passing one another for the third time, they started with small talk, an awkward introduction, and their relationship blossomed into a full friendship. Seeing Melissa's buoyant mood that morning lifted Eréndira's spirit, and she found herself smiling at her, otherwise, sullen classmates. Some, caught off guard, bashfully smiled back, while others awkwardly averted their eyes like they didn't know how to respond.

Lunchtime arrives, and, sure enough, Rosalee and Luisa bring their friends to the back of the library. This time the group has grown to about fifteen students. Melissa is late which makes Eréndira nervous. Nonetheless, conversation revolves around the latest movie, how they are doing in classes, and their plans for the following weekend. When Melissa finally comes around the library corner, she stops dead in her tracks at the sight of the large group of students sitting in a circle at her sacred lunch space. Eréndira sees the startled look on Melissa's face and waves her over. The girls in the group automatically scoot over to make room.

Melissa sits down next to Eréndira and quietly asks, "Is this the surprise you were telling me about?"

"Yep! And there's more!" Eréndira then turns to Luisa, "So, Luisa… can you tell Melissa what you were all thinking of starting here on campus?"

Luisa puts up a finger to signal that she must finish chewing the food in her mouth. After several deliberate chews she swallows, then enthusiastically answers, "Yes. It is a club. Anyone can join and we have enough students who have said they want to be in it."

"Okay," Melissa says. "What is this club about?"

Luisa takes the napkin from the box lunch and wipes the corner of her mouth. "It's about showing kindness to others."

Rosalee adds, "It doesn't have to be just nice things for other students. We can also help people in the community or even in other countries."

"Like what?" asks Melissa.

One of the others, Pavinder, chimes in, "Like when there's a new student, we can make sure that there is a buddy assigned to the student. Someone who helps the student find their classes, sits with them at lunch… just until they feel comfortable to be on their own. It's not like they must become our best friends, but just so they feel welcomed."

Another, Trinh, adds, "Or like when that family lost their home in a fire. They were recent refugees from Afghanistan. They lost everything. We could have helped by raising money for them to get into an apartment. They needed first and last month's rent, plus a deposit. That would have been close to $3,000. A lot of money for a family who have already gone through so much. I bet lots of people have extra furniture, clothes, and stuff in their garages they don't use. This could have been donated to help them get back on their feet."

"Why do you want to do this?" Melissa asks.

Luisa takes this one. "It is needed. Sometimes people need a reason to do the right thing. It might mean showing them ways to be better."

Trinh continues, "We don't want you to think that we don't like this school. It's that there is such a big focus on getting good grades. This doesn't make for well-rounded people. It feels a bit too competitive."

Pavinder, "That's right. We do care about our grades, but getting good grades isn't all we care about."

There is an observable pause for Melissa and Eréndira to take in what they've heard. Finally, Eréndira breaks the silence.

"You care about people." Everyone nods in agreement.

Pavinder quietly replies, "Yes. But it isn't enough just to say that we care. If care is not shown to others, then how do they know they matter? Simply caring does nothing."

"So…" continues Melissa, "You want to make a positive difference." Again, all nod.

"Besides," Rosalee offers, "What's the point of just going to school every day, class after class, homework every night, the same old thing. We can all get A's. But making someone else's life a bit easier… that is truly an accomplishment. Plus…" Rosalee looks to the others for assurance.

Pavinder urges her, "Go ahead. They should know."

Rosalee continues, "Well… our school has one of the highest suicide rates in the county." Rosalee's words hang in the air. The mood suddenly turns dark.

Startled by this revelation, Eréndira asks, "How do you know this?"

Trinh explains, "I am interested in being a psychiatrist, so I did an assignment on mental health for one of my classes. I interviewed the Director of the Suicide Prevention agency. That's where I learned that our district has the highest rate of attempted and completed suicide in the region."

"Holy crap. That's awful." Melissa reacts.

"And tell them the rest." Pavinder prompts Trinh, who looks down, reluctant to give words to what still needs to be shared.

Luisa picks up the thread at this turning point, "Susan and her friends have been hostile to many. The kids they go after might have a visible disability, walk with a limp… thick glasses… that sort of thing. Others, like me, don't speak the best English. Or maybe don't wear the most up-to-date clothes. Whatever it is, they find something to belittle."

"Kids have committed suicide because of them?" exclaims Melissa.

"No, no, no. Not all." Rosalee shook her head and went on to clarify. "Some, when they can't take it anymore, transfer to another school. There are others who have tried. When it gets to that point, then the adults finally listen and let them transfer. There have been some who have stuck it out but," Rosalee stops short of saying more and looks downward.

Melissa and Eréndira scan the others—Pavinder, Luisa, Trinh—to see who will complete what Rosalee hinted at, but no one is making eye contact with anyone else. Then, Eréndira's eyes fall on a student who has not spoken at all. In fact, even prior to this exchange, this student has been particularly quiet, even when the others make efforts to include her. The quiet one sits still, staring down at her food. The others see that Eréndira's gaze has fallen on the quiet one. They all turn to this young woman who now has tears streaming down her face. The group remains silent as the tears turn to sobs. Eréndira and Melissa give each other side glances, unsure of what was said to bring her to tears.

Eréndira asks the young woman, "I haven't really gotten to know you. What is your name?"

Wearing a dress speckled with yellow daisies, she says her name, but the sobs make her words indiscernible.

Trinh, seeing that Melissa and Eréndira are unable to understand, chimes in, "Her name is Daryna. Her name, in Ukrainian, means 'God's Gift."

Pavinder wraps a sisterly arm around Daryna's shoulder.

Trinh adds, "Her sister's name was Iryna which means 'Peace."

Eréndira repeats the word that Trinh stated to be sure she heard it right, "Her sister *was?*"

Trinh confirms. "Yes. *Was.*"

Eréndira softly says to Daryna, "I am so sorry."

Melissa quickly adds, "Me too."

The bell rings and they all slowly get up, but they don't leave. The group of students, except Eréndira and Melissa, gather around Daryna. They hug, hold, touch, soothe, and console her. She accepts their offering of comfort and wipes her face with a tissue that has been handed to her. Another student picks up her backpack from the ground and another her lunch box, placing it on top of her own so she can return them to the cafeteria. Eréndira and Melissa, the two who know Daryna the least, step forward last and each place a hand on her shoulder.

Melissa offers, "We'll see you here tomorrow for lunch Daryna. And let's see what we can do with this club we're starting up."

Daryna furiously nods her head, catches her breath and gets out a discernible, "Thank you. Thank you so much. I wish someone would have stuck up for my sister...." Her voice trails off.

Knowing that saying more would just kick off another bout of sobbing, Daryna abruptly walks away and toward her next class. The rest of the group, other than Rosalee, surround her and accompany her like a protective flock.

Rosalee confides to Melissa and Eréndira, "Daryna tried to stick up for her sister. But, I guess Iryna couldn't take it anymore. It was all too much. As it is, their family fled Ukraine because of the war. Their father and older brother had to stay behind and fight against the invading Russians. They don't even know if they are alive."

"This is ALL so wrong!" Melissa exclaims trying to contain her emotions.

Eréndira asks, "So what is the administration doing about these mean girls?"

Rosalee shrugs. "Not much. Sometimes they call the girls in to"—Rosalee does air quotes—"'discuss' reports of bullying but these girls pretend like they don't know anything. They put on the false charm in front of the counselors, but as soon as they get out of the counselors' offices, they double down on their meanness on whoever reported them. What is worse is that these girls' parents defend them, and they act like their daughters are saints. They come in touting their daughters' grades, being on cheer team, all the stuff that doesn't matter. If admin does anything more, the parents threaten to sue and then say they will no longer donate to the school's scholarship fund or for the new performing art center. In the meantime, these girls keep making 'the outsiders' lives miserable. No one cares what harm they cause."

The three, Eréndira, Melissa, and Rosalee, arrive at the point in the hallways where they will have to go separate ways. Students rushing to their respective classes sidestep them and Rosalee adds, "Now, with what happened between you and Susan, the energy on campus has changed. You had the courage to step up to the bully. I know it's been hard on you but even though people might not be saying anything, they are glad you did what you did." She says no more, turns around, and heads for her own class.

Melissa says to no one in particular, "That's just plain evil." She turns to Eréndira, "But it seems like they need you."

Eréndira, not enjoying the weight of so much expectation falling on her, promptly replies, "We all need each other."

Melissa smiles. "That's right. Okay. Gotta go." She gives Eréndira the peace sign and says, "Iryna."

"What?"

"Peace! Remember… Iryna means PEACE in Ukrainian!"

Eréndira watches her friend disappear into the crowd of students.

For the rest of the day, Eréndira's head spins over the intense experience at lunch. *How tragic*, she thinks to herself, *that a young woman whose name means 'Peace' took her life because the world she lives in is so hostile.* Wars in other parts of the world are out of Eréndira's control, but those who are impacted—the refugees and victims of aggression—certainly deserve compassion. Considering what Daryna and her now dead sister, Iryna, have gone through, it makes Eréndira's own troubles with Susan seem miniscule. Yet, she still doesn't see herself and her situation as a catalyst for confronting the hostility on campus. Punching out Susan was just a reaction in response to her physical provocation. It *was* self-defense. In this moment, as she thinks about Iryna, her anger toward Susan intensifies.

When Eréndira gets home, she sends a text to her Naníta.

"I'm home now Naníta. Can't wait 2 C U. Have much to run by U."

"Glad you made it home safe. Miss you. Have something to show you. Hope you can come up this weekend."

"Miss U 2! Will ask Mom & Dad ☺. Is it OK if my friend Melissa comes?"

"Of course! 😘."

Eréndira smiles. "❤ it, Naníta! You are learning to use emoji! 😆"

Naníta sends final text, "👍😌"

"I get it. Buenas Noches! 😊"

Over dinner, Eréndira shows her parents the book that Melissa's mother checked out from the University library.

Verónica observes, "Melissa's mother must work on campus to get to the library so quickly. Where does she work?"

"She works in one of the Dean's offices. Something having to do with keeping the professors organized."

Verónica raises her eyebrows. "Wow! She must have superpowers! Keeping professors organized is like herding cats!"

Victor chimes in, "You can say that again!"

Swatting Victor's shoulder, Verónica exclaims, "HEY!"

Victor leans in toward Verónica, "I wasn't talking about you, of course."

With a warning look and a half smile, Verónica huffs, "Humm!"

Eréndira, amused by her parent's bantering, cuts in, "Well… while the two of you figure that out, I'm going to get to my homework and check out the notes Melissa left me."

Eréndira takes the dinner dishes off the table, rinses them and puts them away in the dishwasher before her mother calls out, "Don't worry about the rest, Eréndira. You and your dad have been so good taking care of me with my late nights on campus. Go ahead and get to your homework and that journal. I'll clean up the kitchen."

"Thanks mom!"

Eréndira bolts up the stairs with the Font journal in hand and dives onto her bed. She opens the book and places Melissa's notes right next to it so she can follow, page by page, the clues that her friend left for her.

The first page number Melissa listed is well into the 500+ page translated journal… page 331. Eréndira carefully turns the thick, stiff pages. Aside from Melissa's recent use of the book, it appears that the book has not been in circulation for some time. The last check-out date stamped was January 29, 2002.

Melissa's note on the list next to page number 331 simply reads, "Cayuco—Launch." Gently turning until she gets to page 331, Eréndira finds Melissa's Post-it on the page with arrows pointing directly to a section that reads, "The cayuco is a vessel resembling a canoe or little launch, like those of the Channel, used by the Indians farther up the coast. It is made of several pieces without nails, and the extremities end in a point with a piece hollowed out as if with a chisel, judging from the cutting and the signs which were seen on the inside of the point."

Eréndira sighs and says out loud, as though speaking directly to Melissa, "Okay. So, the Indians had canoes. So what?"

The next page number listed is 375. The accompanying notation reads, "Expanse of water over a plain—then the Sierra Nevada." Eréndira, again, carefully turns the pages until she finds another Post-it with arrows pointing directly to script in the translated journal, "Looking northeast we saw an immense plain without any trees, through which the water extends for a long distance, having in it several little islands of lowland. And finally, on the other side of the immense plain, and at about forty leagues, we saw a great Sierra Nevada whose trend appeared to me to be from south-south-east to north-northwest."

Another strategically placed Post-it points to a footnote that indicates that Font and this expedition were camped close to what is now called Pacheco, in the Bay Area. Melissa included another note that reads, "In case you're wondering, Sherlock… 40 leagues is 111 miles. I looked it up for you! de Anza and Font and the people traveling with them were in the East Bay Area, looking toward the Sierras. They were looking over water that was, then, covering the area where Sacramento is now."

Eréndira remembers the shell fossil discovered at Naníta's. *It is not out of the question*, she thinks, *that during the time of Font's expedition that the entire central region of California was still under water and that the top of hills jutting out of the water appeared as little islands. Now, the topography of California has changed and continues to change as does the climate. What Font and de Anza saw with their eyes was that which was above lake level… but there was a lake covering the central region of California … a lake that no longer exists.*

Eréndira moves on to the next page number listed, 382, slowly turning the brittle pages until she reaches the next Post-it that reads, "Men from Sierra Hunting." Melissa made little arrows on the Post-it that point directly to a portion of the journal she wanted Eréndira to read:

"When they (the soldiers) returned they brought the report that they had met more than twenty Indians who came from fishing loaded with four or five salmon each, and that near the campsite whence we set out they found some Indians who came from the Sierra to the plain to hunt, carrying the head of a deer, one Indian being painted the same color as the deer."

Eréndira sits up and rereads the passage. This is the first evidence she has seen showing a connection between the Spaniards and the Sierra foothill Miwok. And rather than the Spaniards being up in the Sierra Foothills, people from the foothills were in the lower elevation where the Spaniards were exploring.

Two pages later, Melissa directs Eréndira to another indication of the California Indian's water navigation capabilities, "….the children and also some women jumped into the water, embarking on their launches, for they had many very well made of tule, with railings, and with poop and prow ending in an elevated point, and all the rails equipped with arched poles as if they served as a balustrade or as a back, and with some small oars they rowed with great facility and lightness of touch."

A few sentences later Melissa directs Eréndira by drawing a set of eyes on the Post-it, "Here we were finally convinced that what was called a river is not a river, but a great sea of fresh water without current, extending through that plain. To it the animals went on their own feet to drink, and we tasted it and found it very fresh and good."

Eréndira reads beyond this last section, where Font defends his reasoning for why he believes this body of water to be a sea, rather than a river as was noted in a previous expedition.

With several references to a great body of water that appears to be a lake, the use of canoes and other water-crossing vessels that women and children easily managed, it appears that this body of water did not stop California Indians from crossing. In fact, the reference to the men who were hunting what appeared to be elk, were noted as Indians from the Sierras foothills. What can be concluded is that since Font saw these hunters, then the hunters most certainly saw Font and de Anza. Furthermore, the village at which Font camped when he came across the women and children was where the Spaniards conducted several experiments to determine whether the expanse of water was a river, which would be difficult to navigate if people were going back toward the Sierras. A lake, on the other hand, would not be as challenging to return from what is, now, lower elevation to the base of the Sierra foothills.

Eréndira has been on kayak trips with her family and knows that crossing a lake is much easier than navigating a river, but it appears—from what she is reading in Font's journal—that California Indians had watercraft that held up even in the ocean. Without a doubt, California Indians confidently transported their families in their watercraft, as evidenced by Font's journal. On page 404, Font summarizes in his journal written almost 250 years ago, "… from these experiments, we concluded and were finally convinced that this mass of water might better be called a freshwater sea than a river, for it has no floods or currents like a river, and like the sea its water is clear and verging on blue, and it has an ebb and flow and little waves on the beach." This, Eréndira concludes, demonstrates that crossing this body of water was manageable at that time.

Melissa's next note says, "Read on to pages 406 to 407," and this is where Eréndira sees, clearly, that de Anza's and Font's expedition were unable to cross what was, then, a large body of water. Eréndira surmises from these two pages that the expedition traveled along the bank of the "sea," as Font called it, trying to find a way to get across the water so they could get to the Sierras. They traveled in different directions trying to find a way, with horses and wagons, but were stymied by thick Tulares "without being able to make any headway toward the Sierra Nevada, but rather getting farther away." The risk of getting across was punctuated by the fact that a deserter of the expedition, being chased by the soldiers, "jumped precipitately into one of those mires, trusting perhaps that he might be able to swim, but was swallowed up and unable to get out, and, as it was impossible to aid him, he remained there, drowned and buried in mud."

Eréndira is reminded of Melissa's essay notes that revealed the Spaniards bad intentions, but to read of a member of the expedition trying to desert and losing his life while trying to get away…. seems to confirm that these people weren't all that nice. She reads on and comes to understand that the edges of the "sea," as Font referred to this body of water, had dangerous sections and people unfamiliar with the terrain could easily lose their lives, as this man did. Yet, California Indians had villages along these same banks. They knew the terrain, sustained themselves on its natural resources, and had the ability to migrate to other locations as needed. This was apparent from Melissa's report of villages appearing to have been deserted, which, in most likelihood, were abandoned when the inhabitants knew that the Spaniards were, once again, intruding onto their homeland.

Melissa's last note read, "So, you see, Sherlock… de Anza and sidekick, Font, never made it up to the Sierra foothills. What I think is that someone from the Sierra Miwok… the hunters? The women and children on that flotilla thing? (It's not like they had texting back then). It was the Sierra Miwok who saw the Spaniards, went back up to the hills (because they could!) to their village and recorded what they saw. How's this for detective work, Ha!!!"

Eréndira falls back onto her bed, looks up at her ceiling, and mulls over the content revealed in Font's journal. There was not only contact between the Sierra Miwok and de Anza's expedition, but the Sierra Miwok had the means to cross the large expanse of water. They were proficient in navigating lakes and oceans. This, she knew, would have to be shared with Nanita! Eréndira checks the time on her phone. It is only 10:00 p.m. "Good!" she says to herself, "Not too late. Nanita might still be up!"

She pulls 'Nanita' up on her iPhone contact list and presses the phone icon. Three rings later, her Nanita's groggy voice comes through the phone.

"Hello Eréndira. Is everything okay?"

"You're not in bed yet?"

"Well yes, I am in bed but when I heard your call come in, I picked up."

"Oh good! You weren't asleep yet. I'm fine, Nanita, but I wanted to let you know that I have a good source confirming that it is likely that the Miwok from your area had contact with de Anza. The guy on the petroglyph."

"Wow! How did you figure this out?"

Eréndira spends the next half hour reading the excerpts from Font's journal.

After listening to Eréndira provide first source documentation that confirms the sighting by the Sierra Miwok of de Anza, Naníta exclaims, "That is incredible! You pieced together valid information that speaks to Miwok agency!"

"Well… I wish I could take full credit, but it was my friend, Melissa, who was using the Font Journal for a report she wrote. She tagged the content that I just read you."

"She what?"

"She earmarked the pages in the book."

"Oh!"

"And Naníta! You should see what Melissa dug up! The Spaniards seemed to have gotten a bad reputation as they came up the coast. There were quite a few times where the Indians were throwing shade on the Spaniards. I'll send you Melissa's notes so you can read them yourself. Ok?"

"That would be wonderful, Eréndira. I'm so proud of both of you for researching and educating yourselves. Sometimes it takes a little digging, but the truth is buried out there."

"Speaking of which, Naníta, you said you had something to show me, too?"

"Oh yes! Speaking of communication…. You think I'm so antiquated in not knowing how to do all this email and texting, but before all this electronic communication, there was rock mail! And I can tell you. The rocks last longer!"

"Rocks? More Rocks, Naníta?"

"Yes. Like you, I took a picture on my phone."

"Send it to me."

"Send it to you? But it's late right now. I'm not going to the photo shop right now. I'm in my pajamas!"

"No! Naníta! Send it to me on a text."

"How do I do that?"

"Ay, Naníta! It is as easy as the emoji's you learned to send. So, this is what you do… on your phone, see where you put the words in when you text?"

"Yes. Next to it is a little tripod like thing. Press on it and then below, you'll see a colorful flower. Press on that and all your pics will come up. Tap the pic and it will go out with your text."

"Wait. You're going too fast. Let me turn on my lamp and put on my glasses." A moment later, "Come again, okay mija but slower?"

Eréndira gathers her patience to walk her grandmother through the steps again. Her Naníta successfully inserts the picture and presses send. Within seconds, Eréndira enlarges the picture and examines it closely. "So, what is it?"

"Ha!" exclaims Naníta. "To me? It looks like a Spanish conquistador."

Eréndira shouts, "Oh my God! It's a rock carving of a Spanish conquistador!"

The rock carving, which can fit in the palm of the hand, clearly depicts a round shield with what appears to be rays extending from the center. The shield is attached to a figure wearing a dark helmet. The face is more difficult to make out, as time and the elements have eroded the features, but, clearly, the person depicted has a beard. On the person's back is some sort of attachment that extends from mid-back to the head, as though for holding arrows or anything else needed by the carrier.

"You see, Eréndira!" exclaims Naníta. "Like I said, 'Before there was e-mail, there was rock mail!' And the California Indians were in communication with others!"

"Dang, Naníta! That is so cool! What a find!"

"I have more to show you but a picture on a cell phone camera won't do it justice. I'll wait until you come up."

"Can't wait…. But Naníta?"

"Yes, Eréndira?"

"I have something else to tell you."

Eréndira shares with her Naníta about the expanded circle of friends that she has made, the circumstances that have brought them to her, the cruel behavior that Susan and her friends inflict on others and its toxic impact on the culture of the school. Then, she also confides in her about the horrible deaths and transfer of students who couldn't put up with the bullying. She shares the story about the Ukrainian sisters and finishes with, "And tomorrow, Susan returns to school, and the Vice Principal, Ms. Foster, is likely to bring us together to try and make good. But from what Rosalee, Luisa, and the others shared, Susan and her friends put on an act in front of adults and then go back to being cruel when adults aren't paying attention." Eréndira catches her breath before proceeding, "Naníta, I despise her more than I did before. The good news is that these new girls that I've gotten to know, they want to start up a club... sort of a counter force to the nastiness. They seem to want me to head it up... because I have been the only one to take on the bully. I just feel so confused over this. I don't know what to say tomorrow because all I want to do now is punch her out again. How does that make me a candidate to head up a club that does 'kind' things?"

Naníta thinks for a while before saying, "Do you regret punching Susan?"

Eréndira considers how to answer. "I regret coming to this school."

Naníta hits back, "You're not answering the question."

Eréndira takes an even longer pause. "Well, you've taught me not to use violence."

"Yes, but in self-defense. And that is what you did, but what do you think would have happened had you not stuck up for yourself?"

"She would still be picking on me... and she and her friends get mean... like cruel mean! They pull on people's backpacks, call them names. Spread vicious lies."

"Ok. So. Your reaction became an inflection point."

"A what?"

"It's a moment in which the current of life changes because of an event that prompts change. It forces people to stop and think. Rather than just having life go on in dysfunctional ways, it gives pause and a chance to reflect on what is happening. And the outcome could be positive and it can be negative, but that depends on what you do. Think about it this way; under regular circumstances, we live our lives peacefully, but when challenges present themselves, the way we respond reveals who we really are, and your response can have more impact than the challenge itself."

"That's a lot to take in, Naníta."

"It is, Eréndira. But don't forget after whom you are named."

"That's right! You'll have to tell me more about her when I get up there."

"You and the Princess are cut from the same cloth. Tomorrow…. I know you'll do what is right."

"Thank you for the vote of confidence, Naníta, but I am still not sure what that is. Any words of wisdom you can share with me? What thoughts as to what Princess Eréndira would do?"

"You're already doing it."

"What do you mean?"

"Let me see if I can name a few of the things. Like the Miwok… they communicated who they saw and warned others. That is agency. You and Princess Eréndira both demonstrated agency as well."

"Okay. Tell me more."

"Well…." Naníta pauses, and collects her breath and proceeds, "First, let's consider that both of you have faced circumstances not of your choosing and not of your making. Nonetheless, you both stood up to aggression. Your actions brought people together. You spoke truth to those who were willing to hear it. Remember, silence is complicity, but you both spoke up and acted against malice. I am sure the Princess would be very proud of you. You carry her spirit and are applying her strength and wisdom in these times."

Eréndira weighs Naníta's observations. The circumstances are different—what Princess Eréndira faced during her life was likely, much more dangerous. But, there is a cost for the nastiness that appears to be endemic in current times.

All Eréndira can say, quietly, as she takes all this in is, "Wow— that's so much I don't even know where to start…"

"Smudge yourself like I have shown you, cleanse your soul… go in with pure heart and long vision."

Tears well in Eréndira's eyes. She has been carefully distracting herself from this conflict with her extra-curricular activities and research. Tomorrow, however, will come no matter how much she detests its arrival, and she will not only have to come face-to-face with Susan—a girl whose nose she busted a little over a week ago, but who Eréndira's loathes even more because of her heartless tormenting of others.

Eréndira takes a deep breath and says, "Okay, Naníta. I'll remember to smudge myself tomorrow."

"And I will say a prayer for you. I will ask the spirits of the Ancients to guide you through this. You are confronting dark energies that still reverberate around us; abuse and exploitation take many forms. Rising above these forces requires connecting with one's higher self."

Eréndira takes another deep breath. "You're right, Naníta. Thank You."

"Oh, yes… one more thing occurred to me about what you and the Princess have in common. You both learned to master the enemies' weapons to defend the vulnerable."

"What? What do you mean by that?"

"Long story. We'll discuss later. I just remembered that one of my kitties is still outside. I need to get her in before the neighborhood skunk family comes by for their nightly visit. Good night, Eréndira."

Eréndira sees her screen go dark as her Naníta rushes off to call in one of her three cats.

As Eréndira waits for sleep to overtake her, she wonders what Naníta meant when she said that she and the Princess mastered the enemies' weapons. Like that wasn't enough to think about, the image of the rock depicting a Spanish soldier lingers in her mind. Another mystery... *Who made it? What was it doing up in Sierra Miwok territory?*

It Was 1521

The final days were coming. Chiefs, lords, and governors from the four quadrants of the Purépecha Nation gathered on the patio in front of Cazonci Zuangua's home. They were not allowed to see him prior to his passing on to the next world but had come, nonetheless, to pay their respects. They left gifts in the vestibule that bore the Cazonci's insignia. When he drew his last breath, the crying of those closest to him, the women who had attended him and his home, alerted those assembled on the patio that the Cazonci's time on earth had ended.

One by one, the lords, starting with highest rank, entered the deceased Cazonci's room and gathered around the lifeless body. Some gasped at the sight of the Cazonci's disfigured skin, ravaged by a disease for which there was no cure. Others stood stoically with stiff jaws and faced their deceased leader. The tortured state of his body portended their situation.

Each lord took their turn bathing their former ruler's body. Several wept as they dressed him in fresh clothing. The first item placed on the withered body was a thin undershirt worn exclusively by the lords, followed by a leather war coat. They distributed the adornments that were to be ceremoniously and tenderly arranged on him. A white fishbone necklace was placed around his neck, small golden bells on his legs, turquoise stones on his wrists, a braid of feathers and then a collar of sacred turquoise. Large gold earrings reserved only for one of his status were inserted in his ear lobes. Two gold bracelets on his arms and a large turquoise lip-ring completed the deceased Cazonci's final dressing.

Once their revered Ruler was fully adorned, the Lords, once more, surrounded him and slipped their hands underneath his body. In unison, they carefully lifted and placed him on top of wide boards covered with varicolored blankets. Additional blankets were placed upon the body to appear as though he was merely sleeping in a portable, makeshift bed. Two poles were placed under the boards, while his head was wrapped in blankets and draped with additional jewelry. The final possessions to make the journey into the next world with him were his tiger-skin quiver and his bow and arrow, which were reverently laid on top of the still body.

The Lords took hold of the poles, lifted the seemingly sleeping Cazonci, and carried him from his home for the final journey. The scent of white copal preceded the somber procession of forty people, each representing a skill or craft useful to the Cazonci while he was alive. They walked ahead of his body as he was transported to the patio of the great temple where a pyre, made of layers of pine, stacked atop one upon another, awaited.

The procession marched to the sound of trumpets and circled the pyre four times. He was placed on top of the piled wood while his relatives sang, and the blaze was set. Throughout the night the Lords stoked the fire. When dawn arrived, only ashes remained of the Cazonci. His remnants were wrapped in blankets and placed in a grave at the foot of and under the first step leading to Curi-caveri's Temple.

The walls of the deep grave, two and a half fathoms (15 feet) wide, were lined with reed mats and round gold and silver shields. The Cazonci's remains were placed on a wooden bed on the floor of the grave. After all his earthly belongings had been secured along with him, beams were placed, crisscrossed, over the opening of the grave, topped with boards, and then plastered over. After the ritual was completed, all who touched the body immediately bathed for fear of contracting the disease that killed the Cazonci—the same disease now devastating the people of the kingdom.

Tucked away on a secluded island, Eréndira spent hours at a time sitting on the shore. Though she and her mother were hidden away, updates of the Cazonci's final days arrived through messengers. When the solemn trumpet blare made its way across Lake Patzcuaro, Eréndira knew what it meant. She stood, waded into the water waist deep, and cried in solitude. Every bone of her body yearned to be by the Cazonci's side, but it was his dying wish that she and her mother be whisked away as quickly as possible. The Cazonci's intention was not to distance himself from his favorite niece but to protect her and her mother from this deadly disease and from the threat of foreign intruders whose intentions were still unknown.

As the forlorn sound of the Cazonci's death reached the island, Sesasi ran to the shore facing Tzintzuntzan. It was there that she found Eréndira shedding tears onto the still lake. Sesasi stepped into the water and embraced her daughter.

"Oh, Amámba! The Cazonci has been like a father. So many see him as some distant and untouchable ruler, but he always demonstrated his care for everyone, but right now... being hidden away like this feels like punishment!"

Sesasi, with her arms around her daughter, explained, "Yes, Eréndira. I can see how you would feel like that. Our being brought here was his last act of love and kindness. A good leader makes wise decisions to maintain the kingdom and protect its people. Think how important it was for him to ensure that you survive these difficult times."

Eréndira gently held her mother's words. She considered his intentions that she survive the scourge of this illness and, perhaps, of what was yet to come. When she was but a child, the Cazonci shared many stories with her like that of Princess Hapunda. There was always a lesson to learn. Often, the message conveyed that evils manifest in many ways, but responding in a like manner is not always best. Even though the Cazonci prepared Eréndira to engage in battle by training for countless hours with her Uncle Anini, he also made sure that she developed the capacity to respond from a well-tempered nature rather than be reactive when confronted by evil.

Eréndira turned to her mother, "You're right, Amámba. He has been a guiding force in my life; his wisdom, planted in my heart, remains."

The following day, a messenger traveled across the lake and delivered further news of what transpired in the Purépecha Nation.

"Greetings, my Princess," he addressed Eréndira and bowed to Sesasi, "A pervasive foreboding takes hold. The Lords have learned that intruders, called acacechas, those who wear hats and caps, have strengthened their forces with the alliance of Tlaxcalan soldiers. Our warriors have yet to encounter the acacechas, but it is apparent that these intruders brought weapons and terms of war that we have yet to encounter. Our warriors who had been sent by the Cazonci to investigate what was transpiring within the Mexica kingdom saw, firsthand, the destruction of the Mexica nation. They reported a lingering stench from a bloody 75-day siege of the Mexica empire capitol, Tenochtitlán and, with their own eyes, witnessed the ferocity of 900 acacechas and a hundred thousand Indian warrior allies."

Eréndira, having learned military strategy, determined that the summary given by the messenger was incomplete. One must know the full nature of one's enemy, what they are capable of, their motivations, their weaknesses, as well as their strengths. In this way, she would be able to understand how to best respond. She asked, "Tell us more. I want details as to what our warriors observed."

The messenger nodded and then proceeded, "The Purépecha warriors who bore witness returned with many stories of weaponry which no one had ever seen. One battle took place in an expansive valley between a thousand Mexica warriors and the invading acacechas. From a distant hill our warriors heard one thousand Mexica warriors, lined up row after row, blow their conch shells in unison. This, a frightening and bone-chilling sound, instills fear in the fiercest enemies but the acacechas responded with thunder from their large sticks. The sound roared across the valley and leveled battalions of Mexica warriors."

"That is strange. Sound sent by sticks kills warriors?"

"Somehow, Princess. It may not be the sound but something that comes from sticks that leaves their enemies bloodied," offered the messenger.

Eréndira surmised, "Like an arrow from a bow. It appears that hand-to-hand combat with the acacechas is only possible if a warrior gets past their sticks."

"That is correct, Princess, but whatever comes from their sticks cannot be seen. Yet, it decimates its victim."

Eréndira considered how battle must be conducted with beings who possess this type of weaponry. After a few moments, she asked, "And what, at this time, say our Lords?"

"The older Lords of the Empire, those who survived the disease, gathered. They discussed who the next Cazonci should be, and they turned to Cazonci Zuangua's oldest son, Tangoxóan. They said, 'Sire, you must be our King. How can this house remain deserted and be-clouded?' Tangoxóan, despondent over the death of his father, was reluctant to assume the position. He responded, 'Do not say this, old man; let my younger brothers do it and I shall be as a father to them, or let it be the Master of Cuyacán called Paguingata.'"

Eréndira knew Tangoxóan well. Besides Uncle Anini, Tangoxóan was one of her father's favorite sons of the late Zuangua. He was of strong nature but also caring and sensitive. Given the tumultuous times in which they lived, she could see why he was unwilling to assume the role. There was tremendous danger for whomever became Cazonci. He knew that the outcome for whomever assumed the position of Cazonci may be ill-fated.

She prodded the messenger further, "So what next? What came of the Lord's decision for replacing Cazonci Zuangua?"

The messenger proceeded, "The Lords, in distress, looked at one another not knowing what to do. They needed to confirm a leader who could direct us all during these times of crisis. One Lord spoke up and said to Tangoxóan, 'What are you saying, Sire? You must be the king. Do you want your younger brothers to take the seigniory from you? You are the oldest!' Reluctantly, Tangoxóan conceded and told the Lords, 'Having been importuned, let it be as you say, old men; I want to obey you. If perchance I do not do well, I beg you not to harm me, but gently separate me from the seigniory. Take heed that we are not to dissemble and listen for what is said about the strange people who are coming, for we do not know who they are. Perhaps the days that I shall have this charge will not be many.' With that, he dismissed all the lords but one… your father, Timas."

Sesasi observed, "Timas was the former Cazonci's most trusted advisor. During these uncertain times in which warfare may be imminent, it is wise that Cazonci Tangoxóan consults with him.

Should the acacechas approach us as they did the Mexica, it is a priority that the people be protected."

The messenger and Eréndira took stock of Sesasi's last statement. Her words conveyed that the Purépecha Kingdom's most precious treasure was its people. Seeing how the disease had penetrated the young and the old, they were now all under threat of devastation.

"What then," asked Eréndira of the messenger, "has my father set in motion?"

"Apparently, Princess, your father, Timas, is carrying out the orders of our departed Cazonci Zuangua. It is well known that Cazonci Zuangua always had a soft spot for you, Princess Eréndira! That is why you and your mother were brought here, but now the rest of the Royal Family must be protected."

"It is very possible," Eréndira suggested, "that the Mexica may convey who the members of the Royal Family are. Now that they have been dominated by these outside intruders, they might try to gain favor with them by handing over any information they have about us."

Sesasi looked to her daughter, "You are saying that all of the members of the Royal Family could be targeted by the acacechas, regardless of how they are received by us?"

Eréndira nodded, "Yes, Amámba. We did not offer the Mexica alliance against the acacechas when they came to us. They have more reason, now, to turn the acacechas against us."

"You are your father's daughter."

"Correct, Princess," the messenger added, "Your father knows that Cazonci Tangoxóan's life may be in peril but not just him… also the lives of his brothers. For this reason, your father proposed to the Cazonci Tangoxóan that he announce a decree that his brothers and their families be put to death…"

"What?!" shouted Sesasi. "What say you? Timas suggested to the Cazonci that he kill his own brothers to avoid having them killed by the enemy of our enemy?!"

The messenger began to respond to the unbelieving and irate Sesasi, but it was Eréndira who calmly responded, "It is but a ruse, Amámba. While the homes of the Cazonci's brothers are vacated, it will *be said* that the Cazonci had them killed." Eréndira emphasized the words *be said*. She recognized the importance of words and that even false words have bearing.

Sesasi, who began to understand, then asked, "And what reason would be given for such an unprecedented act?"

"Not so unprecedented." Eréndira explained, "It is known that we have no tolerance for drunkenness, nor for adultery and treason. So, this is what can be done…. As the families are quietly taken to a hidden location as was done with us, it is announced that, perhaps, that the brothers have been sleeping with the women of Cazonci Tangoxóan's household."

"Ah!" exclaimed Sesasi, "That would be believable as several of the Cazonci Tangoxóan's brothers are not married so the temptation of tasting that which is nearby is not totally out of the question."

Eréndira, pleased to hear her mother understanding ways of thinking to protect without having to resort to violence added, "Yes! Or another possibility is to plant a rumor that they were planning to remove the new Cazonci out of jealousy so, to eliminate the threat, the Cazonci eliminates them! In this way, the acacechas, the Mexica, and those within the Kingdom who might betray the Royal Family, will cease to target us like prized deer."

Sesasi, coming to terms with the ruse and its consequences, said, "So be it. I do pray that this danger will pass because with this plan, it is likely that Cazonci Tangoxóan might not ever see his family again. This, being a great sacrifice. As is, he mourns his father and now, he must feign condemning his own blood relations to their death. Either way, he will mourn them."

"As we speak," the messenger offered, "Timas is already carrying out the ruse and setting up a counteroffensive. We don't know what these acacechas want of us. It appears they care not for the lives of those they encounter on this land but only what the land, itself, has to offer. They seem to have a sickness, craving only gold, silver, and pure domination."

"Very well, so we know what drives them," interjected Eréndira. "For this reason, my father will devise plots within plots. He will see to it that our people do not suffer the same fate as the Mexica. Upon your return, convey to Cazonci Tangoxóan and my father that I am ready to serve the cause of preserving the lives of our people. The royal family is being attended to, but we must also protect as many from the kingdom as we can. I have understood from earlier reports that Moctezuma, ruler of the Mexica, had, prior to the arrival of these intruders, sent women, children, and soldiers into hiding in a remote location. There, they were ordered to remain regardless of the outcome between the acacechas and the Mexica. Even though Tenochtitlán has been decimated, Moctezuma protected the greatest treasure… their culture. It would be an honor to do the same for the Purépecha."

The messenger bowed to the Princess and her mother, Sesasi. Before departing, he and the men charged with navigating his canoe were provided food and water. Having restored their stamina, the men furiously paddled back across the lake to deliver the messenger carrying Princess Eréndira's message.

As Princess Eréndira and her mother watched the canoe disappear, they exchanged ideas of how to create a 'fog' like the one that shielded Princess Hapunda during her escape from invading Chichimecas. Already, Timas was setting in motion the 'vanishing' of the Cazonci's family, his brothers, extended family, and as many Lords and their families as possible. But what was told to others as to the reason for their sudden disappearance, and what was in truth, reality, was a fog of subterfuge to most. *How many more*, Eréndira wondered, *can I save should the acacechas come to our lands with an insatiable lust for precious metals and death? What other sacrifices will need to be made to preserve the lives of my own people and perhaps others on this continent?*

Multiple canoes cut through the dense Lake Pátzcuaro fog and arrived on the secluded island just as the sun peeked over the eastern horizon. Eréndira greeted the canoes carrying Timas and Cazonci

Tangoxóan's extended family. No sooner had the first ripples been cast as they made their way to the island that the prescribed rumor had been released in the wake of the family's exodus; that the Cazonci's brothers had been executed for alleged moral misconduct. The fabricated cloak of protection for the Cazonci's brothers claimed that the brothers were charged with intent to carry out treason. This explained the disappearance of the brothers' families, who were subsequently banished from the Kingdom, escorted to lands far beyond the boundaries of the Kingdom and left to fend for themselves.

None of this being true, of course, but it was the proposed narrative to account for the sudden absence of so many people related to the new Ruler, Cazonci Tangoxóan. With so many unimaginable events destabilizing the kingdom—the death of Cazonci Zuangua, an incurable disease taking the lives of young and old, and the emergence of the acacechas—the executions and banishments of the Royal family could blend in as seemingly natural outcomes in the highly unusual and chaotic times. The existential disorder during overwhelming uncertainty made the ruse that much more believable.

Upon hearing of the arrival of the canoes carrying Cazonci Tangoxóan's brothers and their families, Sesasi left the island camp and ran to the shore. As Timas disembarked, Sesasi wrapped him in a full embrace while Eréndira received and welcomed the Cazonci Tangoxóan's extended family.

Timas stole a few moments to hold Sesasi then turned to those left on the shore and requested the audience of the warriors, the Cazonci's brothers, and the women of the royal family. With Sesasi and Eréndira on either side of him, Timas addressed the assemblage of Purépecha royal refugees who, up until this point, had not had this major disruption to their lives explained.

"The Mexica, our traditional enemies, have been besieged by a terrible disease for which they have no cure. As you know, the same disease has fallen upon our own people, and none of our healers have been able to cure those who have contracted this sickness. Perhaps worse than this malady are the acacechas who seem to follow this illness' deadly path. These threats compel us to respond with measured caution. For this reason, Cazonci Tangoxóan, out of concern for your safety, commanded that you remain here. We will seek to learn who these strangers are, what it is they may want from us, and, more importantly, how to ensure we do not suffer the same fate as the Mexica."

Anini cleared his throat before speaking, "Uncle Timas, we thank you for giving us the cause for being swept from our homes in the middle of the night without explanation. I can understand that the women, children and elders must be protected, but wouldn't we, the warriors who are here… me and my brothers, as advisors, best serve our brother, the Cazonci, by being by his side?"

Timas called Anini to the front of the gathered group and placed both hands on his shoulders.

"Your allegiance to your brother and to the kingdom is noted, but at this moment, it is believed that the Cazonci ordered the execution of you and your brothers."

The assembled members of the royalty gasped in unison. Anini looked to his brothers, Tirimarasco and Azinche, whose expression of disbelief reflected his own.

Tirimarasco voiced their collective shock, "What is this Uncle Timas? To be cast to this remote island for our protection is one thing, but to be declared dead, it is another. Executed at the command of our own brother? This is outrageous! Tangoxóan would never conceive of such an act!"

Timas, stern in his composure to this point, suddenly broke out with a big grin, an expression incongruent with the sentiments of the moment. In return, those assembled peered at him with tremendous confusion and silently wondered, *In the midst of all this chaos, has Timas gone insane?*

No one spoke a word as the displaced family attempted to make sense of what had overtaken Timas. They turned to one another for an answer to his inappropriately foolish composure, but it was Eréndira and Sesasi who understood why Timas was smiling. The mother and daughter turned to one another and exchanged a knowing glance. The rest of the family members looked to the faces of those around them who, without warning or explanation, were all whisked away from their warm beds in the middle of the night to a remote island in the middle of Lake Pátzcuaro. Then, one by one, starting with Tirimarasco and Azinche, familiar with the history of Purépecha military strategy, scoffed and embraced one another. Once the group had come to an unspoken understanding, they nodded to one another and Timas did not need to explain. Anini addressed his Uncle Timas on behalf of the group.

"We understand Uncle Timas. And, when you are ready for us to come back to life, we will wholeheartedly serve my brother and the Purépecha people. But, while we play dead here on this island, we will prepare for whatever comes and do whatever is asked."

Timas acknowledged his nephew, "Thank you Anini." To the rest of the assembled people, Timas offered, "Thank you all. While here, look out for one another and be vigilant. For now, I must head to the borderlands where I will gather our warriors and notify all of how we will respond to this threat. Women, children, and elders will be sent back to this island and out of harm's way. Prepare for their arrival."

Timas turned away from the group, taking Sesasi and Eréndira with him to have a private conversation. As soon as they were out of hearing range from the others, Sesasi addressed Timas.

"Please, Timas. You are going to Acámbaro, aren't you?"

Timas solemnly nodded. Eréndira silently witnessed this rare emotional exchange between her parents.

Sesasi continued, "I know I ask much of you Timas, but please, can you bring back my family to this island where they will be safe? My father can serve as one of the guards and even my mother can shoot an arrow as well as any warrior. They could both serve just as well here as they can at the border."

"Sesasi. You and Eréndira have united our kingdom through the warmth and devotion extended between our communities. Because of this, your taáte, Irepani, will always place himself where he is most needed in protection of you and all the kingdom. Your amámba, Parakata, I doubt she would consider leaving his side, especially in these dark times, but if there is any way to convince them to seek sanctuary here, I will send them. But you must know,

Sesasi," at this moment, Timas pulled mother and daughter, one in each of his arms, closer to him, lowering his voice he said, "Eréndira, you must know that this mysterious illness, tepari pamangarata, has fallen heavily upon our eastern border, the direction from which these acacechas are now. Be prepared, for I don't know who or what I will find there."

All three held their emotions in firm as they fervently hoped their loved ones would have escaped the wrath of this disease.

It was Eréndira who finally spoke, "Taáte, may I come with you? Tatíta Irepani has trained me to fight in battle and Uncle Anini has fine-tuned my skills. We have spent many days and nights on this island mastering the weapons. I can use these skills if I am by your side rather than confined to this island."

"It is much too dangerous for you Eréndira. There are people I will be speaking to who already know my rank with the Royal family. Once you are seen with me, in any capacity, you would be in even more danger than any other young woman in the kingdom. If caught, you could be used as a pawn. You could be tortured for information. You would be defiled in front of us. How could we bear such things?"

Eréndira stood defiant in front of her father, not wincing at any of the possible outcomes should she be caught by their enemies.

Sesasi broke the silence, "He is right, Eréndira. You would serve valiantly at the front line and it is also true that you would be targeted. You are needed and you have trained, but your time will come. Please be patient and let your father and the Cazonci figure out a plan. There may be a place and a time for you to serve beyond the shores of this island."

Eréndira's disappointment was apparent. She knew she could be of assistance but felt suffocated by that cloak of protection. Timas read her frustration, remembering how he, as a young warrior, wanted to give more but was always expected to wait until he was told that he was ready to take on more responsibility. The time finally came. He considered Eréndira's tender age and he wished it wasn't so, but, it may be possible that with all that had befallen their Kingdom that, maybe, this was Eréndira's time. *Perhaps*, he thought to himself, *there is a way in which she could assist but kept out of harms' way.*

Timas replied, "I love your courage, Eréndira. The messenger did deliver your offer… to oversee the cloak of protection to as many of our people, beyond the Royal family. And, if your amámba permits," he motioned to Sesasi, "perhaps you could escort me part way to the borderlands. There, you can wait, with guards, of course. And should I have your Tatíta, your Naníta, or any others who may need to come here for sanctuary, then I can have them delivered to you. Your charge will be to safely escort them back across the Lake or relocate them to the highlands. This would be helpful, and it would free me to return to the capitol and join Cazonci Tangoxóan."

Eréndira's face softened and her shoulders relaxed at the thought of overseeing the safety of others. "Yes, Taáte! I will gladly do as you ask. When do we leave?"

"Now."

Without another word, Eréndira ran to her lodge where she retrieved clothing for the colder evenings, a blanket in which to sleep, and her weapons.

Timas turned to Sesasi and assured her, "Don't worry. I will select the best of our warriors to accompany her. Furthermore, I will ensure that they are encamped in an area well hidden from any enemies. Not only will they be well fortified, they also will have higher ground to see who comes and goes."

Not able to sustain contact with Sesasi's troubled eyes, Timas turned away to assemble his brothers along with several warriors. Huddled away from the rest of the community, he explained to them the next steps to be taken.

Eréndira and several guards would accompany Timas halfway to Acámbaro and make camp in a location hidden from the main roads. The plan was for Timas to proceed to Acámbaro and then on to Taximaroa, the stronghold and nucleus of the Purépecha borderland. In between these two communities he was to stop in Maravatio where he would assess what was transpiring at the border, gather the warriors, and fortify Purépecha boundaries. Once the warriors on the borderlands were organized, Timas would make his way back to Tzintzuntzan where the Cazonci awaited him.

Any people from Acámbaro and the other border communities who were still alive, and not infected with the illness, would be sent back to Eréndira. They, in turn, would deliver to her, and her small, assembled army, updates from the borderlands and further instructions. When Eréndira and the guards ascertained that the roads were safe, they were to escort survivors and refugees to the hidden island in Lake Pátzcuaro. Some, however, would remain in the highlands to help others who were perhaps too weak or ill to travel. Those who were healthy and able would be trained to fight should a counteroffensive be necessary. Despite contingencies established for all the possible outcomes, they prayed that the dark cloud brought by the acacechas passed them without further harm.

Without delay, Timas and Eréndira departed for Acámbaro with a small contingent of warriors. On the way to their destination Eréndira and a handful of the best warriors were safely tucked away in forested highlands where they could catch sight of who came and went. She had been given strict instructions not to attack any acacechas or other allies of these intruders. For time being, the Purépecha had to portray themselves as neutrally as possible until they knew the acacechas' intentions and could assess their strengths and weaknesses. Eréndira's strict orders were to ensure safe passage of the elders, women, and children back to the island in Lake Pátzcuaro. Those who were fit were to remain with her, and she was to oversee their training and preparation for battle.

After giving his daughter one last hug, Timas gathered his warriors and continued the route to the borderlands facing the perilous Mexica nation. To his dismay, before even seeing the community of Acámbaro, the wind carried the ominous drone of wailing. The sound of collective lament sent a chill up his spine as he and his accompanying warriors entered the village's outskirts. Unlike previous visits to this vibrant village, there were no bustling and lively exchanges between residents and merchants. The streets were vacant of vendors and their colorful wares. Instead of the fragrance of roasting chilis and fresh corn tortillas, the repulsive odor of death lingered in the air. Timas and his warriors warily stepped forward as they attempted to make sense of what perpetrated this absence of humanity.

Amid the deserted streets, Timas spotted an unaccompanied and vacant-eyed child of no more than three years, sitting alone outside a home. This unusual and heart rendering sight prompted Timas to approach the entrance of the home. He stepped past the child, who looked up at him, emotionless. Timas pulled up the blanket that covered the entrance and instinctively shielded his nose as he was overtaken with the stench of death. He motioned the warriors to stay back. The scene before him told all. There were several bodies of various sizes wrapped and prepared for burial. Next to the bodies were their meager belongings along with some food and water meant to accompany them to their other world destination. Unable to complete the burial, the body of a man lay curled next to the largest of the wrapped bodies. His face, in death, revealed the anguished disfigurement from tepari pamangarata. In his final moments, the man desperately attempted to wrap the final body, presumably that of his deceased temba. His fingers still clutched the cloth he was wrapping around her body. This, his final act of love and devotion. In the end, there was no one left to attend to him.

Timas stumbled out of the home, gasping for air. The bewildered faces of the warriors reflected Timas' own despair, which he attempted to conceal even as he looked up to the heavens for a response to his prayers. One warrior motioned toward two figures that appeared further up the road, cautiously approaching them. As they got closer Timas recognized one of the two, a Lord accompanied by a servant.

Upon recognizing Timas, the Lord offered the formal greeting between those of stature, "Natsï jámaxaki."

Timas responded, "Natsï jámaxaki. We have come to gather as many warriors as possible and ensure the safety of those who have survived this scourge." Timas motioned to the child—the family's sole survivor of the disease.

The Lord sadly explained, "Yes, he is one but for a handful of children who have escaped this unfathomable illness. There are more children and others who are hidden away in the outskirts of the community. This one continues to leave the safe zone. We are watchful of this one but he escapes our vigilance and returns to his home. As you can see, he is the only survivor of his family. We came looking for him." The Lord looked to the child who sat, motionless as a sentry, at the entrance of his family's home, and continued, "Unfortunately, some of the people charged with administering final rites and ensuring proper burial succumbed to the illness. Such was the case of this child's father. Those assigned to searching for any survivors and any items that would be of use in the safe zone found the child here."

Timas looked down at the child who had apparently been living off food and water that he managed to scavenge from the bodies that never made it to burial. In these dire circumstances, Timas wondered who else of Acámbaro was left. He turned to the Lord and requested, "Take me to the survivors."

The Lord bowed his head in acknowledgement of the request and motioned for the servant to pick up the child, who gave no resistance. As the group retreated to where those living were sequestered, the child looked over the servant's shoulder and yelled back to his deceased parents and siblings, now slumbering eternally in what was once a joyous home, "Pauani jamberi." *See you tomorrow.*

The group ascended into the higher elevations of Acámbaro, where those surviving had banded together. As expected, Timas was greeted by a small force of warriors who had been spared of the illness. With a sigh of relief, he readily recognized Sesasi's father, Irepani, but was taken aback by his physical presence. Though not showing signs of the disease, Irepani looked withered, as if the life force had left him.

Despite his condition, Irepani stepped forward and openly welcomed Timas and his accompanying warriors, "Terútseme je ixu!"

Timas took Irepani in both his arms, surveyed the encampment of several hundred people from Acámbaro who were making meals, sharpening their swords, macanas and spears, while others organized small groups, recognized by their covered faces, to locate and bury those who had passed and awaited burial. Hauntingly, the sounds of mourning encroached upon these daily and mundane tasks, reminding everyone that the shadow of death touched their lives.

Irepani led Timas into a small home that had been temporarily converted into a military headquarters. Timas looked for signs of Irepani's lovely temba, Parakata.

Sensing that Timas was searching for her, Irepani explained, "You look for Parakata but she is not to be found amongst the living. She was one of the first to cross over. Fortunately, there were still enough of us at the time to perform the final rites. But the same fate awaited the rest of our children and their children. Here in Acámbaro, I am the last left of our lineage."

Timas looked upon Irepani with disbelief. This illness presumably brought by the acacechas had devastated Sesasi's entire family, less, her father, Irepani.

Before Timas could say anything more, Irepani explained, "Those of us who were guarding the perimeters of the community were mostly spared. We thought it best to gather those surviving together, quarantine, and remain vigilant." Irepani gave Timas a few silent moments to process the loss of Sesasi's entire family. Then, he proceeded, "Timas, tell us what word do you bring from Tzintzuntzan? My daughter, Sesasi, and my granddaughter, Eréndira, do they live? My blood and that of my beloved Parakata runs through their veins. They are all I have left in this world." Irepani looked pleadingly at Timas as he said, "Please, Timas. Tell me that they still live."

Promptly, Timas answered, "Not to worry, my friend. Both are safe and await you. Sesasi is on an isolated island. Eréndira is in the forested highlands, not far from there, where she is to escort survivors from the borderlands back to a secluded sanctuary. I have come to organize our warriors from these lands and offer you passage to safety."

Irepani gave a sigh of relief. With that, he announced with greater strength in his voice, "Knowing Sesasi and Eréndira are safe gives me reason to live and to fight. Timas, I must go with you and carry on my duties in service to our people. I will accompany you to Taximaroa. There are many here who can return to this sanctuary island and join Sesasi, but there are also warriors here in Acámbaro who will fight to their last breath. Perhaps they can remain in the highlands where Eréndira is now sequestered."

Irepani's words steeled Timas' confidence. With Irepani, a loyal and experienced leader of countless battles, by his side, and an expansive and proactive plan in place, he did not feel as overwhelmed with having to confront the unknown. Furthermore, Eréndira's presence in the refugee camp representing the Royalty and the military, would lift the people's spirits. He turned to Irepani and announced, "You speak the words of a leader. Tomorrow, we leave for Taximaroa."

Timas and his warriors were fed that evening, but the exuberance of a vibrant people was missing as they grappled with the loss of so many of their loved ones. Sleeping that night in Irepani's temporary home, Timas missed Parakata's essence. Her warmth, humor, and sensitive nature permeated the soul of the community. Her passing left a dreary void.

As for Irepani, he was like the child who returned to the bodies of his deceased family. His eyes reflected a hollowness in his soul, but, unlike the child, his actions projected an anger that sought vengeance for the deaths these acacechas had brought with them. At first, it appeared to Timas that Irepani barely had the will to breathe air into his lungs, but now he saw the dual motivation of vengeance for the deaths and protection of his surviving daughter, Sesasi, and granddaughter, Eréndira. This fueled him, so as Irepani sharpened his weapons he locked the image of Sesasi and Eréndira in his mind. In this way, he felt reason to continue living but, more importantly, for fighting.

Dozing off to the sound of Irepani sharpening his macana, Timas shuddered when he thought of Sesasi. Within several days, she would learn the news delivered from Acámbaro that her dear mother, her siblings, and her siblings' children were no more. The news will engulf her with sorrow, but Eréndira, he knew, would channel her grief. Despite Eréndira's gracious temperament, there was a side of her that could ignite with a consuming fury-seeking relief.

Timas let his body and mind give way to overwhelming fatigue and much needed sleep. The next day, and the days after, would most certainly be without any opportunities to replenish his well-being. This, he knew, because now that the acacechas had arrived, there would be no rest, no comfort, no safety for anyone.

Timas did not know, as he slipped into slumber on the outskirts of Acámbaro, that Hernan Cortés had expanded his ambitions and had set his sights on Purépecha Territory. With Timas and Irepani prepared to leave the following morning to galvanize the warriors on the borderlands, the Cazonci was left, alone, to respond to what was to come.

It came by way of a messenger sent by the acacechas who were now sequestered in Taximaroa. The exhausted courier notified the Cazonci that the acacechas requested safe passage into Purépecha territory. The delivery of the message followed established inter-tribal protocols and rules of engagement which meant only one thing… the Mexica were cooperating with the acacechas. This was the price the Purépecha would pay for refusing alliance.

The Cazonci heard the request and became enraged because the acacechas not only wanted access to Purepecha territory, but they also presumed that the Cazonci would personally receive an envoy. These acacechas believed themselves to be equal to and perhaps superior to the Cazonci who was expected to acquiesce to their request. Still despondent from the loss of his father and mourning the fact that he would, most likely, never see his brothers and his family again, the Cazonci deliberated his response. Reluctantly and inevitably, he understood that it was his responsibility to deal with these strangers, and he must do so without the counsel of his brothers or his trusted Uncle Timas. While he had many of the kingdom's lords at his fingertips, their suggestions were not only divided, but the loyalty of some was questionable.

The courier, noting a soured change in the Cazonci's countenance, nervously waited for a response. The Cazonci, tapping an arrow on the ground as his father did during such exchanges, surmised how badly the Mexica alignment with these acacechas could harm them. The Mexica's revenge on the Purépecha would, undoubtedly, result in sending these invaders and their wrath at them. To make matters worse, they were likely exaggerating Purépecha treasures to entice these invaders into attacking. The appearance of this courier meant that the acacechas were cautiously assessing, for themselves, Purépecha confidence in their military might.

Once the Cazonci came to these conclusions, he determined it was best to receive the envoy while projecting superior Purépecha military prowess during their visit. *Perhaps*, the Cazonci resolved, *a dual show of force and of generosity would stave off acacecha aggression*. In this way, the Purépecha would convey that they are more formidable people than the Mexica. He finally rendered his well-considered response to the exhausted courier.

"After you have rested, carry this message back... 'The envoy may come. I will receive them.'"

The courier took the Cazonci's response to the acacechas, who were waiting in Taximaroa. In the meantime, the Cazonci's commanders prepared the people of Tzintzuntzan for the arrival of their guests. The finest gifts were gathered from throughout the kingdom and accommodations were prepared in advance, so while Timas and Irepani departed Acámbaro to gather forces along the border, the Cazonci set out a feast for the three acacecha guests who arrived in Tzintzuntzan on horseback.

As was custom and like the tribes from Veracruz, the Cazonci honored the three acacechas with gifts. Upon their heads were placed wreaths of gold. Round golden shields were hung from their necks, and they were each presented gourd dishes, leather war jackets, and blankets. The three acacechas indulged in bountiful kaúikua, warm bread, and an array of fruits unknown to their palette. They were most impressed, however, with evidence that confirmed the presence of gold and other riches. They also took a liking to the Purépecha women but during the feast, where they saw the women dancing with full physicality, maintained a respectful distance.

To impress upon the acacechas, as well as to instill fear in them, the Cazonci called upon his people to demonstrate their mastery of the bow and arrow. The hunters, painted for the occasion, struck out on a deer hunt and returned with five which were presented to the guests. In his calculations, the Cazonci assumed that concurrent demonstrations of graciousness and strength would temper any malicious intentions. Little did he know, however, that the gifts only encouraged these strangers to discuss amongst themselves that they would most certainly return, but not for reciprocity, but pillaging. By the end of the evening, after being treated to the best of Purépecha hospitality, the three acacechas whispered among themselves of how this vibrant city of 40,000 held sufficient people to, ultimately, serve their purposes …. *as slaves.*

After several days of feasting and observation, the three acacechas prepared for their departure from Tzintzuntzan. They had gathered sufficient information to report back to their comrades in Taximaroa. Though they were inebriated from drinking so much kaúikua, they were, more so, drunk with greed. Their visit had aroused, even more, their lust for material riches.

Before leaving, the acacechas asked the Cazonci for two women of his court to accompany them on their return trip to Taximaroa. The Cazonci was reticent, at first, until the acacechas explained that they have had no female companionship to temper their ill-learned language and habits. They expounded on their predicament as soldiers who have been deprived of the presence of beautiful and poised women, such as those in the Cazonci's court. They emphasized how having the companionship of such refined women would alleviate their boredom by enhancing what would, otherwise, be dull interactions amongst themselves. Plus, they suggested that this would establish a relationship of mutual trust between the Purépecha and, as they call themselves, the Spaniards.

The Cazonci considered the custom of building alliances between families through marriage but recognized that alliances with these acacechas in this manner was out of the question. Yet, to deny the request would be considered discourteous. For this reason, he consented and called upon two young women from his extended family to accompany these men on their journey back to the border town of Taximaroa.

Being doubtful of the acacechas' intentions, while also attempting to appear gracious, the Cazonci offered several male porters to accompany the envoy on their return. He politely explained that these strong young men could carry provisions and the many gifts, making the acacechas' trip more comfortable. Antonio, the acacecha who served as the primary spokesperson for the envoy, declined the assistance, giving the explanation that their horses carry heavy loads. The Cazonci insisted that the women would not leave with the acacechas unless the porters accompanied them. The acacechas feigned appreciation. The Cazonci secretly planted a skilled warrior amongst the porters.

The two young women, seeing themselves as ambassadors of their nation, excitedly dressed themselves in their most regal attire and jewelry. Never having travelled beyond the boundaries of Purépecha territory, they saw themselves as symbols of a new alliance with these acacechas who had conquered their traditional enemies, the Mexica. Furthermore, under the protection of these acacechas, they would be the first Purépecha women to fearlessly and triumphantly step onto the territories of their enemies. The two young women took pleasure in imagining how their appearance on Mexica territory would mark the beginning of a new era in which Purépecha might, in alliance with the acacechas, hold reign over the Mexica.

After a full day's travel to the border town of Taximaroa, the three acacechas unmasked their true intentions. To the surprise and shock of the Purépecha women and the porters, two of the acacechas dragged the two women from the shared campfire onto the side of the road and assaulted them as vile men do. While two acacechas had their way with the women, the third pointed his harquebus at the porters while keeping a lit stick close at hand. The women screamed as they were brazenly defiled. The porters, frozen in fear, had heard of the potency of the thunder stick but had not witnessed its capacity. The most they could conjure was to yell at the Spaniards with a sarcastic sneer in their voice.

"Tarascue! Tarascue!" *Relative! Relative!* They were indicating that their women were being taken by the acacechas as though they were their relatives, when they were not.

The disrespect of the women revealed to the Purépecha porters that these people were disingenuous. They had shown one face to the Cazonci in Tzintzuntzan, and now had revealed who they really were. In this way, they were even more dangerous than an enemy who shows himself. The women's overwhelming humiliation and cries for help compelled the one warrior planted amongst the porters to act. He pulled out a knife and ran toward the two acacechas in an attempt to defend the women. This prompted the acacecha on guard to light the harquebus' wick and shoot the Purépecha warrior in the back. The thunderous sound and the sight of the warrior being lifted off his feet and propelled forward with a gaping hole emerging through his body terrorized the rest of the porters. They immediately sprung into flight toward Taximaroa.

The sudden discharge stopped the rapists in mid-assault. They scrambled from the bushes, pulling up their pants and reaching for their weapons. While the harquebus is effective against one opponent, it is slow to load and fire. By the time the acacechas gathered themselves after the chaos, the porters were well out of range and running with such speed that the Spaniards let them go. They rolled the dead warrior's body off to the side of the road, hastily dug a shallow grave into which they dumped his body and covered him with bushes. They returned to the women, but the women were nowhere to be found. They escaped during the melee.

Knowing well the various routes connecting the communities within the Purépecha Nation, the porters quickly made their way using alternate routes to Taximaroa. They avoided the main road where the acacechas would likely catch up with them on their large beasts. On the outskirts of Taximaroa, they encountered Timas, Irepani, and the small contingent of warriors who had earlier left Acámbaro and were destined, also, for Taximaroa.

"Timas! Timas!" shouted one of the porters, Erandi, who recognized this close relative of the Cazonci.

Timas, startled to encounter anyone on these obscure trails, stopped in his tracks and looked upon the disheveled porters running toward him. The guards accompanying Timas drew their weapons and stepped between Timas and the approaching porters. Irepani pulled out his macana and positioned himself by Timas' side.

Timas signaled to Irepani and the guards to lower their weapons. He quietly told them, "I recognize these men. They are porters from the Cazonci's household. What, however, are they doing here on the outskirts of Taximaroa looking as they do?" To the guards he instructed, "Let one come forward and attend to the others. They look as though they have been through a battle."

The one porter who had called Timas by name stepped forward and stood before him.

Timas asked, "What is your name?"

"Erandi, Lord Timas."

"Why, Erandi, are you here on the outskirts of Taximaroa and so far from Tzintzuntzan appearing as you do?"

"I... We..." He motioned towards the others who arrived with him, "escaped the acacechas." Timas's heart jumped. He knew, immediately, that the fact that a porter from the Cazonci's household has had contact with the acacechas meant that he was already being outplayed by these intruders.

The young porter, Erandi, gathered his composure as he told what transpired in Tzintzuntzan since Timas left.

"A courier sent by the acacechas from Taximaroa arrived in Tzintzuntzan. The acacechas were seeking the Cazonci's audience. The Cazonci agreed to the request. The man making the request is referred to as the marques del valle. His name is Cortés. Then, three acacechas arrived, on large deers. One acacecha is called Antonio. Over several days, they were feasted, given gifts, and bore witness to the might of Purépecha hunters. Upon their departure, these men requested to have two women from the Cazonci's relatives accompany them back to Mexica territory that is now under acacecha control. The Cazonci insisted that porters accompany the returning envoy. The reluctance to accept the assistance of the porters is now clear. They didn't want us with them."

Erandi hesitated. He looked down at his feet and began sobbing.

Timas lost his patience. "What? What happened? Tell me now. We do not have time to waste, for there will be more sorrow if we do not act quickly!"

"I am so sorry, my Lord." In between sobs, Erandi choked out, "We were into our second day on the journey back to Mexica territory by way of Taximaroa when the acacechas took the two women and viciously took turns violating them while one kept pointing the fire stick at us. We didn't know what to do. We had heard of the ferocity of the fire sticks. We kept shouting 'Tarascue! Tarascue!' One of the porters was a warrior, planted amongst us by the Cazonci … he attempted to defend the young women but the acacecha carrying the long stick set fire to it and with a deafening thunder the warrior was lifted off his feet and landed dead on the ground. The roar that came from the fire stick made a hole through his body. We ran, Lord Timas! We ran! I'm so sorry. We didn't know what to do but to run! We feared they would pursue us on their beasts. They had demonstrated how these beasts are trained to attack and kill. We took alternate paths to Taximaroa that the acacechas would not be familiar with and their beasts would not be able to travel. And now, we find you. I am so sorry."

Erandi released his terror in a stream of tears. The assembled men standing with Timas looked down upon the porter who had fallen to his knees, unabashedly screaming and sobbing. For several minutes in which no one said a word, Erandi discharged the horror he had witnessed and escaped.

When it was quiet, Timas asked of him, "Why do you apologize, Erandi?"

Erandi, exhausted and with head bowed, breathed heavily. He quietly whispered, "Because my Lord. Because. I secretly loved one of the young women. I knew I could never have her for I am a mere porter. But I felt like such a coward. I froze when the women were suddenly taken onto the side of the road. I did nothing. All I could do was shout at those wicked men. Then, I ran. I ran and ran and ran. The warrior was no match for these acacechas, but at least he died showing his courage. But what did I do? I ran. Like a coward."

No one spoke. Timas and his assembled warriors felt for the young porter who was trained to serve, not to fight. Erandi's unabashed shame caused them to avert their eyes. They were embarrassed by his display of self-loathing because it served as a chilling reminder of the question, *How will you respond to an outrage committed in your presence?*

Irepani broke the silence. "Erandi… the young women? What became of them?"

Erandi looked up at Irepani whose looming presence induced a quick response. "I wish I could tell you. I am so ashamed. I didn't bother looking back. Once we started running, I was afraid to look back. I feared the fire stick and what they make the beasts do. We abandoned these two young women. We did nothing to defend them." Erandi hung his head low.

Timas continued, "You made the right decision, Erandi, given the circumstances. Knowing what you have told us, we can mobilize. So, tell us… How far back are they? What do you know of them?"

"There are three. One of them is called Antonio. Each has a large deer. One of the deer is pure white. They were given many gifts by the Cazonci that they will likely not part with. We had been charged with carrying these gifts. Likely, they will have put these gifts on the backs of their deer, which means they will be on foot. They are on their way back to Mexica territory by way of Taximaroa. I would say that they are not that far behind us. A half day's travel, at most."

Timas said, "That is good to know, Erandi. If you think of anything else that would be useful, tell us." To one of the guards he instructed, "Tend to Erandi. Make sure he is cared for."

Timas then turned to the rest of the assembled guards and said, "The war has started. The acacechas have made their intentions clear though they do so in the most cowardly manner. They put on a false face before the Cazonci and then attack our women. I know what we must do. Two of you go directly to Taximaroa, along with the porters, and tell any of our people you can what has transpired.

Then, instruct them to hide the women, the children, the elders. The rest of you come with me and Irepani. We will strike first."

Timas turned to one of the porters accompanying Erandi, "You! You will serve as messenger. Go to Acámbaro and report what we now know. Then, proceed to Princess Eréndira's encampment. She is to be particularly vigilant, but her orders are to remain where she is. I will send a warrior with you."

With that, the porter now-turned-messenger bowed to Timas, and with a warrior leading the way, proceeded on the path back to the sight of the Purépecha counter offensive.

February 1552 had arrived. Timas and Irepani assembled their small contingent of warriors in the mountains outside the valley community of Taximaroa. They prepared an ambush on the acacechas, who would most likely travel the prominent route—the only route known by these acacechas that would take them back to Mexica territory. The young porter, Erandi, remained at Timas' side.

Irepani addressed the warriors, "In case these intruders deviate from the known route, several of you will be strategically positioned throughout the mountains surrounding Taximaroa. You are to ensure that these three acacechas do not slip by us. If you see these intruders on another route, send your fastest runner to alert us so we can change location and join forces. We will intercept and kill them but save one. The gifts given to them in Tzintzuntzan are to be returned and, if possible, we will capture the animals that accompany them."

The warriors nodded, indicating they understood what they were expected to do.

Timas turned to Erandi, "Tell us everything you remember about the acacechas. You and the other porters have had the most contact with these strangers and we must know our enemy if we are to understand how to best engage them. What of their thoughts? Their habits? Their weapons? How do they control the large deer?"

Erandi, regaining his self-confidence, recognized that his time spent with these strangers could be of use. In the events leading to this moment, he had witnessed these three men accept the Cazonci's generosity, but then they turned around and defiled two young women of his family. With what he has seen, he was but one of a few who knew the acacechas' true nature.

Erandi recollected his observations and then offered, "What I can tell you, Lord Timas, is that these strangers do not like water."

Irepani, who had been looking down at the incoming path, turned his attention back to Erandi. "What? They don't like water. How do you know this?"

"What I can tell you, Irepani… and Lord Timas, is that they smell awful. Even their large deer do not reek as they do! I don't believe these acacechas bathe."

"I see." said Irepani. "Perhaps we will smell their approach before we see them?"

"Well… it may be possible, but you may hear them even before smelling or seeing them. They wear metal armor so that each step is accentuated with a disquieting clanging. They have metal swords and their fire sticks are deadly, but it seems that these sticks cannot strike with multiple bolts of lightning. If that was the case, me and the other porters would be dead. That is what I have concluded now that I have seen them use it. They must light the stick each time for the lightning to come out."

Erandi shuttered as he recalled the gaping hole that the fire stick made through the warrior's body.

"And what of their large deer?" asked Timas.

"They are large, yes, but they are trained and respond to the commands of the person mounted on them. When we travelled with them, they demonstrated their control over these large beasts. They mount the animals, holding tight to the body with their knees, and by controlling the head, the beast turns this way or that way." Erandi attempted to mimic the movement of the acacechas holding reins and directing their mount. Then, he offered further observation, "Most impressive was how the animal rears up on its hind legs and kicks forward with the front legs. Unbelievably, the animals can shift their weight so that it pushes itself high off the ground, kicks with the front legs and then while still in mid-air, the back legs send a ferocious kick at anything or anyone behind them. The acacecha, showing off their large deer, made it spin with alternating kicks going forward and then backward. Here. Let me show you!"

Erandi got on all fours and mimicked what he saw. Timas and the others, with raised eyebrows, watched this awkward display. They tried to imagine what it would be like to confront a huge beast following such commands. Truly, warriors attacking from every direction would suffer injury, if they were at the receiving end of one of the kicks.

Irepani, voiced what others were thinking, "It does seem, Erandi, that these beasts are trained to cause great harm. Perhaps, in our ambush we must first attack from a distance and use spears, bow and arrows. We maim them, then move in for hand-to-hand combat."

"Yes, Irepani, that would be best, but there is more to the circumstances. The animals only do these movements when they have the acacecha on their back directing them. Otherwise, they are tame and docile. The animal is controlled by their head."

Timas raised his eyebrows and looked to the others, "Did you hear that? Control the head! This is good information. The beasts can only harm when they are mounted! Proceed, Erandi! What else can you tell us?"

Erandi, gaining confidence continued, "The provisions and gifts that we, the porters, carried were weighty. I do not expect that the acacechas would abandon the many gifts, especially those of gold. Without porters they will likely use their large animals to carry everything. This means that the acacechas will probably be on foot."

This brought a smile across Irepani's face, who then addressed the others, "Perhaps, in this encounter, we will have the upper hand. If the acacechas are not on their beasts, then we need to be sure that they do not mount them."

Erandi offered, "Also, one last thing. While these acacechas do not appear to like water, they do consume vast amounts of kaúikua. They were very intoxicated when we were with them."

"Even better for us," said Timas.

After Erandi's briefing, Irepani and several warriors took their positions on either side of the path. Erandi kept watch alongside Timas, listening for anything unusual that would signal the approach of the three acacechas and their large deer. The morning dragged on with warriors giving one another hand signals as their only source of communication. Other than the sudden appearance of a coyote giving chase to a speedy rabbit, there was no movement or sounds in the forest. The path, in full view, remained eerily quiet as though anticipating what was to come. The afternoon sun cut through the pines bringing needed warmth. A fire would have been welcomed, but its smoke and scent would give away their presence, so the men remained huddled behind fallen trees, the brush, and boulders. Their eyes and ears remained fixed on any movement that signaled the approaching acacechas.

After several hours, Erandi's eyelids grew heavy. He had not slept for several nights and wondered how these older men were able to hold up while he, much younger, was barely able to keep his head up. Just as he began to doze off, he heard a distant clambering, mixed with the synchronous rhythm of steps. Angry tones attached to slurred speech rumbled in the distance. The three acacechas were casting fault on each other for losing the women and blaming the one who killed the warrior for not killing or at least controlling the rest of the escaped porters. The word, "Tarascue" could be heard being tossed back and forth between the three belligerent acacechas.

The sound of the acacechas' language sent a rush of adrenaline through Erandi's body. The jolt forced him to stand as he turned to face the road where he could see, at a distance, the approaching acacechas. He accurately predicted their condition; weary with feet dragging and shoulders slumped. Their burdened beasts were led with a leash attached to the head as they steadily walked straight into a Purépecha ambush.

The hair on the back of Erandi's neck stood on end. His breath came rapid and more shallow. He quickly turned to Timas, who was still and silent, poised like a jaguar prepared to attack, watching the approaching intruders. Without looking at Erandi, Timas motioned with one hand for him to crouch down.

As planned, the awaiting Purépecha patiently waited until the acacechas were almost past them. Timas noted the disrespectful way in which these acacechas passed through Purépecha lands, after having committed an atrocity against their women and murdering the warrior. He concluded that these acacechas were either completely clueless as to the repercussions that were due them for their actions, or they were innately arrogant. Perhaps both, because they carelessly gave away their presence without suspicion or fear.

Hung over, dehydrated, and hungry, the acacechas had placed all the provisions and the gold gifts on their horses. Feeling tired, hot, and queasy, they had also taken off their armor to make walking, of which they had become unaccustomed, a bit easier. This, however, made them even more vulnerable to the Purépecha warrior's weapons. Erandi, not seeing the two women with these acacechas, prayed that they did not suffer the same outcome as his friend, the dead warrior, and that they made their escape.

After the call of a hawk cut through the trees, an arrow plunged through the shoulder of one of the acacechas while a spear lodged in the thigh of another. The bewildered acacechas were quickly surrounded by the Purépecha warriors, who emerged like swift shadows and closed in on the acacechas from every direction. Quick swipes of macanas across the necks of the two injured acacechas took their life force. Several warriors also thrust their spears into the fallen acacechas, just to be sure that it was possible to penetrate them when they were without their armor. The one acacecha left standing, Antonio, was thrown to the ground. The attack was so sudden that he did not have time to reach for his weapons. The Purépecha warriors took turns pounding him with their clubs, but he was allowed to live.

The huge deer, frightened by the commotion, became skittish. The Purépecha warriors had observed how the acacechas easily led the animals, who appeared just as weary as their masters, by holding the leash that controlled the head. After several unsuccessful and frantic attempts to grab the leashes the warriors finally took hold, careful to stay clear of the animals' hooves, for they had heard how, in battle, Mexica warriors were trampled by these huge beasts.

Antonio, bleeding from cuts on his head and body, was pulled to his feet. He recognized Erandi and called out to him, "Tarascue! Tarascue!" Antonio mistakenly thought that by repeating the word that he heard the Purépecha porters cry, over and over, while the women were being raped, that he was endearing himself. Little did he realize that the term was used by the porters to call out the acacechas depraved behavior. Antonio's use of this word, without understanding the context in which he first heard it, confirmed to Erandi that these acacechas have no regard for the morals of their people.

Timas did not know what to make of this strange man who, as Erandi had warned, reeked. He commanded the warriors to bound Antonio's hands and tie a lead rope to him, but the warriors were repulsed by Antonio's stench. They stalled as each hoped that the other would be the one to respond to Timas' command. Finally, Erandi stepped up and tied up the surviving acacecha. The other men gingerly approached the horses and relieved them of the burden they carried. The provisions and gold gifts were stowed away on the side of the road to eventually be returned to Tzintzuntzan. Once the horses were free of their load, Timas had the warriors throw the bodies of the two dead men over the animals' backs.

While Irepani held the leash to Antonio's large white deer, Timas attempted to mount the animal but slid off on the first try. After several tries, in which he jumped up and swung his leg around, he successfully mounted the animal. Antonio, watching his horse being commandeered by Timas, continued to shout, "Tarascue! Tarascue!"

Irepani kicked Antonio in his privates, causing him to double over and fall to the ground.

"That," Irepani said to the man writhing on the ground, "is for the two young women you violated and the young man you murdered. Tarascue!"

Irepani held the leash to the white deer that carried Timas while the other warriors led the other two animals carrying the dead acacechas. Antonio, bound and gagged, was also led by a rope like a domesticated animal. The Purépecha envoy, uplifted by the victory of this one encounter, continued on the path to Taximaroa. Without having to say a word, they also knew that this marked the beginning of what could only become an escalating conflict between the acacechas and the Purépecha Nation.

After winding a few miles through the mountain pass, Irepani turned to Timas, atop of the animal, and asked, "You have a plan?"

"Yes, my friend," responded Timas. "This animal, I will gift to Eréndira. She is capable, fearless, and it will make her more mobile."

"You think well, Timas, as we face these unknown enemies."

Irepani envisioned Eréndira riding this seemingly docile large beast. He had trained her in the art of weaponry. Anini furthered her skills. The deceased Cazonci endowed her with military strategy. If she could also conquer this beast, then she would be fully prepared to lead. With each step toward Taximaroa, despite the animal's bound master walking alongside, it became apparent that these animals were not innately ferocious. While the Purépecha had heard stories of the ways in which their animals trampled warriors during battle, it became apparent that these animals were ready to serve whoever held the reins.

With one hand holding the leash, Irepani reached back with the other and rubbed the animal's long neck. The animal did not reject but, instead, received this gesture of affection with an appreciative snort. In this moment, Irepani and Timas came to recognize that this animal, used as a weapon by the acacechas in battle to kill, was not only tame but also trained to respond to the intentions of the person commanding it. Irepani looked up at Timas who, with each passing moment, looked more relaxed upon the back of the large animal.

Irepani continued the conversation, "Much rests on Eréndira and the next generation. So much is unknown to us, but if our people are to survive the scourge of these acacechas, she will need to master and conquer their weapons to undermine their intentions."

"Exactly. First, I will deliver this poor excuse of a man with his dead brothers to his people. I will be sure that they see me atop this animal. In this way, they may see what becomes of those who bring their poor manners to our land and… that we do not fear their large beasts."

Irepani gave the horse an additional pat, and the other warriors, leading the two animals carrying the dead bodies, took note. They followed Irepani's example and cautiously touched the long manes of the animals before running their hands along the long necks. Timas nodded to them, encouraging their attempts to get acquainted with these animals.

As Timas continued to consider the future and what it had in store for Eréndira, he told Irepani, "You know, there is a young man who has his eye on Eréndira. Before these acacechas came and disrupted our world, his family sent an envoy to inquire about her."

Irepani, hearing this for the first time, exclaimed, "What? I had not heard of this! Who is this? How did you and Sesasi respond? Wait! More importantly… how did Eréndira respond?"

"Your last question being the most vital—is name is Nanuma. As soon as she had completed her Changing Woman Ceremony his family inquired about her. He is well provided for by his family, but that is exactly the problem. She does not have confidence in his ability to stand with her, as her equal. He acquiesces to his family's wishes, and they have not proven themselves to be in solidarity with us during these trying times. Prior to evacuating the royal family to the island, we had consult with the Lords of the land. This young man's family immediately voiced the desire to side with the invaders… to offer immediate alliance without vetting these people or seeing who they were and learning of their intentions. Eréndira had already seen them for what they are. Their loyalty follows the strongest wind. Nanuma comes from a family that would surrender the Kingdom without a fight, which shows weakness."

"Any young woman with Eréndira's character and training deserves someone equally strong."

"That's right. Eréndira has a strong spirit, deserving of someone to match her. She is not one to be controlled like these animals. And now that we know what we know of these intruders, I don't count on his family to stand with us. Eréndira had even asked me and Sesasi, 'How is it that Nanuma's family oversees a whole province and derives their support from the people but are not willing to defend these same people?'"

"She has a good point!" exclaimed Irepani. "If she sees that Nanuma's family lacks courage to stand with the Purépecha Nation… it would seem that he would also lack courage to stand with her."

"That is right, my friend. Their loyalty is unreliable. And for that reason, this animal goes to her and not to those who lack the courage to do what is necessary to defend our people."

Irepani and Timas punctuated their shared understanding with a nod. Before sunset, this small group of warriors entered the outskirts of Taximaroa. Once rested, the victorious Purépecha warriors demonstrated to the few Purépecha still left in Taximaroa how the large animals could be controlled. They paraded around the two dead acacechas to prove the outsiders' vincibility.

The bound one continuously howled, "Tarascue! Tarascue!"

After Timas rested, he mounted what was previously Antonio's white horse. He led Antonio by a rope tied around his neck while also holding the leashes of the two horses carrying the dead cargo. He rode into Mexica territory, arriving at a hill overlooking the entrance of what was formerly the Mexica capital. Acacecha sentries, from a distance, spotted the solitary man, sitting atop the white horse. Unbelievably, they also saw that this man was leading, by leash, two other horses burdened by the weight of their dead comrades and holding the leash of a bloodied and half-crazed Antonio. The man on the horse peered down at the acacecha sentries. He said nothing but released Antonio's leash and pushed the dead Spaniards off the horses. The bodies landed with a thud.

Antonio bolted away from Timas shouting, "Son Tarascues! Tarascues!" As Antonio reached the acacecha sentries, he fell to his knees. He said one last time to the sentry who stood before him, "They are Tarascan. That is what they call themselves." Then he fell face forward, an arrow lodged in his back.

The sentries looked up the hill where Timas continued to sit, stoic, on the horse, daring them to retaliate. After several tense moments, during which it became apparent that the acacecha sentries would not be raising a finger, Timas rode off. The other two horses obediently followed behind him on their leashes.

Timas quickly covered the distance to Eréndira's hideout at the fast pace of the horses. Panicked at first sight of a man on the back of the beast, the people adjusted their reaction upon realizing that it was Timas confidently riding this animal and leading two more. He dismounted and handed the leash of the white horse to Eréndira.

"This is yours."

He handed the other two leashes to nearby warriors, who looked at the animals with disbelief and stifled fear.

After eating and bathing, Timas gathered the people of this hideaway and told the story of all that had transpired. Eréndira then informed him that they already knew the extent of these acacechas' treachery.

She motioned to one of the dwellings, "Two young women of the Cazonci's family arrived here. They are not well." She didn't need to say more.

Timas asked his daughter, "These are the two who escaped these evil men?"

Eréndira turned her head away and averted her eyes, conveying the shame of what the acacechas had done to the two young women. This told Timas everything he needed to know.

His jaw stiffened as he told his daughter, "Tell them that they have been vindicated."

With no further words, Timas gave Eréndira a parting kiss, a long hug, and then mounted one of the other beasts. He headed to Tzintzuntzan, where he would notify the Cazonci of the treachery and intentions of these vile acacechas. Together, they would devise a plan to ensure that the Purépecha did not suffer the same fate as the Mexica.

July 1522 had arrived. Eréndira spent long days training refugees from the border communities and surrounding villages to fight in battle. She fulfilled her duty of transferring elders, children, and women to the remote islands of Lake Patzcuaro or to the secluded and inaccessible mountain regions. The displaced people from the borderlands added to the growing army of warriors, now numbering in the thousands. Eréndira was determined not to disappoint all those who had invested in her own preparation for what was yet to come. She delivered care and encouragement to all.

In the evening, while others prepared their final meal of the day, she devoted herself to the care of Tekéchu—the name given by the Purépecha to the large white deer. Erandi, with the knowledge he had gained through observation, had been charged with assisting Princess Eréndira with mastering the animal. Many of the lessons hinged on trial and error.

One evening, Erandi tightly gripped the white horse's leash as Eréndira mounted. She then loosely held the reins while balancing herself on the animal's back. Several weeks of slow gallops and quick turns bolstered Eréndira's confidence. When she was ready to attempt the more advanced techniques used in battle, she cued Erandi to let go of the leash and step aside. Despite the weight of responsibility for the Princess' safety, he let go as he was told.

With Erandi clearly out of Tekéchu's path, Eréndira lightly nudged with both knees and the animal began to saunter. A pull on the rein to the left made Tekéchu's large head turn in that direction and the body followed. A sudden pull to the right and the animal suddenly changed direction again. With a constant pull in either direction, Tekéchu spun in a tight circle. When Eréndira pulled the reins back toward her own body, the animal stopped.

"Now," Eréndira said to Erandi, "This is elementary. Let us move on to the attack moves."

Erandi guided Eréndira as best he could, recalling the maneuvers demonstrated by the acacechas. At a moment when she thought she may slip off, Eréndira quickly applied extra leg pressure. Unknowingly, this signaled the animal to rear up and stand on its hind legs. She quickly slid off the animal's back and hit the ground with a thud. Erandi, still frightened at the enormousness of this animal when it reared up, feared that it might trample the Princess, or even fall backward and crush her. He rushed to her, grabbed her arm, and dragged her away from the perceived danger.

Eréndira, windless and dazed, looked up at Erandi who still had a hard grip on her arm. Tekéchu, back on all fours, turned around to see what had happened. Upon locating Eréndira on the ground, the large muscular beast slowly stepped in her direction and lowered its large head to nuzzle Eréndira's face, leaving a trail of slobber. Eréndira and Erandi laughed with relief at this demonstration of care from this animal whose presence terrified most of their people. Eréndira got up and shook off as much mud as she could.

She turned to Erandi, "Let's try this again."

"Are you sure, Princess?"

"Of course, I am sure. This animal responds to commands given by the rider. When I tightened my knees, it immediately reared up! It was only doing what it thought I wanted it to do. It has been trained to do this."

"You're right!" exclaimed Erandi. "The acacecha did make the animal rear up. I guess you figured out how to signal the animal to do that."

"Let's try it again! This time, I will lean slightly forward into Tekéchu's body when it tilts."

Erandi knelt on one knee, positioning the other as a step, and Eréndira climbed back onto Tekéchu. This time, she prepared herself for the moment the beast would rear up. She commanded it to saunter for a bit, took a deep breath, and then squeezed with her knees as she did before. As expected, Tekéchu reared up. Eréndira leaned her upper body toward the animal's head, but the angle was so severe that she instinctively threw her arms around its neck. When Tekéchu's front legs hit the ground, the force sent Eréndira flying into the air, and she landed face down on the ground once more.

Erandi, again, rushed to Eréndira's side. She looked up with her face completely covered in mud. It was an awkward moment, and Erandi did not know how to comment on such a humbling experience. He offered his honesty, "Princess, I don't remember the acacechas demonstrating this."

Eréndira sat up, wiped a handful of mud off her face, and then hurled it at Erandi, smacking him on the chest. He was not sure how to respond. She stood up, gave him a mischievous grin, and wiped more mud off her face. He could see that she was preparing to throw it at him so he turned and ran.

She chased him shouting, "Of course that wasn't what was supposed to happen!"

Tekéchu stood alone, looking puzzled, and then strolled off in search of fresh grass.

The next day, Eréndira tried again. She envisioned in her mind what commands could signal Tekéchu to execute the maneuvers that Erandi spoke of, particularly the one where Tekéchu would spin while kicking with its front and back legs. Most certainly, the Purépecha would have to engage in battle with these acacechas, and she must be prepared to lead them when the time came. Mastering Tekéchu as an additional weapon would elevate their cause.

Committed to her duties, the deep pain from losing her dear Parakata and the entirety of her mother Sesasi's family, less her Tatíta Irepani, fueled Eréndira's fury. She channeled her rage toward this enemy, who had disrupted the hard-earned peace her people had only recently gained. Though her father had given her strict instructions not to attack until told, Eréndira embraced her role as a symbol of resistance within this burgeoning community of warriors-in-training. During the day, she bolstered the soldiers' morale as they trained together. At night, they prayed to Kurikaweri, God of war and of the sun, for strength and courage. She regularly reminded them of their victories against the Mexica and how her Taáte and her Tatíta, with but a handful of warriors, defeated three acacechas and captured the three large deer.

Riding atop Tekéchu, she rained words of encouragement on Purépecha recruits as they refined their skills with multiple weapons. Young and the old looked up at her with pride as she, atop the white four-legged beast, rode by at full speed, her black hair flowing behind her, and shouted, "We are Purépecha! We do not submit to these outsiders. Who are we if not the ones who defeated the Mexica, over and over? No intruders will hold dominance over us!"

She rode to the outskirts of the holdout, where the metalsmiths forged weapons and shields of copper and silver while others gathered large quantities of food to feed the warriors, the metalsmiths, and all who spent their days preparing for battle. To them she shouted, "What other people than the Purépecha possess such skill? Look at our people working as one! We do not just give away our land to those who come and say, 'give it to us!' We protect our women, our children, our elders, our land! We are not cowards!"

Erandi, with his rich knowledge of multiple routes between the Purépecha communities, was conscripted to keep watch of the activities on the 60-mile route between Tzintzuntzan and Taximaroa. He was also entrusted to carry messages between Timas in Tzintzuntzan and Eréndira at her hideout—several days' travel between them.

After delivering the white Tekéchu to Eréndira, Timas reported to the Cazonci that, despite his demonstration of Purépecha force and hospitality, the three acacechas had assaulted the young women and killed the warrior who attempted to protect them. This, in turn, required Timas to enact swift retaliation that would, most certainly, provoke the acacechas to respond with force. Timas calculated that the acacechas next move would be to appear in Taximaroa. For this reason, Timas cleared Taximaroa of any remaining Purépecha inhabitants and sent them to Eréndira, who ensured their safe passage to the islands or to the highlands.

Taking all these circumstances into consideration, runners were immediately sent to all the communities to rally the Purépecha for war.

The Cazonci, upon hearing the news of the atrocities from Timas, held his head with two hands. "What? Timas… are we to do? They came here! Those deceptive animals! They gratefully took our gifts, and then proceeded to violate our women. I am a fool!"

"No, my Cazonci. Do not doubt yourself. How were you to know? Now, we see them for what they are and must prepare accordingly."

"Yes. Yes. But I can tell you, Timas, that there are Lords amongst us who will be quick to avoid war. They will want to negotiate or, worse yet, suggest that we submit ourselves to an alliance with these intruders."

"Let us then see who, amongst us, is with us and which ones are not to be trusted. We shall test their fidelity. I know, myself, that I have had doubts over Nanuma. He continues to irritate Eréndira with overtures of his devotion to her, but I have yet to see him or his father step up to declare solidarity with our Nation in the face of this threat."

"Eréndira, a treasure, is not one to waste upon the spineless. Similarly, I, too, have doubts about some of our closest advisors."

"Name me one, Cazonci, and we shall devise ways to pull the weeds from our garden."

"It gives me tremendous sadness to say his name as one to distrust, but my adopted brother, Don Pedro Cuiniarángari. His words reflect fear but, more so, his own self-interest."

"Our behavior during hardship reveals true character. Let us see how Don Pedro responds to a test of his loyalty. I will send him to Taximaroa with the task of ascertaining what has transpired since I delivered the two dead acacechas and a half-crazed Antonio to the acacechas. I will have him observed so we can see how he engages with these intruders. Ultimately, we will learn where his allegiance stands."

The Cazonci considered this tactic and looked upon his uncle. "So be it, Uncle Timas. Let us see if we can flush out those amongst us who, eventually, cannot be relied upon. Better we know now, so we can plan accordingly."

Timas instructed Erandi to deliver a message to Eréndira. She was alerted of Don Pedro's directive to travel to Taximaroa, where it was anticipated that the acacechas were already gathered and waiting. She was tasked with preparing armed forces, who were to remain hidden from view while observing Don Pedro's movement from Tzintzuntzan to Taximaroa.

As predicted, after Timas delivered the two dead acacechas and fearlessly killed the third in front of the sentries, Cortés took this as an ominous message from the Cazonci himself. Cortés did not know that this was the cost for violations committed by the three acacechas who attacked the two young women and killed a Purépecha Warrior. In response, a furious Cortés dispatched Captain Cristóbal de Olid and 200 acacechas to Taximaroa.

Don Pedro, carrying out the directive given him by Timas, set out for Taximaroa. In the meantime, Eréndira gathered the people of Ucareo, Acámbaro, Araro, and Tuzantlan. Thousands of newly trained warriors hid in the forest along the 60-mile route between Tzintzuntzan and Taximaroa. They waited patiently for the right time to strike.

Keeping watch on the route, Eréndira caught sight of Don Pedro on his way to the abandoned city of Taximaroa. He was accompanied by another principal, Nuzundira. Eréndira nimbly dodged behind trees and boulders, keeping the two in her sight. She was advantaged by the elevation of hills and mountains rising above the well-worn trail.

After hours of tracking Don Pedro and Nuzundira, she saw them cross paths with another principal, Lord Quezecuapara. When Timas had previously instructed all to leave Taximaroa, Quezecuapara had insisted on delaying his departure. He wanted to be certain that any of his community who were out hunting or had yet to return from nearby travels were alerted to immediately pack and find their way to Eréndira's hide out. Unfortunately, he was one of the few Purépecha left in Taximaroa when Cristóbal de Olid and his soldiers arrived. He witnessed their bloody wrath upon the few

Taximaroa inhabitants who remained and was the only survivor left to speak of the acacechas vengeance.

Don Pedro greeted the approaching Lord, but Quezecuapara did not answer with the formal reply.

Quezecuapara gruffly asked, "What are you doing here?"

Don Pedro, noting Quezecuapara's bewildered state, calmly explained, "The Cazonci has sent me to gather the war people from the villages of Taximaroa, Ucareo, Acámbaro, Araro, and Tuzantlan. Other Principals have been sent to other regions of the province to gather the war people."

Quezecuapara scoffed and said, "Go ahead if you wish. I do not want to say anything, but all the people of Taximaroa are gone or dead, Don Pedro." With that, the Lord of Taximaroa picked up his stride, as though acacechas were snapping at his heels. He continued down the road to Tzintzuntzan without even a farewell to Don Pedro and Nuzundira.

Eréndira watched the encounter from a distance but could not hear the exchange between Quezecuapara and Don Pedro. She stilled her heart, taking slow and measured breaths as the interaction unfolded. Above the gentle breeze whistling through low brush, Eréndira caught the tenor of heated words between Don Pedro and Nuzundira. She couldn't discern what they were saying, but their body language conveyed disagreement between the two. It was apparent that the information received from Quezecuapara had disturbed them. Abruptly, Nuzundira broke away from Don Pedro and followed Quezecuapara on the path back to Tzintzuntzan.

Don Pedro threw up his hands and yelled at Nuzundira. The wind carried only a few of Don Pedro's angry words—"…chémsï…" something about being fearful…"jurhájkuni…" abandoning.

Nuzundira yelled back, again, with only the loudest words carried by the breeze, "…uarhíni ióni…" He was telling Don Pedro that he wanted to live longer.

With that, Don Pedro furiously stomped the ground and continued alone down the road toward Taximaroa, without Nuzundira by his side.

Eréndira turned to Erandi who had stood by her side watching the scene unfold. She commanded, "Go back to my father. Be careful not to be seen along this main route. Report to him what we just witnessed. Don Pedro encountered Lord Quezecuapara, fleeing Taximaroa. He communicated to Don Pedro that Taximaroa is not safe. Nuzundira chose not to continue with Don Pedro, but Don Pedro chose to proceed. He plans to give himself over to the acacechas."

"Yes, Princess. I will deliver the message."

Erandi ran for a day and a half until he arrived in Tzintzuntzan. He notified Timas of what transpired on the road. Anticipating what was to come, Timas approached the Cazonci with a plan of protection for the leader, while establishing counter offenses at various fronts.

"Cazonci, it is apparent that the loyalties of some are fraying. You must leave while you still can and let our military speak for the kingdom."

Cazonci Tangoxóan, overwhelmed by the enormity of what was unfolding, understood that there were inevitabilities. He challenged Timas, "How can I? The Cazonci? Leave Tzintzuntzan? I will look a coward!"

"That is not my intention, Cazonci. You must go underground and let our war people confront these intruders. You must also recognize that we have Principals amongst us who cannot be trusted. By hiding you away, we can see, of those who remain, where they truly stand. Do they stand with us, the Purépecha, or are they going to, like other nations of this land, give themselves over to the acacechas? You are of no use to the kingdom dead, but we can certainly make them believe that you are."

"What? I am to disappear?"

"Yes… just as your brothers and their families were suddenly 'gone' we will stage your disappearance. We know the intentions of these acacechas… they lust for gold… silver… so we can feed them what they crave, but we must protect what is irreplaceable. We have taken steps to preserve the lives of our people, but, next, we must feign your suicide by drowning and leave not a trace of your body for the acacechas to harm. In your absence, the Lords who will stand for our people will become known, but those who do not will likely acquiesce to these vile men. Eréndira, as well as your brothers, have gathered warriors from throughout the province. They wait patiently for the right moment, allowing us to clearly see who our enemy is—even if the enemy is amongst us. Then, we will know who we are fighting."

The Cazonci lowered his head and took several deep breaths. "Subterfuge. I see. Fear has gripped the hearts of our Lords. Now, we must not only outmaneuver the acacechas but also enact a scheme that will flush out the weak amongst us."

"That is right, Cazonci. From what Eréndira has reported, Don Pedro's loyalty is highly questionable."

The Cazonci tightly shut his eyes at this information. He put one hand over his heart, as though he had been stabbed. He had hoped that Don Pedro would prove himself to be a loyal advisor. The realization that Don Pedro was heading straight to the aca- cechas confirmed Timas' assessment as painfully accurate. In the moment, the acute betrayal of one of his closest advisors loomed larger than his fear of these acacechas.

Having dispatched Erandi to warn her father of Don Pedro's actions, Eréndira, with the advantage of speed riding atop Teké- chu, quickly intercepted Quezecuapara and Nuzundira on their way to Tzintzuntzan. Quezecuapara immediately recognized the white large deer Princess Eréndira rode. It was the same animal that Timas rode when he had arrived in Taximaroa after ambushing the three vile acacechas. His eyes filled with tears as he took in Prin- cess Eréndira's masterful control of the animal's every move. This, a welcome sight to push away the memory of blood-thirsty acacechas bludgeoning his fellow Taximaroans.

Together, Quezecuapara, Nuzundira, and Eréndira traveled to the village of Yndeparapec. They met with Captain Xamando, who was informed of the death inflicted by the acacechas upon the people left in Taximaroa. Nuzundira added that Don Pedro, despite knowing of the acacechas' penchant for death, still chose to proceed to Taximaroa in hopes of entreating them into an alliance.

Captain Xamando, in private consultation with Eréndira, asked, "What shall we do? We cannot just sit here and let these outsiders come to Tzintzuntzan unimpeded."

Eréndira knew she was charged with protecting the lives of thousands hidden away in the mountains, on islands, and in the forests. For this reason, her father would not want her to prematurely stage an attack.

"As you know, we have many whose lives we protect," she replied. "We also have many prepared to fight. You, Captain Xamando, have made your heart clear. Stage a reception of our military here. In this way, should the acacechas arrive, they will see our courage and know that we do not fear them."

Captain Xamando accepted Princess Eréndira's appreciation for his willingness to step forward, despite not knowing what or who they would be encountering. "Thank You Princess. I know of your father's strategies. And my guess is that there will be waves of battles raining down upon these acacechas. I have many warriors at my disposal. Return to the mountains, and I will cut off any incursion that may be headed to Tzintzuntzan from Taximaroa."

"You speak well, Captain Xamando."

With that, Eréndira returned to her hideaway, where Erandi awaited her. He reported Timas' plan to have the Cazonci feign his own suicide—a tactic designed to reveal the Principals' fidelity to the Purépecha Kingdom.

Eréndira and a line of warriors returned to their positions and kept watch to see what would transpire for Captain Xamando and his gathered men. Within a few days, it was not the acacechas who appeared on the road but, instead, it was Don Pedro returning from Taximaroa and on his way to Tzintzuntzan. Five Mexica and five Otomis, allies of the acacechas, accompanied him. As Don Pedro made his way down the road, he motioned to his ten companions to stay put. He then proceeded, unimpeded, to Tzintzuntzan, where he came upon Captain Xamando and the force of 8,000 warriors. The sight of the army sent Don Pedro into a panic.

He ran straight to Captain Xamando shouting, "Separate your men and go away from here. These people who are in Taximaroa—

they are called Spaniards. They are not angry, but they are happy. They have asked me to give the Cazonci a message. It is a message directly from Cristóbal de Olid, commander of the Spaniards. He is asking the Cazonci to receive him in Quangaceo."

"How could this be?" asked Captain Xamando. "If what you say is true, why would Quezecuapara, who came ahead, throw fear into us and tell us that these Spaniards, as they call themselves, killed everybody in Taximaroa?"

Don Pedro, looking to placate the captain, responded, "I don't know. Quezecuapara refused to talk to me when I met him, but the Cazonci must be getting impatient for he awaits my return. I bring him this good news. At dawn I am going to the city with the people who accompany me."

What Don Pedro did not convey to Captain Xamando was that the Spaniards had not only taken him hostage while he was in Taximaroa, but Cristóbal de Olid had also hung two Mexica men in Don Pedro's presence as a warning. While the two bodies dangled from a tree, Olid had smiled wryly at Don Pedro and said, "Tell the Cazonci not to be afraid, that we shall do him no harm." The interpreter, Xanaqua, had conveyed Olid's words to Don Pedro, but also added, without Olid's knowledge, "Go, Sire, at an auspicious time, and tell the Cazonci not to make war, that the Spaniards are very generous and do no harm, that the blankets, corn, gold, and silver he has should be hidden away, for the Spaniards will take it all as soon as they see it. This is what the Mexica did. They hid everything."

Don Pedro, grateful for the interpreter's warning, answered, "What you have told me is enough. You have been very generous in what you have said, and I shall repeat your words to the Cazonci."

What Don Pedro did not know, however, was that the Cazonci had already hidden away vast amounts of the treasures, and, more importantly, he had safely hidden many Purépecha people. This, as was also done by the Mexica, to preserve as many lives as possible.

Captain Xamando allowed Don Pedro to proceed to Tzintzu-ntzan, but also sent a runner to tell Eréndira of the message being carried to the Cazonci from Cristóbal de Olid. He also sent word that these people called themselves Spaniards, and that they had every intention of making their way to the Purépecha Capitol. In the captain's estimation, Eréndira must prepare her gathered forces to engage this scourge that had come upon their people.

Eréndira, her father, Timas, and the Cazonci sat near a smoldering campfire in July 1522. They were hidden away in the western highlands, some thirty miles from Tzintzuntzan in the forests of Uruapán. She noted the Cazonci's solemnity, which was understandable given the mounting tension since the acacechas disruptive presence arrived and the illness that raged and continued to take lives. What she noticed most, however, was how much he had aged since taking on his service as leader of a people confronted with never-before-seen tribulations. He appeared distant, though he was only an arm's reach away. The heavy silence between their three bodies was broken only by the crackling fire and the crashing of a nearby waterfall. She stoked the fire and turned to the Cazonci.

"I am happy that you made it here safely, to our Huatápera, our meeting place."

The sound of Eréndira's voice snapped the Cazonci back to the present moment. He took in his surroundings, as though refamiliarizing himself.

He responded, "This has been our meeting place for generations. It is where we come for sanctuary. The constant sound of water landing upon the rocks soothes the soul. It reminds us that while our lives are finite, the elements will continue even when we are no longer here. That is reassuring."

Eréndira focused her attention on these sonic rhythms. Despite the playful melodies of water rushing upon rocks, she perceived a looming darkness upon the Cazonci's soul. As leader of the Purépecha, he was not only a target of the acacechas but also possibly sought by members of his own tribe, motivated by fear or the opportunity to side with the acacechas. Since learning of Don Pedro's betrayal, he was deeply troubled that the enemy's identity was not only unknown but could also include those he had trusted. This instability and unpredictability elevated the Cazonci's vulnerability. Similarly, it had altered Eréndira's perception of her own world. As she had often visited the Huatápara, she shivered at the thought of the earth's natural rhythms being disrupted. It felt as though they were experiencing... a foreboding cataclysm.

In trying to make sense of it all, she asked the Cazonci, "The lords were with you at every turn in Tzintzuntzan. How did you manage to break away from them?"

"As you can imagine, Eréndira, it is always your father thinking ahead. We staged a final night of feasting, in preparation for my feigned suicide, but while others imbibed, I only pretended to drink. When the others were inebriated, I had all the fires extinguished and slipped out a secret back door with the women. Some of the lords followed. Those who stayed behind... well, we will see how they respond once Don Pedro and his new friends, the acacechas arrive."

Eréndira took stock of the division occurring among their own people. She turned to her father, "What are your thoughts, father? Do you believe many of the Lords will abandon Purépecha sovereignty and give their loyalty to the acacechas?"

Timas mentally tallied the various lords and silently recounted his recent interactions with them. "We shall see. If they are loyal, they will go along with the plot that the Cazonci has died. Otherwise, any betrayal that reveals that he is still living will endanger not only the Cazonci but everyone in the kingdom. We may need to feed these acacechas' hunger for gold, but we will not submit the lives of our people."

"In the meantime," the Cazonci cut in, "Eréndira, one bit of news to give you is of Nanuma." Eréndira crinkled her nose at the name of this pesky suitor. The Cazonci took note of her reaction but continued, "He sent his father to speak to me, directly, asking that I arrange for your marriage."

Eréndira scoffed and looked at her father with such indignation that Timas looked away. She then responded to the Cazonci, who looked at her with astonishment, "I apologize Cazonci. No disrespect to you. I have already conveyed my feelings to Nanuma. As of recently, I have seen children faithfully serve the Kingdom with a level of courage that Nanuma could learn from. He knows that he must demonstrate more than just the wealth derived from the people of his family's region. Once he proves he is worth more than the precious stones he wears, I will consider."

The Cazonci raised his eyebrows, taking in Eréndira's definitive rebuke of this young man from a prominent family. He turned to Timas who smiled and shrugged before he said, "Nanuma is with Don Pedro at this moment. The acacechas make their way to Tzintzuntzan so we will see how Don Pedro, Nanuma, and the others respond."

Timas confirmed, "Our most trusted courier, Erandi, has been charged with watching over what transpires in Tzintzuntzan. He is far enough to not be seen but close enough to observe the movements of our people and the acacechas."

The Cazonci turned to Eréndira, "I hope that our Lords do not disappoint us. If we become a divided people, we will have more difficulty in overcoming what has come upon us. But you, Eréndira, are young, brave, and have many years ahead of you. I wish for you to have a long life and, perhaps, raise a family with someone who truly loves you. May Nanuma demonstrate his worthiness to be your uámba and may your children flourish in a world filled with peace."

Eréndira studied the fire while she mulled the Cazonci's words. Given the ominous circumstances overshadowing their lives, the hopeful blessings he offered felt unattainable. She stoked the embers with a stick until flames re-emerged, mirroring a fire in her own soul. With measured words she responded respectfully. "We shall see, Cazonci, how the lords and Nanuma respond.

Then, we will know where their loyalties lie. And then, *I* will know how to respond.”

Timas sensed his daughter’s mounting anger. He reached out and took Eréndira’s hand in his. She turned her full attention to her father.

“Know, Eréndira, that not all have the capacity to hold strong when faced with adversity,” said Timas. “Some are not well rooted. A powerful wind comes and, like a leaf, there they go. They stand for nothing. For that reason, they become slaves to the wind. We may be disappointed by them but we shouldn’t be surprised.”

Eréndira studied her father’s weathered hands, holding her own with a sense of assurance but also urgency. She wondered how much longer she would have the security of a father who always cleared the path before her and a mother who calmed her when obstacles in the path seemed insurmountable.

“You, father, and so many others have prepared me to lead. I have had guidance and training. You can count on me.”

Timas met the eyes of the Cazonci, who gave him a nod before fixing his gaze back on the glowing embers.

“We had hoped you would never have to use the training,” expounded Timas, “but it is likely, Eréndira, that you will have to strike when the time comes.”

Eréndira, wide-eyed, was in disbelief. Her training had prepared her for battle, and she had even been entrusted to train others. Yet, her father’s approval of her judgement to put that training to use marked a new level of responsibility. With much of the royal family dispersed across the kingdom, she was strategically positioned with many newly trained warriors ready at her command, best suited to lead thousands into battle.

The Cazonci affirmed, “You always had a special place in my father’s heart. He saw something in you, an unwavering fearlessness and clarity of spirit. That is why we know you can do this.”

“And,” added Timas, “we do not know what comes next, but we do know that you will make the best decision when the time comes for you to save as many as you can.”

Eréndira stated firmly, “That I will do. You have taught me well.”

While the Cazonci sat safely around the fire with his closest confidants in Uruapán, Cristóbal de Olid weighed conflicting reports as to the Cazonci's status and whereabouts. Some Lords told him that the Cazonci had fled Tzintzuntzan and abandoned them. On the other hand, Mexica couriers, sent to investigate on behalf of Olid, reported back that the Cazonci had drowned himself.

Considering the news of either a dead or fled Cazonci, Cristóbal de Olid seized upon the absence. He surmised that, without their leader, the Purépecha were not only weakened but in chaos. With bolstered confidence, Olid announced to his men, "I have decided! We have done well. Our presence has destabilized the Purépecha. We must take that city!"

Don Pedro, left in Tzintzuntzan with his brother, Huizizilzi, to deal with what may come, heard of the approaching acacechas. He was unnerved, however, hearing that they were not outfitted for peace, as he had been assured by the interpreter, but rather, for war! Admitting to himself that the acacechas lied to him, he and his brother hastily donned their war outfits and gathered what war people they could in the immediate area. Nanuma, the young man seeking Eréndira's favor, joined them. They proceeded to Apupato, a place about a mile and a half outside of Tzintzuntzan, where they drew a line against the approaching enemy consisting of 300 well-armed acacechas and 5,000 Tlaxcalan allies.

Infuriated by the double-crossing Olid, Don Pedro confronted the acacecha upon what could potentially turn into a bloody battlefield. Don Pedro and Olid, backed by their armies, stood face to face. Erandi watched from a safe distance.

Don Pedro challenged, "What is your purpose for coming? I was told to deliver a message to the Cazonci that your people come in peace and not to fear. Yet, you killed the few that remained in Taximaroa and said it was in retaliation for one of ours killing the three men in your envoy. Did you not know that these men violated two of our women and killed one of our warriors trying to protect them? This, your men did after being treated so graciously by our Cazonci. You are not who you say you are. You come to destroy."

Captain Olid feigned a smile. With one hand, he motioned to the army behind him—many on horseback and every one of the acacecha soldiers carrying fire sticks. He answered, "We do not want to kill you. Come quickly and join us, or is it you who wants to make war against us?"

"That is nonsense. We have not provoked you. It is you who have come on our land wreaking havoc and destruction," answered Don Pedro.

Captain Olid, offering the most charming smile that he could muster, "It appears there have been transgressions on both sides. Let us put these minor transgressions behind us. Put down your bows and arrows and join us. In this way, we can ensure that there is no more loss of life."

Don Pedro turned to his brother, Huizizilzi, and had a private exchange. The two then turned to Nanuma, who had positioned himself at the front line of warriors, waiting for the command to defend their province. From afar, Erandi could see that there was a terse exchange between the three. Nanuma stepped away from Don Pedro and Huizizilzi toward the acacechas, alone and as though looking to provoke a battle. He took a long look at the acacechas and the imposing army of allies accompanying them, then returned to Don Pedro and Huizizilzi, shaking his head. Don Pedro turned to the thousands of warriors who stood behind them and commanded them to drop their bows and arrows.

Erandi's heart dropped the moment the Purépecha warriors' weapons hit the ground. He felt humiliated having witnessed such a gutless surrender. Watching Nanuma meekly retreat and lay down his arms left Erandi fuming. More so, he knew what this lack of courage meant for Eréndira, who Nanuma desired to have as his témba. He would have to deliver this disappointing news to her, but first... he had to get to the Cazonci and Timas. They would be heart-broken by this cowardly submission of Cazonci's own Lords. Carrying the weight of the events, Erandi ran with urgency to reach Uruapán where the Cazonci, Eréndira, and Timas waited.

The Spaniards, accompanied by Don Pedro, entered Tzintzuntzan and took quarters in the temples and in the houses of the chief priests. There were almost no women left in the city. Knowing the reputation of these men, most were evacuated in advance with only a meager few remaining, provided with guards, to tend to the Cazonci's home. This left the Lords and the old men to attend to the full army of invaders who, during their stay of six moons (twenty days for each moon) consumed the food, bread, chickens, eggs, and fish.

While they were waited on by the old men, the acacecha soldiers plundered the Cazonci' quarters, where they found twenty chests of gold and twenty of silver in round shields. A few of the Cazonci's women bravely confronted the young acacechas stealing the Cazonci's treasures, beating them with canes. The acacecha soldiers, intent on not dropping their stolen treasure, covered their heads and ran, rather than fight with the women.

The women ridiculed the few Lords left in Tzintzuntzan, taunting, "Who are you who wear the precious lip-rings of valiant men? You are useless in defending the gold and silver that has been carried off by these acacecha thieves! Shame on you!"

The Lords chastised the women, "Do not harm these men. They are gods and what they carry belongs to them."

The women scoffed and looked upon the cowardly Lords with disgust. In turn, the Lords no longer made eye contact with these women who fought more valiantly than they did, for they, unrooted, had succumbed to the wind.

Olid, satisfied with the plunder, ordered Don Pedro to deliver the loads of gold and silver to the Marquis del Valle, Hernan Cortés, who waited in Mexico City. Upon Don Pedro's arrival, Cortés examined the loot and beckoned Don Pedro to stand before him.

"Come, Don Pedro! Surely, what you bring me is just a small amount of what the Purépecha possess."

Don Pedro, kneeling before Cortés, spoke with head bowed, "It is an offering, of course. For you. A token of our friendship."

Cortés shouted, "Nonsense!" Don Pedro writhed at Cortés' angry voice. He had witnessed the cruelty inflicted upon the Mexica for the slightest offense. The decomposing bodies of two Mexica men still dangled from a tree in Taximaroa—this being their punishment for merely having burned wooden fences in one of the temples.

Cortés continued, "Don't take me for a fool, Don Pedro. Surely, their Cazonci knows where the treasure has been hidden. Why did you tell me that the Cazonci had drowned himself? They say he is hidden in the mountains. Two Principals, afraid of our might, disclosed his whereabouts. This, that you bring me, is merely a token to distract me."

Don Pedro, caught in the contradictory reports of the Cazonci, began to weep. He was sure that his body would soon be hanging just like the two Mexica rotting corpses. In between sobs, he managed, "I have not deceived you, Master! Please believe me. I only seek to bring good relations between our people. Perhaps it is true as they say, maybe he got out of the Lake somewhere and crawled onto some remote island."

Cortés grabbed Don Pedro by the hair and yanked his head up so they were eye-to-eye. "Do not weep. Go back to your country. Tomorrow, I shall give you a letter, and in three days you shall go and tell the Cazonci to come and see me. He is not to be afraid. He is to come to his houses in Mechuacán. The Spaniards will not harm him!"

Don Pedro departed the following day for Tzintzuntzan. Cortés lined Don Pedro's pockets with turquoise and jerky for the journey. He was accompanied by two Spaniards and his brother, Huizizilzi. Once they arrived in Tzintzuntzan, Don Pedro called for the presence of the remaining Lords and chiefs.

"See what the acacechas have given me!" He showed them the turquoise gifted by Cortés, himself. "They call themselves Spaniards. They only seek to establish peace with us. You must convey this to the Cazonci whose whereabouts we do not know. The Master of the Spaniards seeks his audience as his guest."

The Lords were not sure whether to trust Don Pedro but were pleased, nonetheless, with the message delivered on behalf of Cortés. One offered, "We will tell you where to find the Cazonci, but you must send your brother, Huizizilzi. Only him. No acacechas… Spaniards, as they call themselves."

Don Pedro agreed to the conditions, and with that Huizizilzi departed for Uruapán, flanked by two Spaniards who escorted him partway. Under the agreement with the Lords, the Spaniards stayed behind before Huizizilzi arrived at the exact location where the Cazonci was hidden. In the end, even the compromised Lords did not want the Spaniards to know of their sacred meeting place.

While Huizizilzi and the two Spaniards made their way towards Uruapán, the Cazonci and Timas had already been apprised by Erandi of all that had transpired in Tzintzuntzan. Running out of tactics, the Cazonci convinced Timas that the best way to engage the enemy was to turn himself over to the acacechas. His feigned suicide had revealed which Lords were to be trusted and which were cast about with the wind. The Cazonci reasoned that by planting himself amid the enemy, Timas, Eréndira, and an alliance of trustworthy lords and warriors could then regroup.

By the time Huizizilzi was spotted climbing the path up to Uruapán, the Cazonci had made peace with the fact that he must submit himself to whatever the fates had in store for him. He might lose his life, but if Timas and others could recover from their tribes' splintering and stage a strong resistance with those loyal to the Purépecha Kingdom, his sacrifice would have meaning.

Erandi alerted the Cazonci of Huizizilzi's approach. The Cazonci immediately rose from prayer and prepared to meet him. Timas and Eréndira quickly took hold of their weapons to follow him, but the Cazonci motioned both to stop.

"You must not come. You must not be seen. If anything happens to me, you will be the next target."

Timas immediately rebutted, "Cazonci. I served your father and now I serve you. Huizizilzi knows that I represent the might of our warriors. Let him see me. Then, he will know that you still command the force of the Purépecha people."

"That would be a rational conclusion in rational times, but these are people who do not think in our way. Yet, stay a bit behind. Should Huizizilzi be here to deceive me, then, your weapons will be of use."

The Cazonci turned to Eréndira and said, "But not you, Eréndira. Watch from as far as possible, and do not be seen. Your faithful and courageous Tatíta, Irepani, is, at this moment, seeking alliance with the northern Chichimecas of Cuinao. I am sorry that Nanuma has not proven himself worthy of you. For now, remain hidden. Your mastery of Tekéchu may serve a greater purpose. You will know what to do when it is time."

Reluctantly, Eréndira conceded. With Erandi by her side, she scampered up a side trail to observe, from behind a rock cropping, the interaction between the Cazonci and Huizizilzi. The latter walked directly up to the Cazonci as he descended the mountain trail.

When they were face to face, Huizizilzi bowed and said, "Sire, let us go to the city, for two Spaniards have come for you, and I hurried ahead to tell you. Do not be afraid, take heart."

The Cazonci, attempting to throw suspicion away from Timas, replied, "Let us go, for I do not know where I am nor why I was brought here by those who have treated me with such rancor, for they are not my relations. As I was leaving, those Principals told me that they had wanted to kill me. What shall we do?"

Huizizilzi smiled, but the Cazonci did not return the feigned gesture. Instead, the Cazonci wordlessly walked past him down the trail toward the two Spaniards. Upon seeing the Cazonci, the Spaniards embraced him and attempted to assure him.

"Do not be afraid, for no one will harm you as we have come for you."

The Cazonci, not believing a word they said, merely responded, "I am ready to go."

Eréndira was consumed by dread as she witnessed the Cazonci lead Huizizilzi and the two Spaniards away from Uruapán toward Tzintzuntzan.

She turned to Erandi and said, "Come… let's go back to the Huatápera. Our world is unraveling right before our eyes. We must speak with my father to see what plan he has devised to subdue these acacechas and get back the Cazonci." She took Erandi's hand to lead him up the path back to the Huatápera but he resisted. She turned around to face him.

"I am sorry, Princess. I already have my orders. I am to discreetly follow the Cazonci to see where he is taken. Then, I will report back."

Eréndira realized, in that moment, how much she had come to depend on Erandi. His loyalty. His patience. His trustworthiness. She looked back down the mountain toward the trail where she could see the Cazonci disappearing into the distance with two Spaniards and a disloyal Principal. The sight of their leader walking away with their enemies was excruciating. To make matters worse, she had no words for what she felt at the threat of not having Erandi, her confidant, by her side. She realized she was still holding tight to his hand. He hadn't pulled away, but out of respect, bowed his head, acknowledging her status. She let go. He lowered his eyes and quickly departed for the path in pursuit of the Cazonci and his captors.

As Eréndira watched Erandi follow a deer path toward Tzintzuntzan, she wondered how she, a young woman who had lived but sixteen years, could turn the tide of what had fallen upon her people?

Disarming Susan

Eréndira has not stopped dreading the arrival of this day. She sits in the small room outside Ms. Foster's office and waits for the face-to-face meeting with Susan to begin. She had smudged herself before leaving her house that morning—like her Naníta told her to do. Counting down to the meeting, she breathes slowly and evenly to stave off waves of anxiety. Still, she is annoyed because she has been called into the vice principal's office during her choir class. With the first concert of the year right around the corner, and Eréndira having a prominent solo in one of the pieces, she can't think of a worse time to miss rehearsal.

While Eréndira focuses on her breathing, students walk the hallway past Ms. Foster's office entrance. Some simply slow down, while others come to a standstill so they can peer through the plexiglass window separating the office and the hallway. Apparently, the word is out throughout the campus. This meeting between Eréndira and Susan has been circulated and built up on social media like a western movie showdown. Eréndira does her best to ignore the gawkers.

Ms. Foster's secretary, Lola, gives Eréndira an assuring smile and offers, "Would you like some water or anything?"

"No, thank you." Eréndira politely declines.

Lola's phone rings. She picks up and says, "Okay. Will do." Lola gets up and addresses Eréndira, "Come this way. Ms. Foster is ready for you."

Eréndira gathers her backpack and walks into Ms. Foster's office where three chairs are situated in a triangle facing one another. Ms. Foster motions to Eréndira to take one of the seats.

"Where's Susan?" asks Eréndira.

"She is on her way." Ms. Foster answers as she also sits down in one of the chairs.

Lola re-enters a few moments later to let Susan in, who plops into the vacant chair, looks directly at Ms. Foster, and completely ignores Eréndira.

Ms. Foster opens the meeting, "Thank you both for being here—"

Susan curtly interrupts. "I didn't have a choice."

"Well, yes. You do have a choice. You could have not shown up, but you did, and you now have a choice in how you respond." Susan indignantly pitches her chin up and glares out the window past Ms. Foster, who continues, "My first question for both of you is, 'What would you like to see come out of this meeting?'"

Eréndira gives a side glance toward Susan to see if she will say anything, but Susan sits stoic with her arms crossed. Eréndira thinks of the inflection point that her Naníta talked about. She also remembers her mother saying something about how there are three things that can be counted on—day, night, and the truth. Both have tried to instill in her an understanding of the world that transcends cruelty and brutality. *How do I apply what I've been taught?* she silently asks herself.

Ms. Foster, growing impatient, prompts, "Neither one of you have anything to say?"

Susan scoffs.

Ms. Foster continues, "Well, in that case…"

Eréndira blurts out, "No! Ms. Foster. I have something."

"Okay, Eréndira. What would you like to say?"

Eréndira remembers that her Naníta talked about the importance of one's words. She doesn't want to waste the opportunity she has by just spewing out a bunch of meaningless words. She wants to be like EunMi who takes her time to give a thoughtful response.

Eréndira asks, "Can you give me a moment?"

"Of course."

Susan rolls her eyes.

Eréndira realizes this is her moment to make a difference. With all the nastiness and fabricated nonsense that Susan and her friends have caused through their actions and their words, they have created a cloud of disarray and divisiveness that makes day-to-day existence at this school an unnecessary hell for many students. This is Eréndira's opportunity to expose this truth. She thinks about Daryna's sister, Iryna, who could no longer tolerate the ugliness, and she thinks about Rosalee and Luisa, who endure daily mistreatment when they have done nothing to harm others. The truth is, Eréndira concludes, that everything Susan spreads is all fabricated nonsense.

She turns to Susan and asks, "Do you spread lies about people because you are miserable, yourself?"

Susan sneers, "What are you talking about? You don't know what you're talking about!"

"Well," Eréndira thinks for a second before proceeding, "I have not been here that long, but I never see you smile. You do laugh, but you laugh *at* people…never *with* people. It seems like you are a miserable person."

Susan's face turns red. Her bulging eyes shoot daggers at Eréndira, and then she yells at Ms. Foster, "This girl is talking crazy stuff! I thought I was here so I can get back in school!"

"Yes, that's right, to some degree. You are allowed back at school, as you've served your suspension. But it's what happens once the two of you walk out that door, and the relationship between the two of you, that I am worried about."

"The only thing to worry about is she needs to keep away from my boyfriend and keep her fists to herself!"

Susan's agitation is over the top, but Eréndira knows she may not have another chance to speak her truth.

"That guy you say is your boyfriend? I'm not interested in him. I never was. He's a player and everybody knows it. He's not good for you or for anyone else. He just told you that I made a move on him because he was pissed that I couldn't care less about him. And you believed him."

Susan rolls her eyes before retorting, "That's a bunch of bull-shit, but that doesn't matter anyway. I'm not with him anymore." To Ms. Foster, she says, "Okay. That's it. So, can we go now?"

"No!" says Eréndira. "I still don't know why you are the way you are, and why you treat others the way you do."

Susan blares at Eréndira full on, "WHAT are you talking about!!!?"

"I don't understand why you must be mean to people. It's not just how you provoked me, but even before I got to this school, you start stuff with everyone. You, and those girls you call friends… you could do so much good for others, but instead you make people's lives a living hell when they have done nothing to you. I want to understand what makes you act like that. All I can figure is that something happened to you that makes you so miserable that it spills out onto other people."

Susan's face reaches a crimson red. She turns to Ms. Foster, who sits quietly letting Eréndira carry the session, directing her next question, "Are you going to let her talk to me like that!?"

"I asked you both what you wanted to get out of this meeting. You didn't answer but she did."

Susan looks like a caged animal, unsure of how to escape this emotional confrontation. She gets up.

"I'm out of here! This is bullshit!" She opens the door with such fury that it slams against the wall and storms out of Ms. Foster's office.

Lola gets up and cranks her head to peer into Ms. Foster's office. Ms. Foster gives her a nod of assurance. Lola gently closes the door.

Ms. Foster, turning to Eréndira, says, "Whew! Sounds like you hit a nerve."

"Sure does." Eréndira takes a deep breath and starts to get up.

"Wait a moment, Eréndira. Can we talk for a bit?"

Eréndira sits back down, figuring she doesn't have a choice, given it is the vice principal's request.

"I know your short time here has been rocky, but I hear how you've made connections with some of our students who are looking to make this school a better experience for everyone."

"Yea. They want to start a club."

"I heard. What a wonderful idea. They are already making strides! There will probably be a lot of students who will want to join."

"Yea, maybe."

"I wonder…. How did you learn to handle yourself?"

"What do you mean?"

"The way you addressed Susan. It was disarming."

"Well, my parents and my grandmother talk a lot about spirituality, so that's something I draw from. On top of that, I took a psychology class last year. We talked a lot about self-esteem and pathologies and stuff like that. It's one thing to know this stuff from a book and from class, but another to see it in people. I'm no psychologist, but it seems like Susan's pretty messed up."

Ms. Foster sadly smiles. "Yes. She has some work to do. We'll see what happens with her. In the meantime, I am asking you that if there are any more problems, please come to me first."

"Maybe see about talking before having to use my fists?"

"Yes. Something like that!"

"Will do." Eréndira picks up her backpack and starts for the door, but then turns and says, "And thank you."

"For what?"

"For trying to make things better. In some schools… the adults don't delve into the problems. They just suspend kids, and they don't ask any questions. Kids know this, so they don't bother going to adults. But you are trying to get people to be better and fix the problems. That's a good thing."

"I appreciate that, Eréndira. The bell just rang… I wouldn't want to keep you from any more of your classes. I look forward to hearing you sing at the upcoming concert. Your choir teacher told me you've got quite a voice!"

Eréndira blushes and politely says, "Thank You," before departing through the door and waving goodbye to Lola as she walks through the front office.

With the sound of the bell, students stream through the hallways. To her surprise, she finds her friends gathered outside the vice principal's door, waiting for her in the hallway.

Daryna steps forward and says, "We heard you had your meeting with Susan today. We wanted to make sure you're okay."

"I'm doing great. I'm so glad you're here though."

Melissa interjects, "It didn't take long for word to get out. Susan was running through the hallways crying and ran off campus like her ass was on fire. We were worried. Thought maybe you punched her again."

Luisa adds, "Not that we think you can't handle yourself, but we thought we should show up to make sure you're okay."

Eréndira inhales deeply. She takes a moment to reflect on the exchange she just had with Susan and realizes that her words surely touched a nerve. By asking her to explain her behavior, Eréndira forced Susan to confront something about herself that she didn't want to admit. Ms. Foster said that Eréndira's words were 'disarming' and, ultimately, the truth that Susan couldn't openly confront about herself forced her to run.

With her friends standing around her wondering what transpired, Eréndira explains, "I'm not sure what is going on with her, but I hope she starts to think about changing how she treats others. At least, that is what I hope for."

One-by-one, her friends step up and give her a hug. Daryna loops her arm through Eréndira's, and they walk her toward her next class. As they pass other students in the hallways, they greet, by name, the ones that they know and smile at the ones they don't know. When they get to the door of Eréndira's next class, Rosalee pulls out a draft for a flyer and shows it to Eréndira.

"Check this out!" Rosalee enthusiastically prods. "It's the flyer for our new club, the Peacemakers!"

Eréndira takes hold of the flyer. "Wow! How'd you come up with this name?"

"We already got into the middle of some stuff!" Luisa proudly states.

"What stuff?"

"With the stuff happening in Gaza. There were words between some of our Palestinian and Jewish students. We took a page out of your book to head it off."

"You punched everybody out?"

"Noooo!" Luisa exclaims, while everyone starts laughing at the thought of their group punching out two whole groups of students. Luisa goes on, "Pavinder and Trinh took the leaders of each group aside—the ones that were getting ready to go to blows—and calmed them down. We got them to agree to meet separate from everybody else egging them on. You know how people just want to see a fight. Once we got them to talk without an audience, we were able to get them to agree for now, to at least not turn to violence with one another here."

"Wow! I guess this is what Ms. Foster meant. When she and I were talking a little while ago she brought up this club and said you were already making strides. Those were her exact words! Nice job! But where did you learn to do all that?"

Trinh replies, "I'm taking conflict resolution training at my church."

Melissa chimes in, "What do you think of that? Great skill to have, huh?"

"Yea, but what about all their friends who still want to go to blows?" Eréndira casts some doubt.

"Not a problem." Pavinder adds, "We're going to bring them in, with Ms. Foster's help, and get them to come to some agreement with one another. We have to start somewhere."

"Yes," Daryna cuts in, "Supposedly, people come to this country to get away from these old conflicts, make a better life. Instead, people just start taking sides and adding more fire to the hatred. It must stop somewhere."

Melissa concludes, "Instead of taking sides and sniping at each other, we can create a space where people can have sort of new beginnings; a space where there is peace."

Eréndira considers what her friends have initiated and simply says, "You've done good! All I did was react out of self-defense, but you have thought this through in a way that will *really* make a difference. Good on you!"

Eréndira gives each one a fist bump as she departs and walks into her classroom.

Melissa, the last one to turn away and head for her own class, yells, "Don't worry Eréndira. We've got your back!"

"We've got each other's back!" Eréndira yells back.

Eréndira is elated to hear her friends taking such a big step in changing the culture of their school. They are interceding in conflict and doing so without having to throw a punch! She feels a sense of belonging that has not been her experience at this school until that moment. As she sits down at her desk, she notices the smiles of classmates directed her way. One of Susan's friends, who generally gives her a scowl, bashfully smiles at her as well. Eréndira turns to her and starts up a conversation.

It Was the Year 1522

"What am I to do with these?"

Eréndira held a thick cloth bag full of palm sized rocks, each carved in the likeness of an acacecha soldier. She pulled one out to examine it more closely. A bearded face peaked out from under a pointed helmet. A round shield off the shoulder and a satchel attached to the back conveyed the image of an acacecha outfitted for battle.

Behind Eréndira, Tekéchu calmly grazed on fallen leaves. Timas stood before his daughter and looked past her shoulder at the animal she had mastered to the point of being a pet and not just a weapon.

He observed, "This beast has taken to you." As though on cue, Tekéchu strolled up to Eréndira from behind and looked over her shoulder at Timas. Now, Timas faced both his daughter and Tekéchu. Motioning to the bag of rocks, Timas added, "When it is time, you and Tekéchu are to take these north, past Cuinao."

Eréndira, confused by her father's instructions, sought clarification. "Is this necessary? My Tatíta is in Cuinao organizing a counterattack. Most certain he is preparing the people for the coming of these acacechas. They will be forewarned of their appearance and habits."

Timas confirmed, "Yes, he is doing so." Grasping that Eréndira was not fully comprehending the gravity of the instructions, he repeated the directive. "You are to take these north," and then emphasized, "*past* the people of Cuinao. When it is time. Tell all you can of what comes, and they are to tell others. Continue north. Follow the path of the courier who previously warned us."

Eréndira stood in silence. The significance of the directive started to sink in, making the moment feel surreal. She was being instructed to travel beyond the Purépecha Kingdom to places where she had never been and to alert people from other kingdoms. Considering all that had transpired since the acacechas' arrival, it was apparent that her purpose, and that of Tekéchu, might be that they would have to reach beyond the boundaries of their Kingdom and warn others. This, only if the Purépecha could no longer hold back the invasion. This, a last resort. She assured her father that she understood what she was being asked to do.

"The courier came many moons ago and carried the skull rock. A warning of what was to come, and it came. He went north."

The Tekéchu nuzzled her ear, as though assuring her that all would be well. Timas petted Tekéchu's soft ears while providing his daughter with more information.

"Erandi arrived late last night. He is resting now. He reported that the Cazonci is constantly guarded by the acacechas. Their leader, Cortés, claims to want peace. The cost for not submitting to their conditions means the same fate as the Mexica."

Eréndira grasped the gravity of the Cazonci's dangerous circumstances.

"And what of the Cazonci? What will we do to save him?"

Timas slowly shook his head. "The Cazonci turned himself over to our enemies knowing his fate may already be predetermined. Cortés took him to meet with the Mexica's last leader, Montezuma's imprisoned nephew, Cuahtemoc. He courageously resisted the invasion and refused to feed these brutes what they crave most, gold. He killed many acacechas. They, in turn, burned his feet to try to get him to give up the treasures. Now, he awaits execution. The Cazonci was told by Cortés, 'Now you have seen the penalty for what he did, be careful lest you meet the same fate.'"

Eréndira shuddered at the thought of their Cazonci being tortured, but quickly dismissed the image. She considered the unravelling loyalties within the kingdom, which made defeating their enemies even more challenging.

With urgency, she asked, "But Taáte, how long shall we continue to feed these gold-hungry intruders? Our spies have reported that the Cazonci already gave them the gold stored on the islands of Pecandan and Huranden. When that wasn't enough, they were then given the gold and silver on the islands of Apupato and Utuyo."

"Yes," Timas confirmed. "That bought time which kept the Cazonci alive. He was allowed to return to Tzintzuntzan, but the acacechas proceeded to dictate terms for the Cazonci and our lords' existence. They are being allowed to remain in their posts, as figureheads only. All the land in our Kingdom will be redistributed to these invaders."

Eréndira's blood boiled at the audacity of these intruders. They controlled the life of their leader and now claimed all the land for themselves.

"How can that be Taáte? This is not a state of peace! They want to make slaves of us on lands that have been home to us for many moons!"

"That is what the acacechas want, but we will do everything we can to maintain our sovereignty and our way of life."

"A counter offensive?"

"Yes. We will strike when it is opportune, and we will continue to protect as many people as we can. Should our plans fail, Eréndira, you and Tekéchu must leave and warn others. Go as far as you can and distribute the acacecha images to all you encounter. The courier from the tribe of first encounter gave warning with the skull rock, but now we can describe them to others. If you can return... do so, but know that it may not be safe for you. Your Tatíta Irepani and I will ensure that as many of our people, and of course, your mother, will be safe from harm."

Eréndira stroked Tekéchu's mane. She let the inevitability of traveling to distant lands turn over in her mind, along with the possibility that she might never see her family again. Just as the Cazonci had surrendered himself to the enemy to buy time for counteroffences, she may also have to sacrifice her life to warn others beyond their kingdom of what threatened their existence. That night, she would ask Kurikaweri to guide her and all those under her command. She would pray not to have to take the journey north but instead to defeat this scourge that had infiltrated their kingdom.

Without further words, Timas turned and walked away from his daughter. Recognizing the dire circumstances for the Purépecha people, he did not know when or if he would see his daughter again.

Eréndira shouted out to him, "Uembekua!"

Timas stopped, turned back to her, and, with a faltering voice, softly replied, "I love you, too."

While Timas, Irepani, and other allied Purépecha Lords planned counter offenses, Olid learned of more riches in the lands south of the Purépecha kingdom. These lands were out of Cortés' reach, so Olid headed for Honduras with the intention of establishing his own colony. He took Huitzitziltzi, Don Pedro's brother, with him, believing that holding Huitzitziltzi hostage would keep the Purépecha from causing trouble while he was away. He did not realize that his absence would avail the opportunity for the Purépecha to strike. Once Cortés heard of Olid's rebellion, he gave chase to his renegade commander and left Mexico City behind. The vacuum of Spanish leadership enabled the Purépecha to enact their counter offensive.

Eréndira and her Tatíta Irepani met on the outskirts of Tzintzuntzan. She brought newly trained troops from Uruapán, and he led assembled warriors from Cuinao. Standing shoulder to shoulder, the warriors pounded their shields in unison to notify their foes of their arrival. The Spaniards, made docile by an abundance of kaúikua, commanded their Tlaxcalan allies to repel the threat. Haphazardly, the inebriated Tlaxcalan warriors ran out to meet the attack.

At the sight of Eréndira riding the white Tekéchu with a mass of furious Purépecha warriors behind her, the Tlaxcalans abruptly turned around and ran back to hide in the dwellings they had been occupying.

Eréndira, bearing her sword, gave chase and shouted, "Run, you cowards! You have sided with our enemies and now you will pay!"

She directed Tekéchu to trample down several Tlaxcalans, and with one sweep of her sword cut down several others from behind. The Purépecha warriors did not follow her in attack but cheered with each fallen enemy. After maiming several more Tlaxcalan warriors, she stopped short of Tzintzuntzan's outskirts and shouted at those still fleeing Tekéchu's hooves.

"What is this? You send cowards! Leaves blown by the wind! Send those who wear thick skins! Send your masters who you obey like dogs! We will show you how to eviscerate them!"

Eréndira returned to the assembled Purépecha warriors, who shouted their approval, their spirits lifted by their Princess's display of courage. She rode Tekéchu back to her Tatíta Irepani's side, who beamed with pride. He nodded his approval as she dismounted and then stood triumphantly at his side, facing their occupied capital, Tzintzuntzan, waiting for acacechas to appear. The Purépecha warriors pounded their shields in unison. The wind carried their angry voices and alerted all for miles around of the impending battle.

After witnessing the Tlaxcalans retreat, the acacechas appeared for battle one-by-one. They were unorganized, and, though a few managed to get off a few blasts from their fire sticks, they were unable to regroup quick enough to repel the Purépecha warriors closing in on them from all sides. The acacecha soldiers, barely sober enough to put on their body armor, were quickly encircled, outnumbered, and succumbed to slicing macanas.

Acacechas and Tlaxcalans who were too frightened to confront the surprise attack heard the screams of their compatriots and fled. They grabbed weapons and food as they escaped on the roads leading to Taximaroa. In the wake of the short-lived battle, the Purépecha warriors seized upon the bodies of the Spanish soldiers and stripped them of their 'skins'—the body armor.

Timas, who had inserted himself back into Tzintzuntzan prior to the attack to protect the Cazonci, watched the enemy flee from the doorway of a home in which he had hidden. He gathered his weapons, and, with other allies by his side, he walked the streets of Tzintzuntzan to ensure that every outsider had been expelled. Once he was confident that the intruders had been banished, he whistled above the din of the few remaining villagers who had come out to relish the Purépecha victory.

Irepani heard Timas' high-pitched whistle. This was the signal for Irepani to enter the city limits with a small detachment of warriors, and for Eréndira to return to Uruapán with the warriors she had trained. That night, the Cazonci, Timas, and elated Purépecha warriors danced on the steps of the yácata pyramids in the 'skins' of the deceased acacechas. Eréndira and the thousands of Purépecha Warriors under her command burned wood to honor Kurikaweri for their first victory.

What Timas didn't know was that Nanuma, Eréndira's rejected suitor, had been hiding, undetected, in Tzintzuntzan. Nanuma, told by the frightened Tlaxcalans of the young woman on the back of a white beast, knew immediately that this must have been Eréndira. He had heard that her father, Timas, had captured the animal, along with two others, during the ambush of the three Spaniards who had defiled the two Purépecha young women.

Hearing of Eréndira's appearance on the beast made Nanuma want her even more. He figured that, as his temba, she would be compelled to lead the Purépecha military in alliance with the acacechas. However, seeing her father in Tzintzuntzan dancing in Spanish soldiers' body armor meant only one thing: he, with full cooperation of the Cazonci, was coordinating the counter offenses. Nanuma figured that if he could eliminate her father, she would be compelled to marry him and concede to acacecha rule, so he set his plan in motion.

In the dead of night, while the Purépecha Warriors and Timas were fast asleep, and the Cazonci slumbered in his quarters, feeling the weight of conquest temporarily lifted from his shoulders, Nanuma snuck out of Tzintzuntzan in search of the escaped acacecha soldiers and Tlaxcalan warriors.

Several days later, Eréndira was awakened by Erandi in the early morning hours.

"Princess. I am so sorry." Erandi was breathless and said no more.

The startled Princess bolted out from under her covers, half dazed from being pulled out of a heavy sleep.

"What is wrong, Erandi? What brings you here at this hour? The sun has yet to rise."

Erandi stammered… not knowing how to deliver what it was he must tell her. Eréndira gave him a few moments but she sensed what he was about to say.

"Speak now!" she commanded.

"Your father, Timas, has been killed."

Eréndira said nothing. She tried to regulate her breathing through the gut punch of this information. Erandi, too, remained silent. He didn't know how much of the details of her father's violent death he should share with her. He had been in Capaquaro, which was where Timas had relocated to after the successful counterattack in Tzintzuntzan. In the middle of the night, Erandi awoke to tremendous commotion. He ran through the open doorway to see forty Tlaxcalan warriors clubbing Timas as he was dragged through the village streets. Timas struggled against the beatings, but there were too many to fight off. The blows didn't stop, even after Timas's head was crushed. Erandi stood frozen as he watched the brutality. Timas's body, battered beyond recognition, was hauled down the streets for all to see. Nanuma walked slowly behind the vicious mob, wearing a satisfied smile. This would be the one bit of information that Erandi would share.

"Princess… it was Nanuma who ordered his death."

Eréndira nodded. "That does not surprise me. And my Tatíta Irepani? What do you know of him?"

"Irepani is in Cuinao. He is evacuating the people. A traitor, Cuaraque, betrayed the Cazonci and told Guzman, who is now leading the acacechas, that the Cazonci is seeking alliance with the people of Cuinao and planning to attack him and his forces. The Cazonci… he has been arrested."

Eréndira felt another gut punch.

"What of my mother?" asked Eréndira, struggling to regulate her breathing.

"She is safe, Princess. Your father made sure of that."

Eréndira turned her eyes to the star filled sky, looking at nothing but seeing everything.

"I know what I must do, Erandi."

"Yes, Princess. Your father, anticipating this moment, told me to deliver this last message: 'You must go on… you and Tekéchu.

Leave while you can and warn others. Warn others beyond the Kingdom.'"

"Yes, Erandi. That I will do, but there is one last battle I must lead."

"It is much too dangerous for you, Princess. They know who you are—you and Tekéchu are known by all. You will be hunted."

"I will be hunted regardless of what I do, but, before I leave, I have one last task. Tell me, Erandi… where is Nanuma?"

"He is on his way to Taximaroa, gathering more acacechas and their allies to take back Tzintzuntzan."

"We must intercept them. Wake up the warriors and tell them to prepare. I will get Tekéchu."

Erandi hesitated. He was certain Timas would not have wanted Eréndira to put herself at risk. Eréndira saw Erandi standing in place rather than responding to her command so uncharacteristically shouted at him.

"NOW, ERANDI! We are losing time!"

Erandi bowed his head, backed away from her, and proceeded to wake up the warriors. He knew that she had singular instructions to warn others, but he was not able to stop her. He knew what she intended to do. She would intercept Nanuma and kill him.

On the same road that Timas had ambushed the three acacechas and secured Tekéchu for his daughter, Eréndira and a thousand warriors caught up to Nanuma and his followers. The Purépecha warriors remained hidden, with only a single hill visibly separating them. Eréndira instructed her warriors not to harm Nanuma. She would be the one to enact justice.

Nanuma and his followers spotted Eréndira on Tekéchu atop a hill above them. He smugly smiled to himself and said to those with him, "Look! The Princess has come to her senses. She comes to ask my forgiveness for rejecting me." The men behind Nanuma laughed. Nanuma instructed them, "Wait here. The Princess has some pride. I will not completely shame her." He walked toward Eréndira as she made her way, atop of Tekéchu, down the hill toward him. They met halfway.

"Hello my Princess!" Nanuma bent at the waist in a mocking bow. "I am so glad to see you."

"And I am glad to find you," she paused before sneeringly saying, "Nanuma!"

"I am so sorry to hear of your Taáte's demise, but it was inevitable. He was manipulated by people who have no understanding of the power of the acacechas. To avert more death, Guzman directed us to cut off the head of the snake."

"I see, Nanuma. I see where *you* stand. But you know… even when you take the head off, the snake continues to move!" With that, Eréndira signaled with her sword held high above her ahead. In that instant, one thousand warriors appeared behind her. As she dropped her sword in one swoop, the warriors charged down the hill and attacked Nanuma's allies.

Nanuma stood in shock as the vast swarm of Purépecha warriors rained down on his small force of soldiers and allies. Even with several bearing fire sticks, survival against so many was improbable. Nanuma didn't move as the Purépecha warriors charged past him and, in a short-lived battle, took out his allies. In the end, Nanuma was the only one left standing.

In the silence after the last sound of sword slashing flesh, Nanuma said to Eréndira, "And now what, Princess?"

"And now, you look upon the one who will make you pay for taking the life of a courageous and honorable man, my Taáte."

"You wouldn't. You realize I am an important man!"

"I would. You *were* an important man only by birthright, but you have committed treason, betrayed our people, and for this, you will pay."

Nanuma slowly realized that Eréndira's warriors had been instructed not to touch him. They stood at attention watching the exchange between the two and waiting for the inevitable outcome. Nanuma surmised that his life rested in Eréndira's hands.

He challenged her, "You wouldn't."

"I will. And I will do it with our enemy's weapon." Eréndira said with tremendous satisfaction.

At that, Nanuma immediately turned and ran toward Taximaroa, hoping she would not have the courage to give chase. The Purépecha warriors laughed at Nanuma, who could not accept his execution with dignity. Eréndira allowed Nanuma a sufficient head start. Once there was considerable distance between them, Eréndira and Tekéchu charged after Nanuma at full speed. The pounding of horse hooves was soon upon him. Within seconds, Tekéchu trampled Nanuma, who landed face down. Eréndira pulled Tekéchu to a full stop, turned him back, and tightly squeezed in her legs so that the animal reared up several times and the full force of his powerful front legs landed on Nanuma's prostrate body again and again.

Eréndira pulled Tekéchu a few steps back from the lifeless form and, once convinced that Nanuma was dead, she returned to the warriors.

"Take off his head and deliver it to his father in Tzintzuntzan. Then, join forces with my Tatíta Irepani. He is evacuating the people of Cuinao. A traitor has revealed our plans. Regroup with him and save as many as you can."

With that, Eréndira and Tekéchu proceeded to the top of the hill where Erandi waited and had observed all that transpired. He held the bag of rocks carved in the image of an acacecha.

"It is time, Erandi. Come with me and Tekéchu." She reached out to pull him up and ride with her. Erandi looked at her outstretched hand.

"I must stay, my Princess. I must serve our people for as long as I can. I will rejoin your Tatíta Irepani, your mother, and the others who remain. You must go. Warn others of this scourge that has come upon the land. Tell them to replicate these images and send them on to others. These intruders will stop at nothing and care for nothing but satisfying their lust. Go, my Princess!"

Eréndira did not want this to be goodbye. She dismounted Tekéchu, faced Erandi, and she said the one thing she could think of to say to this man who had demonstrated tremendous courage and loyalty.

"You are a brave man, Erandi. Uembekua."

With that, Eréndira turned away from Erandi. She pulled Tekéchu's reins so the animal was face-to-face with her. Eréndira placed her forehead between the eyes of the large animal and whispered, "Travel with me, my friend. You were once my enemy, and now we are united. Let us go far, together, until we can go no more."

Tekéchu stepped back and knelt with one front leg. Eréndira grabbed its mane and swung herself onto its back. With her vision clouded by tears, they followed the path of the courier. She and Tekéchu rode north to distribute the bag of rock-carved images.

Erandi did not move, for he was trained to observe and to retell what he had seen. The animal's rippling muscles showed no strain in full gallop and easily carried the young Princess, her long black hair flowing behind her. He watched the Princess and Tekéchu until they fully disappeared into the horizon. He called out to her even though she was well out of sight.

"I will tell others, Princess, of your courage. The children of our children and their children will know of you. You will not be forgotten."

Back on Naníta's Porch

Sipping on Naníta's homemade horchata, Eréndira can't wait to recount for her Naníta the latest events at school. Melissa has come with her to Naníta's but is off toiling away with Victor and Verónica on the property.

"Are you sure your friend Melissa wouldn't rather be up here with us in the cool shade? Seems strange to have a guest come to visit and then put her to work!" says Naníta.

"Oh, no. She was looking forward to it! She says she's always lived in apartments so has never had a chance to do 'yard work.'" Eréndira emphasizes yard work by doing air quotes around the two words. "I think this is the first time she's held a rake!"

"Well, this is more than yard work! It's clearing out fallen branches and raking away several decades of decomposed leaves." Naníta sits with it for a while, looking down toward the back of her property, and sees the three, Melissa, Victor, and Verónica, working together and tackling an area in which she has yet to make a dent. "Well. I think you're right. It's good for her and for me! Your parents flex their brains at work. They look forward to working with their bodies. Does me good too!" Eréndira and Naníta clink their horchata glasses. "So, tell me, what happened after your meeting with the V.P.?"

"Well, I told you what happened in the meeting, but then I learned that Susan wasn't returning to school."

"They didn't let her back in school?"

"She didn't want to return. She went on Independent Study."

"Maybe that's a good thing."

"In what way?"

"Well... from what you're telling me. You posed a question that forced her to look at herself. Rather than talk about the mitote and chismes that she creates, you asked her to atone for her behavior and examine the nature of her spirit."

"Wow. I didn't realize I was doing that."

"I think you did know it but are now understanding the power of your word."

"I think I get it. Like you've taught me. We can use our word for good or for bad."

"Yes, what we put out in the world can cause joy or it can cause pain. Unfortunately, not everyone has learned this so they live in an illusionary world where they value things rather than value people. They speak and do without considering their impact on others."

"It's a way of being."

"That's right, Eréndira. It's a spiritual path and when you are on this path, you will find that you can rise above the mitote."

"I think, Nanita, this created an inflection point, like you said."

"What makes you say this?"

"Well…. Remember I told you about the group of girls who approached me? Turns out, they are a courageous group. They started a club to help people."

"How? What sort of help are they offering?"

"Well, they haven't refined exactly what they are going to do, but, already, they stepped in to break up some tensions between some of our Jewish and Muslim students. Then, we had one meeting to talk about what the club would do and had about fifty people show up!"

"That's incredible!"

"We did a bunch of brainstorming on what we wanted to do. The ideas were everything from assigning buddies to new students, raising money for emergency situations, to even training students to be peer counselors."

"Sounds like you inspired many people, Eréndira! I'm so proud of you!"

"And I'm proud of my friends. Also, I appreciate you so much Nanita. Thank you for being there for me and guiding me through all this."

"My pleasure. And with all that has happened, what have you decided about switching schools? I know that was on the table."

"Yes, it was, but now I'm going to stay."

"You've decided to be part of the solution."

"Yep! I can see positive momentum so I'm going to ride it out."

"Sometimes we are called to take on challenges we never imagined. I know you would prefer to focus on singing, and that's a good thing, but situations like the one you dealt with test character. Valuable lessons can be gained if you're open to learning."

"Speaking of which, I've noticed you're expanding your skills on your iPhone!"

"Yes! You're the one who wanted me to get it. I'll have to admit… I was a bit resistant at first, but I'm learning to have a growth mindset!"

"These are the tools we use today, Naníta! And, remember… you promised to tell me about the Princess I was named after."

"Yes. I did! Shall we begin?"

"Yes… but first, before we forget, you said you had something you wanted to show me?"

Naníta pauses, trying to remember what it was that she wanted to share with Eréndira, then it comes to her.

"Oh yes! Wait here, I'll go get it!" Naníta runs into the house and returns with a palm sized item wrapped in a handkerchief. She holds out her hand for Eréndira to see as she carefully peels away the layers of the handkerchief that covers it.

Eréndira, at the full unveiling, exclaims, "It's a rock! What a fascinating color!"

Naníta pulls out a small flashlight from her pocket and says, "Now, look at this!" She holds the rock up at eye level between herself and Eréndira. The rock, the color of a flame, is shaped like the profile of a skull. Naníta turns on the flashlight and shines it through from her side of the rock which reveals that the rock is translucent.

"Wow! There are etchings on the rock!"

"Yes! What do you see?"

"I see what looks like an owl."

"What does the owl represent?"

"Well, I remember when you first moved here you took down the owl yard art because you didn't want the bad energy here. You said that owls are messengers and usually carry bad news."

"That's right. This rare rock is a fire opal. I looked it up! This type of rock comes from Mexico. Someone took the time to shape it into a skull. What do you know of the skull representation?"

Eréndira thinks on this before answering, "Well, when we do our yearly Day of the Dead Altars, the skulls and skeletons are a symbol of the afterlife."

"What do you think this may portray?"

"Seems like a warning. Like a message that something bad is coming. I wonder how it got here?" As soon as the question leaves her lips, Eréndira recants, "I take that back. I have an idea how it got here. The people from up and down this continent were already connected!"

Naníta looks upon Eréndira and gives her a big smile. "You, Eréndira, are precious. Now, let's sit down and I'll tell you as much as I know about Princess Eréndira. For she, too, rose up and faced overwhelming circumstances."

As Eréndira sits by Naníta's side, taking in the full story of Princess Eréndira, the clouds in the sky gently move closer to the earth. Eréndira and Naníta notice the transformation taking place before them. The clouds reveal the image of a young woman atop a galloping horse.

Oral Traditions Persist.
Princess Eréndira Lives.

To know who we are, our histories must be made visible. Atrocities continue to be carried out in the name of conquest. Cultures are silenced and the people stripped of their language and pushed out from their land. We must unearth our histories. For, when we know our histories, we can embrace our identity.

According to *The Chronicles of Michoacan* (1970), a first-hand account recorded in the early 1500's, the fate of the Cazonci was ultimately left in the hands of the Spaniards. The Cazonci persistently resisted obeying Guzman's orders. Thus, the Cazonci was tortured in the same manner as Cuauhtémoc, the last leader of the Mexica. Along with other Purépecha Lords, he was hung over a brazier full of coals and his feet burned.

Looking to expand their territory, the Spaniards demanded that the Cazonci gather 8,000 men to accompany the Spaniards, but the Cazonci refused to request this of his people. Nonetheless, the call went out from Guzman and 8,000 Purépecha men were gathered and admonished to bring all the gold from their villages. These men were divided between the Spaniards and the Cazonci. In chains and carried in hammocks, the Purépechas entered the lands of the Chichimecas.

With continued pressure to reveal hidden treasures, the Cazonci had limited amounts of the precious metal delivered to Guzman which angered him. Additionally, his captors had heard rumors that the Cazonci was planning another ambush. Subsequently, he was tied to the tail of a horse, dragged alive, and burned. They tied him on a mat hitched to the tail of a horse which a Spaniard was riding, preceded by a crier who shouted as he went: "People, look!

This stupid fool tried to kill us. He has been tried and this sentence was handed down against him: that he be dragged alive. Look at him, see the example. Look, you low people for you are all stupid." After he had been dragged for a time, they untied him from the mat, for he still had life in him, and they secured him to a post. The Spaniards commanded him to tell whether he had accomplices in this foul deed and how many, saying that he alone was to die. The Cazonci replied: "What do I have to tell you? I know nothing." They garroted and strangled him until he was dead. The Spaniards then piled wood around his body and burned it, and Guzman had his servants gather up the ashes and throw them in the river (99).

During his short-lived rule, the Cazonci refused to cooperate with the Spaniards. His silence and denials were acts of resistance intended to undermine the invasion of the Purépecha people. While the Cazonci suffered a brutal death as did countless others, opposition to Spanish incursion continued throughout the America's. The following historically chronicled examples are but a few.

The 1680s saw the Pueblo Uprising in which the many different tribes within what is now called the Southwestern United States cooperated on an attack that purged their land of Spanish rule. This expulsion led to twelve years of autonomy free of Spanish presence. Ultimately, the Spaniards returned and retook the region at the cost of many Native lives.

In what was to become California, thousands of California Indians found themselves captive in Missions that were established up and down the Pacific Coast for the purpose of staving off Russian and U.S. expansion. While some California Indians were able to escape, there were also ongoing uprisings in which their captors, the Spanish padres, were poisoned or bludgeoned to death and the missions burned down. Such as the case in San Diego where the Kumeyaay, outraged by the pattern of sexual assaults on their women, destroyed Mission San Diego and killed the local padre in 1775.

Likewise, 1781 saw an uprising in which two missions located along the Colorado River were destroyed by Quechan and Mohave Indians who killed four missionaries and numerous other colonists.

This rebellion deprived Spaniards of the only overland route into Alta California from Northern New Spain which would later be called Mexico. Military efforts to reopen the road and punish the Indians were met with utter failure.

Another large-scale mission Indian revolt in 1824 saw Chumash Indians violently overthrow mission control at Santa Barbara, Santa Ynez, and La Purisima. Santa Barbara was destroyed when Santa Ynez Chumash torched most of the buildings before fleeing. At La Purisima, Chumash seized the mission and fought with colonial troops while a significant number escaped deep into the interior of the Southern San Joaquin Valley.

In 1810, almost three hundred years after the Purépecha first encountered the acacechas, a growing number of guerrilla bands from the California interior were formed when fugitive mission Indians united with interior tribes and villages. Like Princess Eréndira, these First Nations warriors mastered the intruders' weapons. As they raided livestock and attacked colonial forces, they were mounted on horses.

CAST OF CHARACTERS, SIGNIFICANT LOCATIONS, AND TERMS

Present Day Characters

Daryna: Eréndira's Friend whose name means God's Gift; she comes from Ukraine.

EunMi: Friend from Eréndira's previous school who Eréndira references.

Elizabeth: Eréndira's Maternal Grandmother, also known as Naníta (Purépecha for Grandmother).

Eréndira: Central character.

Iryna: Daryna's Sister. Her name means Peace.

Lola: Front office clerk for Vice Principal, Ms. Foster.

Mama Lupe: Elizabeth's Maternal Grandmother

Melissa: Eréndira's best friend.

Ms. Foster: Vice Principal at Eréndira's school.

Pavinder: Friend of Eréndira's at school.

Rosalee & Luisa: Sisters who attend school and are from El Salvador

Susan: Eréndira's Nemesis

Trinh: Friend of Eréndira's at School

Verónica: Eréndira's Mother, Dean of a College at local University

Victor: Eréndira's Father, State Government Administrator

Historical Characters

Chuperipati: Charged with care of the Cazonci Zuangua's jewelry.

Cuauhtémoc: The last leader of the Mexica.

Don Pedro Cuiniarángari: Adopted brother and advisor to Cazonci Tzintzicha Tangáxoan.

Erandi: A porter and Eréndira's confidante.

Hicharuta Vandari: Chief Canoe Maker.

Huizizilzi: Don Pedro's brother.

Irepani: Sesasi's father and Eréndira's maternal grandfather. Irepani means 'he who lays the foundation for life and home.' He is also referred to as Tatíta, Purépecha for Grandfather.

Nanuma: Son of a Lord who wants to marry Eréndira.

Parakata: Sesasi's mother and Eréndira's maternal grandmother (Nanita). Parakata means 'butterfly'.

Paricuti: Chief boatman.

Princess Eréndira: Central character.

Purépecha: Indigenous people whose empire, prior to Spanish Incursion, covered parts of Mexico and included areas in what is now known as Michoacan and Guanajuato.

Sesasi: Princess Eréndira's mother and common-law wife to Timas.

Tangoxóan, Tirimarasco, Azinche & Anini: Four sons of the Cazonci, Zuangua, with Tangoxóan being the oldest.

Timas: Princess Eréndira's father who is the adopted uncle to the kingdom's ruler. She addresses him as father, in Purépecha, Taáte.

Tzintzicha Tangoxóan: The oldest of the sons of Zuangua, whose name means one who erects many fortresses and is courageous in battle. After Zuangua dies from smallpox, Tzintzicha Tangoxóan becomes the next Cazonci during Eréndira's lifetime.

Zuangua: The Cazonci (Ruler) of the Purepecha Empire.

Significant Locations

Acámbaro: Sesasi's Birthplace which is on the eastern border of the Purépecha Kingdom. Served as a military buffer facing their enemies of that time, the Mexica (aka, Aztec). This city is now in the state of Guanajuato and is where Mama Lupe, modern day Eréndira's great-grandmother was born and raised.

Chignahuapan River: Now known as the Lerma River.

Taximaroa: A community standing at the border between the Purépecha and Mexica Nations. Served as an entryway between the two nations. Is now known as Hidalgo.

Tzintzuntzan, Land of the Hummingbirds: Capital of the Purépecha Nation.

Uruapan: Where the Cazonci seeks refuge to escape the Spaniards.

Terms

Acacecha: Purépecha name for the Spaniard; means people who wear caps and hats.

Amámba: Mother.

Cazonci: Ruler.

Chismes: (*Spanish*) Lies, Gossip.

Cómo: (*Spanish*) How.

Harquebus: An early version of the musket.

Horchata (*Spanish*): Rice Water, a refreshing sweet drink.

Huatápera: Meeting place.

Itzï: Water.

Janíkua: Rain.

Jirestani: Breathe.

Kaúikua: Wine.

Kómekua: Ocean.

Mexica: Also known as Aztecs; enemies of the Purépecha and eventually sought an alliance in the face of Spanish incursion.

Mitote: (*Spanish*) Illusion.

Nánde: Mother.

Naníta: Grandmother.

Taáte: Father.

Tatíta: Grandfather.

Temba: Wife.

Tepari pamangarata: "Tepari pamangarata" can be found in the elaborate dictionaries composed by the Franciscan Fray Maturino Gilberti who lived and died in Michoacán from 1535 to October 3rd, 1585. Tepari, meaning "something hard on the body" (cosa así gruesa de cuerpo) and pamangarata, "exhaustion" (cansalcio tal) might suggest smallpox since the tough lesions described on the body might suggest sores which led to eventual weakness and death among the affected.

Terútseme sani ixu: Welcome greeting.
Tekéchu: Horse.
Tukúru: Owl.
Uamba: Husband.
Uembekua: I love you.

SOURCES

Bolton, H. (1931). *Font's Complete Diary, A chronicle of the Founding of San Francisco*. University of California Press, Berkeley.

Gibson, C. (1970). *The Chronicles of Michoacan*. University of Oklahoma Press.

Juan Bautista de Anza National Historic Trail. 2024, September 9. Anza Trail Foundation. https://anzahistorictrail.org

Princess Eréndira. 2024, May 23. In Wikipedia. Wikimedia Foundation Inc. https://en.wikipedia.org/wiki/Princess_Eréndira

Princess Hapunda and the Patzcuaro Lake. 2016, May 3. In Latinfolktales. wordpress.com. https://latinfolktales.wordpress.com/2016/05/03/princess-hapunda-and-the-patzcuaro-river/

ACKNOWLEDGMENTS

Born and raised in California, I worked on weekends and summers alongside my parents, brother, and several classmates and their families in the fields, harvesting fruits and vegetables. We represented the Mexican diaspora; a people displaced from our homelands and trying to get a foothold in the U.S. While the generation before us worked multiple jobs to leverage hard labor into better opportunities, my generation caught scraps of our history when and where we could: from Elders, extended family, and for me, the serendipitous opportunity to teach for several years at a tribal college while completing my doctorate degree and starting a tenure track position at Sac State.

It is at this tribal college where I first heard about Princess Eréndira. Being insecure about my lack of Spanish fluency, I told my students, many of them who had been born in Mexico, El Salvador, and beyond, that my parents were both born in Mexico but had immigrated to the U.S. when they were very young. They inquired where my parents were from, and when they heard that my father was from Guanajuato—particularly the region of Guanajuato, Chamacuaro, and Acámbaro—I was ushered into an era and circumstances unparalleled by any other accounts of my history that I had ever heard. It was two of my students, Ernesto and Fidelia Rios, who I credit for opening the door for me to learn about this courageous young Princess.

In writing about Princess Eréndira, I had to learn the art of creative writing. During the Covid lockdown, I started to take classes from the Muse Writers Center and repeated writing workshops, via zoom, with Lisa Cooper. Back in California, I had an extremely supportive writing circle with Anne Halley Kel-Artinian, Anna Kato, EunMi Cho, and Kimberly Biddle. Many iterations of this novel were turned over to another group of readers consisting of Joy Jennings Danziger, Koney Austinn, Alexandrea Hernandez, Jill Schneider, and, once again, Anne Halley Kel-Artinian offering her patience and expertise.

Getting this to publication... *my* friend, Dr. Melissa Moreno, introduced me to Dr. Josie Méndez-Negrete. I had hoped to land this first novel with a publishing house where the forces of conquest and colonization were understood. More importantly, I sought an editor who understood the importance of preserving our true history and promoting the voices and narratives of those who watch over us; this, I found in Dr. Méndez-Negrete. Her decision to bring in ash good to give this work of love one last and sound review was a stroke of genius and demonstrated her commitment to the quality of this portrayal.

Finally, to my life partner, Mike, for taking pride in and supporting this endeavor. As we look to recover that which has been subsumed in our ancestor's efforts to survive conquest and colonization, I see the values of care and collectivism in our children, Michael and Lilian... and our daughter's chosen life partner, Aria. May the spirit and sacrifices of our ancestors live on in our grandson, Cyrus, and in those inspired by Princess Eréndira.

ABOUT THE AUTHOR

Rose Borunda started her professional career in child assault prevention and school counseling. After witnessing and interceding on the reverberating impact of historical conquest and colonization, she sought her doctorate degree at the University of San Francisco to gain a larger perspective of the structures that sustain and strengthen subjugation and relational cruelty. With her degree she embarked upon a tenure track position at California State University, Sacramento while concurrently working regionally and throughout the nation with Indigenous and tribal communities. This collective experience furthered her insight as to what exists in our systems and our hearts that fuels or heals the challenges that our youth and nation(s) face today. As a descendent of the Purépecha people, Borunda pivots from scholarly writing as she offers the courage of a legendary historical figure from her tribe —*Eréndira*—and employs lessons from this princess to a young woman of the same name facing challenges in the modern era.

In Borunda's spare time, she enjoys learning from and being nurtured by nature, socializing with growth mindset(ed) friends, performing and offering Native American flute melodies, watching her two children Michael, Lilian, and plus one, Aria, carve a more peaceful and harmonious life for the next generation, including her new grandson, Cyrus. She lives with her husband and kitties in the hills that have been home to the Sierra Miwok for thousands of years.

www.ingramcontent.com/pod-product-compliance
Lightning Source LLC
Chambersburg PA
CBHW060308310726
48976CB00007B/2257